MOTHERS
AND OTHER
LOVERS

MOTHERS AND OTHER LOVERS

Joanna Briscoe

PHOENIX HOUSE
London

First published in Great Britain 1994
© 1994 Joanna Briscoe

Phoenix House, Orion House, 5 Upper St Martin's Lane,
London WC2H 9EA

Joanna Briscoe has asserted her right under the Copyright,
Designs and Patents Act 1988 to be identified as the author of
this work

A CIP catalogue record for this book is available from the
British Library

ISBN 1 89758 081 9 cased
ISBN 1 89758 086 X paper

Typeset at The Spartan Press Ltd,
Lymington, Hants
Printed in England by Clays Ltd, St Ives plc

FOR CAROL BRISCOE, WITH LOVE

ONE

PAULA STRACHAN WATCHED HER DAUGHTER PLAY, AND remained untouched, found her devoid of charm. The small child glanced sidelong to check on her audience, her eyes wild with drama, and Paula felt a stab of irritation that others were oblivious to her guile.

And of course Paula loved Eleanor too, loved her so passionately that she could consume her, fast kisses too feeble to conceal her guilt that a part of her disliked a four-year-old child with dandelion seed hair and an awkward manner. But she picked at her like a scab, unable to leave her until she bled.

It had begun with a mere twitch of resentment when Eleanor was a baby. Eleanor's father would stare into the darkness of her off-centre gaze like someone in a trance, woven into her world, while Paula prepared supper and waited for them to surface. But their mutual fascination never exhausted itself.

The Strachan children were the source of envy and derision. Eleanor, Rolf, and later Poppy, were permitted to swear and address their parents by their first names; they lived in houses featuring bookcases made of railway sleepers balanced on bricks, and hessian lamp shades trimmed with Scandinavian braid; they wore Guernseys before they appeared in colour supplements and Kickers bought in France; they knew how babies were conceived, and were allowed to spray passing cars with the garden hose and air views of a rude or rebellious nature with piping force.

Eleanor's legacy was confusion. She sensed discordance. Her principal crime, she suspected in lucid moments, was that she wasn't Rolf, Paula's bundle, sweet and bad tempered with thick layers of hair, long lashes and a toothless grin. His eyes a glassy dark blue, still wet with the tears of his temper, he'd break into that cheruby beam and Paula would pluck him onto her lap, her rough naughty boy with strong scratched legs who loved her with all the abandon of physical need and a milky devotion beyond.

Eleanor would follow the expanse of Paula's back in a garish Indian shift round the supermarket, terrified that she might transgress. Paula, her shoulders sweating, would turn round and look down resentfully at the gawky web of sensitivities trailing her. 'Oh Eleanor,' she would say, 'you *know* you're not allowed sweet cereals. What's the use of me trying to give you all a healthier life when you just ask for rubbish?'

Later, when Eleanor was seventeen and had blossomed so that her flimsy tufts had become thicker hooks and she knew how to protect herself, she had a sense of coming into her own.

'*Why* do you persistently stuff yourself with such rubbish?' asked Paula as Eleanor downed a Family Size pack of crisps with a mugful of Cinzano.

A memory of the broad back in the supermarket drifted before Eleanor, but she was aware of her slimness under her dressing gown and the secret damp warmth of her thighs as she stretched her legs under the table, and looked bulky Paula up and down and said, 'Mother dear, I feel you're hardly in a position to air your views on the effects of healthy eating.'

Paula tightened her lips.

The Strachans were no longer unanimously perceived as oddities when they moved west to Devon from the flat villages of Somerset. Poppy's OshKosh dungarees were not always laughed at, and Eleanor knew people at school whose parents also had *Jonathan Livingstone Seagull* on their bookshelves. At seventeen, Eleanor was unsure whether she was Debbie Harry or Tess Durbeyfield as she paced over Dartmoor's higher reaches, enraptured by the idea of her own long hair blowing behind her, imagining herself a star of the screen or a fragile milkmaid.

Paula ran a bookshop in a four-storey building where people hired rooms for their own businesses – shoemaking, reflexology, a community magazine – and embezzled coins from the electricity meter. The frozen hall and staircases were painted a violent red, all visible pipes mauve and green, and led to warm smelly rooms high with voices. Noticeboards proliferated. Paula made new friends and wondered how she had ever tolerated living amidst the oozing plains of Somerset, or had stayed at home for so much of her married life, like a cow. People – in twos, in fives – called round at the Centre that housed the bookshop, whereas at home she sat with a novel propped up on the kitchen table, eating too much, alone all day while the woman from the post office walked by and waved and the fields slumped.

When Eleanor was seventeen, she felt as though she were marooned down that lane like a gaudy flower in a swamp. The house was granite sunken into a hollow, a damp grey undulation, its outbuildings rising from dock and corrugated iron.

Trees wept through the kitchen window. Eleanor and some of her friends draped themselves over the table and mimicked people from their class at school. The house eased itself into the slack of a Friday afternoon. The breathings and shiftings of its history had left ill-fitting door frames and sloping floors; human movement radiated extended creaks. The houses in that region had sunk into themselves, whole rows of cottages hump-backed, farms with end walls swollen.

The passage above the kitchen shuddered as Poppy, the youngest child, crashed along it stamping her feet and neighing for the benefit of anyone who was listening. Her distant whinnies volleyed down the staircase. She burst into the kitchen and pawed the floor, lips trumpeted, frowning brows and rolling eyes.

Paula came in with some colourfully dressed friends. Eleanor suppressed a sigh and darted a conspiratorial glance at the others as they abandoned their conjectures on the sex lives of their teachers and sat in a flush of subdued hilarity.

'It's the bloody hippies,' muttered Eleanor.

Paula's friends carried a collective smell, a musky scent compounded by smoke and old wool. Two were ruddy, the other a curdy pale. All three wore bulbous boots in faded primary colours. They were uniformly reticent; when they spoke, they spoke very slowly.

Poppy pawed the floor, snorting.

'Hello, P-P-Paula-a-a-a,' she said in a neigh that tailed off into laughter.

'Hello, Poppy,' replied Paula calmly.

Eleanor and her school friends sat self-consciously. Between their studiedly sleepy gestures and laid-back affectations, there was much darting of looks at the older people in their rusts and reds. Eleanor's mouth twitched with mirth and shame: she grinned slightly at her friends. Paula's guests sat at the table; a tight-knit hostility emanated from the schoolgirls. They were surrounded by birthday presents: enamelled boxes, drifts of

4

underwear, Mary Quant tights, mascara in silly colours. They all had the same glow, the kind of milk and seal flush that comes of youth and a preoccupation with sex. Eleanor's features were still rounded and plump at the nose and not quite fixed. She was reminiscent of standard girls in Victorian portraits, an intensity in the eyes, a brownness, an introspective suggestion. Her eyebrows were marked and dark and defined a face that might have become lumpy once it lost youth. The girls wore jumpers too long at the sleeve. They were nervous behind the disdain.

Eleanor, high on her latest phrases and experimenting with a slight pout, was irritated by the re-appearance of Paula, who had been searching for stage costumes, with an armful of clothes.

'You've got mountains of stuff there,' said one of Paula's friends.

Eleanor cringed. To her eternal humiliation, Paula now perceived herself as a vigorously active member of the community, a facet of her new personality along with her mauve leather character shoes and sporadic assertiveness.

'Look, it's a proper production the kids are in,' said Eleanor, rifling through the pile of clothes that Paula was donating to Poppy's school play. 'You can't give them this decrepit old stuff. How incredibly embarrassing.'

Sweating from her search, Paula clicked her tongue in annoyance. 'Eleanor,' she said. 'There's some lovely old things here.'

Eleanor cast a glance at her friends. 'Oh. I see. It would seem Paula's turned into a style mentor, everyone.'

The friends giggled.

'I wish you tittering snobs would keep out of it,' said Paula.

Eleanor shrugged.

'This is what you can look forward to when your one's a teenager,' said Paula to one of her guests, raising her eyes to the ceiling.

'Oh fuck off and don't be so patronising,' snarled Eleanor.

Paula narrowed her lips. They paled so the freckles around them stood out fishily. 'Listen, just don't *speak* to me like that,' she said, suddenly incensed, shaking in her effort to summon authority in front of an audience. 'You have no idea what you're talking about as usual, but you're so narrow minded you automatically mock.'

'Gosh, we do have self-confidence all of a sudden. Have you recently attended one of your Assertiveness Training workshops on the quiet? Or is it just that you have some guests you can show off in front of, perchance?'

'Leave it, will you please, Eleanor.'

'Well, I think you ought to stop using other people being here as a way of getting at me. It doesn't impress anyone, if you want to know the truth.'

There was silence. Paula made tea. The rain slipped into five o'clock dusk and the overhead light buzzed. Eleanor looked at her school friends and smirked, a surreptitious hiss of laughter through her nose as the ruptured calm drifted and re-settled.

Paula caught Eleanor's eye. She paused. 'I mean, really.' She bit her lip. 'You really are so arrogant, Eleanor. I don't know what – what you think you are, who you think you are. You and your friends . . .'

'God, Paula, can you stop going on at me?' Eleanor sighed.

'How else can I get through to you? You're so hard recently – I don't know where these snobbish attitudes come from. Every-one's either *darling* or a *peasant* . . .'

The school friends giggled.

'It's all just Sixth Form clever-clever stuff.'

'You bitch,' muttered Eleanor, tailing off.

'What did you say?'

'Nothing.'

'What did you say?'

'Sorry,' said Eleanor, shrugging.

Paula pursed her lips.

'Just going to the loo,' muttered Eleanor. She tightened her throat against a clump of tears.

There was a knock on the door. Paula went to answer it. 'I want a word with you later,' called Paula to Eleanor. 'I don't like this racket you're getting into at all.'

Eleanor spun off down the hall to the lavatory. A single tear escaped onto her cheek. When she returned to the hallway, she was momentarily confused. She registered Paula standing by the front door, then realised that she was actually further ahead by the kitchen. She glanced back at the other figure, and saw a woman whose only similarity to Paula was in the colour of the dress she wore; the resemblance had been smudged and brief and now eluded her.

'What's this?' said the woman, catching sight of her. She raised her eyebrows. 'Have you been crying?'

Eleanor's eyes watered as she shook her head. She walked into the hallway, but the woman held out her arms, and Eleanor found herself enveloped in alien warmth, pressing against the bosom of a stranger. She recoiled slightly. 'Your mascara'll run if you cry,' said the woman, hugging her to her.

'It's OK,' muttered Eleanor, her voice distorted against the woman's shoulder. She tried to edge away.

'Selma?' called Paula.

'Just coming.'

'What's the matter, sweetheart?' said the woman.

'Nothing,' said Eleanor.

'What's your name?' She held Eleanor to her still.

'Eleanor.'

'Eleanor, yes. Well, that's very pretty. You've stopped crying now.' She pulled a strand of Eleanor's hair away from her mouth.

She let her go and followed Paula. Eleanor paused in the hall, then loitered by the doorway.

Paula was talking with a note of pride in her voice. Eleanor slipped in to sit by her friends, shielding herself from Paula's gaze. 'And Selma's a friend of mine and my new, well, my new business partner – is that how you'd describe yourself?' said Paula. 'She'll be taking over my days off at the bookshop. This is the friend I've been telling you all about!' she finished brightly.

So when Eleanor was seventeen, it was as though a part of her had died. There was the bright rinsed despair of the moor and a woman who was sometimes kind and at other times showed a species of cruelty towards her. She breathed life into the numb bit and killed it again.

Eleanor was the academic one, Rolf the artistic one, Poppy was the naughty youngest child; thus were their roles assigned by unspoken family lore. Eleanor and Poppy attended state school since they could cope with the system; Rolf had his creativity encouraged at a progressive school.

Eleanor would ride the bus from school along the river road sleepily watching the students from the college hitching lifts to Dartington, the bus that mounted the dry back of the moor and perambulated the lanes daily, shunting the locals like animals back to the high ground. She sat in a slack-mouthed daze as its motion fuelled her fantasies of academic and sexual accomplishment. It was better than her mother arriving to collect her in her VW van and embarrassing her. Her hair would be dirty; she would be grumpy with approaching homework; she thought she was unique nevertheless, and out of the window she imagined London W1, and inside her the penis of Mr Lennock, the glorious English teacher. Her school friends would often come home with her, alighting from the bus by the Tom Cobleigh B & B and tramping down the lane to the Strachan house. Paula would see Eleanor cornering the lane with her friends on their stolid or stalky legs, arm in arm, hair straggling, and think they looked happy. They walked down the lane screaming with exaggerated laughter, despairing in hoity toity voices over other people, over Devon, ignoring the beauties of the hedgerows and the fields as they swept past in a rush of precocious and puerile babble. Such was Eleanor's existence.

Selma Healy was not typical of Paula's friends, who were more commonly earnest and patchouli-scented. She held echoes of them, but the flavour of her was different. She was pale haired and very pale skinned and emphatically womanly in a way that they were not. In her presence the girls were restless and wanted to giggle, but they were paradoxically silenced by her. The more characteristic friends of Paula's became increasingly reticent under the flood of her conversation. As Selma talked, Paula nodded her head, her mouth a small round point of concentration, and Eleanor could see, to her scorn, that Paula looked up to her: she would soon come home expounding her philosophies or wearing scarves of similar design.

The hippy friends started mentioning children waiting at home. Paula wandered out with them to see them off. There was silence in the room.

Eleanor smiled at one of her friends and touched her peroxide hair.

'Shall I do your eyes?' she murmured.

She leant over her, pulled her head taut from the forehead and murmured commands, her pupils becoming dark and blank in concentration.

Selma Healy watched them idly. They were hard with secrets

and sly glances, an acute awareness of themselves. There was a lingering youthful slightness behind fat thighs or healthy bosoms. They dragged back their hair when they spoke and wore too much black eyeliner.

'I wish bloody Paula would leave me alone just for once,' said Eleanor. 'Why is it always me? Stupid sla— what's she got to be so narked about?'

There was a quaver behind her smile.

'I'm not that full of myself, am I?'

'No, I don't think so,' said her schoolfriend.

'And what if you were?' said Selma. 'A bit of self-value is only positive, surely, so value it.'

Eleanor reddened slightly at the unknown adult addressing her. 'Oh, it's not *self-value*,' she said. 'You didn't hear her. I'm snobby, arrogant, vain . . .'

'So why shouldn't you be? You look just lovely, of course you're vain. Well *I* certainly am. Wouldn't it be boring if we were all modest little women?'

'We – yes,' said Eleanor. She drew thin lines under her friend's eyes and spoke compliments in a low voice, soothed her to keep her still as she worked, while the friend closed her eyes and held her head back obediently. Eleanor leant over her face as she added mascara and patted a wetted finger on her mistakes.

Selma was heavy, mesmerised in the Strachan kitchen. The child Poppy was asking people to come and view her paintings on the barn wall. Her bold felt tip designs on wood decorated the kitchen, marked by a signature of a waving poppy. The older girls murmured as they made each other up.

'Oh, your eyes look so much better with mascara,' said Eleanor.

'God!' said the other friend. 'Your eyes look so dark now, your lashes are *massive*. You look like a camel.'

Eleanor stood back to observe her work.

'Make me look like a camel,' said Poppy, bounding up to Eleanor. Eleanor propped her on a stool and kissed her red cheek as she sat, waiting, with her eyes closed. Poppy's warm smell of unchanged flannel sheets and her Parma Violet perfume made Eleanor kiss her again, suddenly almost tearful over Paula and the fact of Poppy's loved cheeks, and she stroked Poppy's hair and the dry patch of skin on her eyelids with her finger before she started.

'Come *on!*' said Poppy.

'You've got sleepy dust,' said Eleanor. 'Shall I scrape it out?' She would have hugged her tightly in her woolly jersey for minutes on end, her private circus, would Poppy not have turned fractious. Eleanor balanced a hand on Poppy's knee to be nearer her face. She saw Selma watching her and became self-conscious.

'Paula's friend wants to be turned into a camel too,' she said. 'Don't you?'

'Well I suppose I should join the herd,' replied Selma.

Poppy lowered herself from the stool with bedraggled pansy eyes.

Selma sat patiently, swinging her leg, waiting for Paula's return. She looked older beside the girls, Paula's age almost. She was pale-skinned and curvy, like a once successful actress. Eleanor turned uncertainly towards her, appearing slim and unkempt beside her. Eleanor's finger nails were rough. The smell of her slightly dirty hair mingled with young cheap perfume, the unwashed hair more appealing than the over-sweet scent. Selma's hair was pulled back off her face in cold sweeps, her eyes stretched tight. She was then aware of her age and the lines to negotiate, the spots on her irises; she breathed through her nose, conscious of her breath up close.

Eleanor sank into a sleepy oblivion as she concentrated. Selma became drowsy in turn. The process was soporific, but her nerves paradoxically flared in anticipation of the next move. Eleanor's fingers were cool on her eyelids, cold eyeshadow, hot concentrated breath on her cheek, then a finger pressed behind her ear to tilt her head and a repeat performance for the second eye. Selma was charged and drowsy; the near professional touch made her feel that measure of lethargy and arousal experienced at the hairdresser's, and she realised she was becoming turned on, and thought then how long it had been since she had had sex, so long, if the mere application of cosmetics could arouse her.

She wondered idly whether such girls as these were still virgins. She imagined the thrusting penis of some local Newton Abbot boy, all Adam's apple and hangdog glint of eagerness, penetrating that narrowness.

The girls talked to each other; Poppy tried to grab their attention.

'So don't forget what I told you,' murmured Selma to Eleanor. 'Vanity's OK. Paula could do with a bit more of it herself!'

Eleanor looked surprised. She snorted.

They were silent. Eleanor applied a final layer of mascara. She blew away stray powder.

'Do you think it's her, then, not me?' said Eleanor.

'I don't know what you mean.'

'Well, I mean, don't you think she –'

'It's usually both people. Not one. No one's fault. If I saw you together I'd probably think you were something of a little madam and she was a bit intolerant – but who knows?' She yawned. 'But you wouldn't want me talking about your mother behind her back, now would you?'

'Naturally not,' said Eleanor. 'Shall I do your lipstick?'

'Lipstick too? Do you want me to be a painted lady? All right.'

Eleanor selected a colour. 'Do you like dark pink?'

'Well, I really don't mind. That claret colour.'

Eleanor was silent. 'But, you know,' she said, 'I can't do anything right. Nothing. So . . .'

'So you give in and do your little brat act. I used to do that too. At least Paula's . . . Paula's a good woman basically. But when you're that age, when you're in your forties or whenever, well then I think suddenly youth, everything, can seem like an insult almost. She's probably jealous that you can stand there wearing clothes like that being outspoken in a way her generation – or,' she shrugged, 'my generation simply weren't allowed to be.'

'*Jealous*? Paula?'

'And why not?' said Selma flippantly. 'Well, you've finished my mouth now. I'm sure it's utterly spectacular, huh? Thank you, Eleanor, with your pretty name.'

She turned to the table and looked through a newspaper.

Paula returned with Rolf, the middle child.

'You'll be here for supper, won't you Rolf?' she asked. 'This is Selma. My son Rolf.'

He shrugged and said he'd see. He murmured something and headed for the pantry. The majority of Paula's friends were vaguely charmed by his handsome surliness, flattered if the young rebel spoke to them, but Selma appeared unmoved.

Paula was radiant and relaxed when her home was warm with activity, friends about the place, music trailed by slammed doors, the children swearing, wheedling, down the phone.

Poppy, bored inside, flouted flimsy rules and appeared in the garden on her pony, demonstrating how she could ride him with no bridle, and ploughing up the sparse autumn lawn.

'My God!' said Paula. 'Poppy, put it back in the field!'

Poppy threw her a V-sign and trotted round the garden on her shaggy pony; Paula laughed.

Plants radiated in mist whitened windows; the house glowed

13

and creaked with footsteps. Back indoors, Poppy displayed her repertoire of dangerous tricks on the Aga rail. In-jokes sucked Selma into the clique. She, the guest, projected herself as the giver; she was bounteous, hugged Paula and told her how wonderful her house was, her hospitality, how beautiful her kids. Paula looked thrilled.

Neighbours were politely wary of the Strachans and their friends scattered over the moor who rhapsodised over dry stone walls and complained about the building of new barns. Their cars were either brand-new or decrepit to the point of wreckage. The Strachans' house was part tiled, part thatched. The thatched section sprouted drifts of vegetable matter and was mocked by the locals who considered thatches fit only for the postcard industry. Tim Strachan talked of horses as a practical means of transport; he wanted to harness the river to hydro-electric power and let the old cow barns out to students or craftspeople. Paula added plots of her own involving moving to Tasmania and avoiding nuclear warfare. Eleanor, Rolf and Poppy were unanimous in their ridicule.

Eleanor was a waitress on Saturdays at the tea-rooms in Widecombe, the neighbouring village, where she read her *Penguin Book of Modern Verse* behind the counter to conceal her shyness and demonstrate her superiority. When she fetched eggs or parts from the blacksmith for her father's lawn mower, weaving through canoning dogs and yards caked with chicken excrement, she glimpsed other houses, and saw only cleanliness, shining floors, electric kettles, curtains with proper prints so different from Paula's hessian drapes and the clutter of home.

There was something sick there, in her parents' house, Eleanor thought, but it was hard to identify. It was as if inertia lay behind those bright schemes, a breed of hopelessness that came of too much money or a suspicion that no one had very much to say to each other. In their search for inner meaning, Paula and Tim adhered to outer realities: spiritual gurus, educational theories. There was a messiness to their existence, in the excesses of their children and in the young couples who lived in the annexe and failed to make their rent payments.

'Why do you always let the annexe out to spongers?' asked Eleanor.

'Oh darling, they're not really spongers, they're just hard up at the moment,' Paula would say, and then look worried and disappointed when the petrol can in the back of her car was found empty.

A woman from Dartington asked Tim if he would sponsor her to set up as a travelling puppeteer.

'So by *sponsor* she means, "Tim whom I hardly know, please will you *give* me a load of money?"' said Eleanor.

Tim pondered the question.

The rottenness was somewhere there at the core. The bloomy fruit – the image of their lives – was rosy, gilded: Eleanor ruthlessly pursued academic achievement; she wore distinctive clothes, though she was afraid to, and pushed herself. Her parents' friends thought her style funny, aesthetic; the neighbours found it inexplicable. And that boy snarled about like a rebel without a cause. Poppy seemed to run wild, could be found trotting solemnly on her horse about the lanes; Paula had her latest hobby in the bookshop.

The darkness lay in twitches, edges. Paula was mystified that Eleanor read so excessively: there was something about that child that had driven her crazy, she had told friends cheerfully, wonderingly when Eleanor was younger; a stubbornness, a need to come out on top; and Eleanor would stay in her room and wipe the expression from her face.

*

Tim and his daughter Eleanor wandered round the moors together, she teasing him about his slow gait and his love of the dry stone walling, he laughing along with her at himself, because for all its sharp edges the mockery was affectionate, and in his passivity he enjoyed the attention it conferred. He imitated Eleanor's imitation of himself. He was like porridge, thought Eleanor, fishermen's jerseys, everything comforting and strong. He was large, slow limbed; he sniffed the air the way his colleagues drank alcohol and drew pleasure from it, and his eyes were blue Scandinavian, and his beard flat brown, and Eleanor had to skip around him because his movements were so slow she grew impatient. And to Paula seeing them come through the gate together, Eleanor leggy in her school clothes, talking intently, hair hooked behind her ears, appearing slimmer and smaller than she was beside Tim, him catching reflections of the horizons in his eyes as he looked around him while smiling at Eleanor's talk, theirs was solid love, theirs was the love. He is the apple tree, thought Eleanor.

They came into the house rosy cheeked and tramping cold air with the exclusiveness of anyone who has sampled virtuous health and returns to find those inside breathing sluggish air.

Rolf had abandoned his homework. Paula was unconcerned, but mildly urged him to take it up. She cast a glance over it, but it was virtually incomprehensible to her, and she asked to hear him play his guitar instead. His hair was dyed black and spiked in moderate middle class rebellion, he wore an old man's jacket sour with sweat and smoke over his pallor, but his fundamental good looks, strong cheekbones, blue eyes and dark brows, withstood the assault.

Eleanor stuck her fingers in her ears with steely focus on her revision. Rolf plucked at the same few chords; Eleanor mouthed conjugations, chewing on the ends of her hair in concentration.

Later they hung in spit-dried points over her shoulder. She hunched herself against the music. So it always was.

Rolf's lips parted in vague surprise if everything were not simple and going his way. He would suck his mother dry, yet it was not pelican blood that Paula fed him, but sticky love. Sweetly given milk that turned rancid under the scrutiny of others.

Off the road that descended from the moor, then rose again the other side of the River Dart before reaching the town of Totnes, Paula's friend Selma Healy now lived with her daughter Louisa and occasionally her husband. Off that barren route with its speeding local and dawdling tourist traffic, its blackberry and cow-parsley hedges rimed with exhaust, a left fork led to a terrace of houses, a gathering called Causton.

Selma Healy had recently moved to Number 3, Causton, her husband continuing to live in the London house when he was not travelling for work or visiting her and Louisa in Devon. While they remained officially married, they were separated for long periods. Selma put Louisa into the local primary school, where Poppy Strachan was a pupil, and continued her work on the book that had occupied her for the past four years, renting an office at the Totnes Centre where Paula had her bookshop, and filling in Paula's afternoons off to supplement her income, and to keep her from an edging loneliness and the burring platitudes of the researcher she had hired.

Selma and Paula quickly became friends. Where Selma's neighbours were suspicious, reserved, the Centre crowd slow and self-absorbed, Paula had always been simply friendly. Selma Healy, in her womanliness, in her articulacy and townish air of differentness, appealed to Paula; and as Paula sat by the two-bar heater in the bookshop serving the earnest drifts of customers who came in or pooling tea rounds with the women from the shoe making company in the back room, she looked forward to Selma dreamily coming down still absorbed in work, mouthing non-sequiturs while caught up in thought, because Selma, in her paleness and self-possession, changed the tenor of the Centre, her register different in a place where clothes were functional, where oaty neutrals mixed with rainbow hues with little in between. Her pale brown hair just touched her shoulders, or she wore it pulled back tightly off her face. She had some Irish and Finnish relatives, she said. She had lived mostly in London. Her voice was lulling, monotonous almost. In her late thirties she had become curvier and finely lined so she was like a bird gone to seed, fine bones supporting slacking flesh. When she turned to Paula and spoke, Paula listened intently, arrested by the monotone in her pleasure at waiting for the inflections.

Eleanor and her friend Karen sat in the Smokers' Common Room at school and giggled about the diminished credibility rating that would result from attending a talk by one of the headmistress's guest speakers.

'If she's an Overseas Development Officer, whatever that means, she's probably some old bag in dungarees,' said Karen.

'Don't be stupid, those do-gooder types have to be pretty smart,' said another friend.

'She's probably some . . . some emasculating harpy with a Charlie's Angels jumpsuit and red finger nails,' said Eleanor.

She was brittle and tear-stained. She had sensed Paula's resentment pooling over the kitchen table when she sat down for breakfast that morning. Paula's hazel, freckle-rimmed gaze followed her as she ate.

Paula, in her large nightie and red flannel dressing gown, felt fat and constipated. The dog smelled damp. Poppy had abandoned her weekly cleaning chore, and grease spotted the window. Paula noticed that Eleanor was sallow and dark-shadowed and held herself stiffly. She estimated that it was about the right time of the month, but she would never ask, because for all that open talk over the years, Eleanor kept herself to herself. Paula sometimes yearned for the kind of daughter who would confide in her about periods and boyfriends, but all she got was stained underwear in the washing basket and a pale look of pain, and the fevered remnants of phone conversations that leaked through from the hall, the odd male name spoken in a different timbre. Even rows were preferable to this slow and intangible punishment, to the friendly indifference punctured with hints and twitches of secret knowledge, because they were at least contact.

Eleanor could shout out in front of her friends in their interminable game of 'Choices', 'Paula, which would you rather do – give Norman Tebbit a blow job or be caught by Doug and Jeannie on the bookshop floor examining yourself with a speculum?' And Paula would dutifully choose and the friends would shriek with laughter. But if, an hour later, Paula asked Eleanor who this Sean was who got mentioned so often, the answer would be, 'Oh, no one,' with a little smile and no eye contact.

Tim Strachan paced around the house preparing himself for work while Poppy and Rolf packed their school bags in predictable morning panic and went off to catch the bus at the end of the lane. Paula kissed Poppy and followed Rolf out with her smile. A fog of nerves hung over the silence.

'What's the matter?' Eleanor asked eventually.

Paula looked at her. The tension was soaked with voiceless resentment.

'Oh–' A sigh. 'Nothing.'

'Have I done something?' asked Eleanor. 'It's me, isn't it? What?'

Paula's lips were pursed.

Eleanor had been a child in a Greek embroidered smock longing for the normality of a pleated skirt and cardigan, trailing Paula through their whitewashed Somerset house with a hungry and defensive gaze. 'What's the matter? Have I done something wrong?' 'Please, darling, don't batter at me,' Paula would say and sip her coffee. Wait. Her lips trembled then went tight with anger. 'I have a bone to pick with you.' Silence. Eleanor, her chest contracting, would want to beg her to tell her what it was. Sometimes she fought back and cried petulantly, but for a while she tried harder and harder to be good, and with every attempt she became more frightened and grew smaller until finally she hoped she looked pale and scared so that Paula could lash out at her as much as she wanted to, and it would be right because she was a martyr whose duty in life was to suffer. Eleanor's fear was shot through with a streak of superiority: why the hell were other people so uptight? Outsiders were intrigued, reluctantly in love with that lavish life. Running wild in the country every summer and trying hard not to irritate Paula, Eleanor's dreams turned rancid beneath the richness, quietly. She read orphanage books and made herself half believe that every stranger knocking at the door was the woman from the children's home come to fetch her and leave Paula and Rolf alone together. Her ecstasy of self-pity turned to dull panic at fresh words of criticism from Paula. Perhaps she actually was going to be given away. Paula: mouth tight, expression closed off. Eleanor wanted to sob, dribble, cry over her dress, cling to her and say sorry, sorry, love me, like me.

'Look, you're all funny this morning,' said Eleanor. 'What's the matter?' A spasm of menstrual cramp spread down her thighs.

'Nothing, really nothing,' Paula said. 'It's just that I never see you,' she said with a nervous laugh. 'I just wish you – wouldn't always be in your room if you're home.'

'I'm *not!*'

Paula smiled in resignation, her lips still pursed.

'But I'm not!' said Eleanor. 'I'm here for supper and I do the washing up, don't I?'

'I said it was nothing.'

Paula cradled her coffee against the edging of her dressing gown, and Eleanor felt the old panic of self-blame. She looked at the speckled eyelids, thought with a throw of distaste that they were leathery like a bat's, but imagined them torn in a car accident or her cutting them with scissors, and had a sudden rush of sorrow. She cried with her head on her arms and her sleeves sodden and said, 'Sorry, sorry,' and hoped Paula wouldn't die, and knew she resented her for studying in her room, for helping in the house, for having been given the freedom that she herself never had.

Eleanor decided to miss the guest speaker. Across a sea of twitching hair and slumped figures, tall windows framed trees drifting in a white afternoon light. She slipped out of the library. The walls of the paved area surrounding the school were mossed and dripping; pre-fabs shone in the wet brightness; pupils traipsed past in groups to classes. She didn't dare go home: the memory of the morning's conversation would flicker between herself and Paula, flints of awareness in the air. She shivered on the High Street and decided she would return for the last lesson to ask Karen whether she could stay the night. And then she saw that woman again. She struggled to recall her identity.

Selma Healy sat in a café with a friend. They were smoking, inclining their heads away from the drift of the smoke, absorbed in conversation. Selma Healy's pallor was emphasised by traces of deep red lipstick, her flat pale skin more surreal under the pool of greasy yellow light. She barely opened her mouth as she spoke, her head tilted backwards so she appeared to look down through her eyelids with an abstracted gaze at some point in the middle distance. Eleanor could not imagine how Paula had made her acquaintance, Paula whose friends' idea of self-adornment encompassed little beyond henna.

The other woman was more tawny and raddled. Eleanor watched them gesture and converse the other side of the glass, and was struck with an unexpected sense of shyness. She walked away and lingered in the High Street, looking into shops. The light in the town became grey. She wondered whether Paula actually hated her.

'Do I spot a camel?' A voice rose on the street behind her.

Eleanor turned.

Selma Healy put her hand on Eleanor's shoulder and said goodbye to her friend in a collision of raincoats.

'Hello,' said Eleanor looking at her.

'Are you walking up this way?' said Selma. She moved her hand onto Eleanor's back, huddling against her on the narrow street.

'Yes,' said Eleanor. 'Towards the top.'

'Aren't you meant to be at school?'

'Well yes, but –'

'I'll walk you back, shall I?'

People jostled against them.

'I was just returning,' said Eleanor, shamed. 'I –'

'Isn't it *cold*?' said Selma.

'Yes,' said Eleanor. She was shivering. She feared she might bleed through her tights and have nothing to change into at Karen's, but she would rather her clothes dried against her skin than return home and feign normality under the knowing gaze of Paula. She wanted to walk alone in the wind and exorcise the essence of Paula. This little known woman by her side made her nervous, her use of make-up and her silence disconcerting. Then she talked, and Eleanor was lulled. The wind whipped her words, so they were ragged and half muted. Propelled by the gritty boom of lorries along the A road to the school the two were gathered in a momentum that fixed itself in Eleanor's memory as flight in its contrast with the usual lunch hour straggle back to school.

'Have you been crying?' said Selma eventually, looking at Eleanor.

'Oh no,' said Eleanor.

'You're probably starting a cold,' said Selma lightly. There was a faint winter blotchiness above Eleanor's lip. Her skin was drained. 'It's hard to feel yourself in the winter. Though you still look beautiful,' she added.

Eleanor shivered. 'No I don't,' she said.

'Yes you do,' said Selma. 'You look lovely.'

'*Me?*'

'Yes, you, madam.'

Eleanor's shoulder muscles unclenched. She stood shivering in an army refuse coat. Her brown hair splayed untidily down her back. Selma touched her arm. 'You're cold. Come on, let's walk.'

They turned away from the road.

'Is it Paula?' said Selma at last.

'No.' Eleanor shook her head.

Selma was silent. She didn't move.

'It's just . . . my stomach hurts,' said Eleanor.

Selma looked at her in silence.

'I'm not going home tonight anyway,' said Eleanor.

'So you've had another argument. Bad?'

Eleanor shrugged. 'I don't know. It was about me and how I'm not . . . something enough. I don't know. I'm supposed to talk to her more or something. But then when I do . . . anyway, I don't think she wants me there.'

'Don't be stupid,' said Selma. 'It'll all have blown over by the time you get home. Act brave. Face it, sweetheart.'

Eleanor smiled slightly. 'I can't.'

'You were a touch rude to her the other week by the sound of it, if I may say, but she thinks you're lovely, she loves you.'

'She certainly doesn't.'

'Of course she does, I know she does, she says so,' said Selma. 'You just can't see it. I'd be so proud to have a daughter like you, so just – come on, forget your last lesson, let's go shopping. You can return to Paula afterwards.'

'No –'

'What we do,' said Selma, putting her hand on Eleanor's back and guiding her up the road, 'is take the short cut to the top of town. Do you like my blouse?' she said suddenly, stopped in the street and turned. She wore a narrow black skirt and an old silk blouse.

'Well – Yes,' said Eleanor.

'Shall we go and buy more?'

Eleanor paused.

'More blouses obviously.'

Eleanor stood there in her slightly faded cotton.

'For me, I mean,' said Selma. 'Will you come and help me?'

'OK,' said Eleanor.

She talked on the street, half to Eleanor, half absorbed in herself, and again Eleanor was lulled, and forgot her fear of the company of older people – of boredom; of her own inadequacy – and relaxed into a cold mental trance as they walked up the road.

Selma took Eleanor's arm, guiding her up a side hill that led to the Narrows, the lane of shops at the top of the town, and into an antique clothes shop where students bought men's shirts, gloves, scraps of silk. The old silks in the shop had taken on the sepia shading of age: Selma's skin was fairer.

'OK, so I want several more blouses, nightdresses maybe,' said

24

Selma, marching in.

She poked into recesses. 'Do you like this one?' she said, emerging with a pile of silks.

'Yes. Nice.'

'A bit more reaction?' she said sharply.

'Well – Yes, well I like the colour. That off-white.'

The watery image of two teachers from the school passed the window; Eleanor instinctively moved behind Selma.

'How about this one?' murmured Selma.

'Well . . . It's exactly the same.'

'It's not. The seaming's quite different. Can you help – these little hooks?'

The shop owner sat in her usual winey haze: middle-aged wives in Totnes were wont to start their own businesses, as had Paula, their own wine bars with Liberty print banquettes, their own natty emporia, until economic reality ended the dream. The owner half smiled at Eleanor from the depths of the shop.

'God save us from becoming Totnes women,' muttered Selma into a pile of blouses.

Eleanor laughed, and hushed herself, but Selma was absorbed in piles of fabric.

'And this one?'

Selma wiped a sleeve across her forehead, black flecks of traffic or sweat making tiny lines across it, the swell of her breasts above her bra visible through limp fabric.

'Yes, but it's all torn under the arm.'

'Is it? Oh, you saved me . . . fifteen pounds. Thank you, Eleanor. So . . . which is best, this or this?'

'Better,' murmured Eleanor.

'What?'

'Oh nothing.'

'I cannot *believe* you are correcting my grammar,' snapped

Selma. She inspected herself in the mirror. The smell of her body, clean sweat, hovered below the flat odour of old silk.

'That's delicate, nice,' murmured Eleanor. Selma pressed her hand on Eleanor's shoulder to balance herself, scrunching her hair, bunching it and letting it drop.

'This is beautiful,' said Selma to the hair. 'This one? This one?'

'Sleeves are rucked.'

They lolled against the door frame.

'But isn't this one sexy?' said Selma.

'If you think baby doll pink is sexy,' said Eleanor.

'Anything, anything, but brown, or sludge, or oats and rust . . . Anything but the uniform of the Totnes Centre. This seething metropolis is hardly a centre of style, is it?' she said within earshot of the shopkeeper.

Selma lifted her arms, and Eleanor obediently pulled a blouse above her head. 'I'd rather look like a Barbie doll than an old hippie in motley garb,' said Selma, leaning against her arm and appraising herself in pale green crêpe. 'Well?'

'Revolting, I think.'

Selma's eyes rested on Eleanor, then she turned away impatiently. 'Well, this?' she said.

'Oh, I love it . . . I really love that one.'

'Do *I* look good in it, though?'

'You look lovely. Really lovely.'

'Thank you.' Selma turned, stroked her hair, held her to her. 'Thank you. Come here. We have to find something for you.'

'Oh no . . .' said Eleanor, 'I . . .'

The crepey warmth of Selma's neck was against Eleanor. Selma held on to Eleanor lightly and studied the reflection in the mirror.

'A present from me to you, for helping me. Or for coming shopping with me. You're good for me. I have to buy you a present. This dress . . . we want something brighter for your colouring. Like . . . this. No. This. You'll look like a sweet kitten in it. Try it on. I'm buying this for you.'

Eleanor stood still and self-conscious in faded cherry-coloured silk; Selma fussed around her, tugging the collar and muttering about covered buttons, her long nails digging into the back of Eleanor's neck as she straightened seams, and she bought them all, a large sagging pile of fabrics with a credit card.

'Now what we have to do,' said Selma, ' – thank you,' she called out to the shopkeeper, 'is get you back through the door of terror – I'll drop you off – and then you just walk in and know that you're really quite clever and really quite gorgeous, and Paula's proud of you. So, Helena Strachan –'

'Eleanor.'

'Eleanor. Remember what I said. Then as soon as a bit of spring arrives, we'll have a white dressy kind of thing on my roof terrace. You can drag along your camel friends, and we'll pose in our dresses and provide a spectacle for the neighbours.'

Selma collected her car and drew up outside the Totnes Centre, the engine ticking over loudly, and kissed Eleanor goodbye, her cheek cold, the smell of powder upon her; and Eleanor realised then that she had been virtually silent, and she wandered about in the wind alone after the car had pulled away, holding alternative imaginary conversations in which she talked prolifically and Selma Healy was both disturbed and intrigued by her. She pictured Selma in her car still suppressing mirth at remarks of such wit that Eleanor was unable to formulate them even with time and the jewel colours of fantasy to play with. Her face was twisted with the intensity of invention, she mouthed snatches of dialogue, and she was stared at as she approached the Centre and entered the bookshop high on ever more brilliant scenarios. Paula looked up at her hopefully, resentfully.

TWO

DOWN THE LANE THAT LED TO WEBBURN, A MILE FROM Widecombe-in-the-Moor, where the Strachans lived, the valley was clotting with growth. Ferns snared the footpaths, the farmers' machinery could be heard in the distance until dark, and the cream tea trade opened its doors for the season.

Eleanor Strachan could tolerate it only by pretending to be a milkmaid. In the spring she was Tess; in the winter a tragic moorland figure, Cathy, Eustacia. Spring was hardest: there was a clear wrung light as a prelude to the high sounds of summer. Wet, diffused breezes filled Eleanor with mild panic, as if losing her grip on an ordered microcosm to an unobtainable world outside, civilisation going on without her beyond the mud and nettles of the lane. Paula thought similarly, but she suppressed it: Tim had almost persuaded her of the glories of the countryside. Eleanor half-heartedly thought of Selma Healy's roof terrace: she caught herself wondering one day whether Selma might be waiting for her, by chance, in the carpark after school, and was embarrassed at the thought, then forgot about it.

Paula survived the country by various means: she pined at times for the town, then told herself she was blessed to be away from it all, this house, this over-abundance of nature outside her window, less barren than the Somerset field, more remote. She had gone through her Lady of the House stage, dreamt of beekeeping, bought a straw hat, joined a tennis club in a village near Exeter; she had been briefly involved with EST; had been a member of a group that was discussing setting up an alternative school in an old church, but had gradually run out of steam. She had sunk into fat, blanketed isolation. Now she had the bookshop, new friends. Wonderful people who had come into the shop and started talking to her.

Eleanor wanted to seal the crack that periodically gaped between herself and the perceived world of adults. Paula's friends would sit around the table, and despite their plodding lack of glamour in Eleanor's eyes, they would fly to heights of sophistication beyond her, lewd and brilliant, leaving her floundering in the shallows. They all had the knowledge of sex. Mature, laughing talks as they drew on cigarettes; a charmed circle of women in their thirties and forties who understood one another through half finished sentences or references that disturbed Eleanor but whose full resonance eluded her. Years ago they had dismissed the doubts that set her nerves rigid. She suspected that Paula excluded her intentionally: suddenly, it seemed, she owned a monopoly on the subjects of childbirth or life in the sixties.

But beyond that, Eleanor scorned them for the humbleness of their achievements, their husbands and mature student BAs, their small businesses and babies. They were vaguely distasteful to her. The room rang with high-pitched voices. They read the *Guardian* Women's Page and rested their chins on their hands to consider an issue; they valued their viewpoints. The lavatory was rank with Blend 37.

*

29

Paula rarely felt wholly at ease. Even at her own party, where the atmosphere was loose-slung, she was an outsider. Having persuaded Tim into an all too rare show of sociability, she wished he would shoulder his share of responsibility for the guests, but he was rooted by the Aga stirring punch, all beard stroking and slow speech. His faintly Nordic attractions were subdued by old corduroy. Paula cast him a look of familiar affection and swallowed the wish to shake him.

She glanced at the taut expanse of her stomach. In one of her more flattering dresses, she drew comfort from a sensation of slimmer shoulders, but the bulk below shadowed her confidence. After eating garlic bread, she surreptitiously negotiated the swell, prodding it painfully as if to punish herself. She listened, half imagining things through the smoke and music, for the door to knock, for the voice of a particular guest. Most people had arrived. She persuaded herself to relinquish her belief that he would turn up, but hopeful nerves flecked any sense of well-being.

There were forty jacket potatoes in the Aga, bulgur, wholemeal pizzas, tahini, tzaziki. Parents of the children's friends drifted in and out of the kitchen; the Totnes Centre crowd hovered together by the table and ate a lot. Paula and Tim's younger set, couples in leather jackets and long skirts, had brought boisterous children called Omri and Clodagh; local photographers and gardeners hung around the punch and talked, as they did every spring, of moving from their council flats into house boats on the river, or of doing up old ambulances and travelling round the country; a few people from the neighbouring houses and farms looked awkward or amused and left early.

A group of boys had arrived. Eleanor was standing across the room watching Sean Kenny. He stood with his crowd in a leather jacket and jeans and fiddled nervously with a cigarette. Men frightened her. She preferred books and photographs. She watched his hands in their unconscious movements and the faintly greasy hair and fine mouth, and longing shivered down her arm to her finger tips like drizzle.

Eleanor wandered away. Paula was talking with a group by the door. She was more relaxed. She smiled at Eleanor and suddenly put her arm round her. They stood there for moments, Eleanor leaning against Paula and Paula hugging Eleanor to her.

Eleanor's gaze flickered from where she stood to the faded denim of Sean's crotch, and again lust plummeted through her so powerfully its effect was almost pain. Her left hand tingled. The world of adults, sex, discomfort. She was aware of wetness on the gusset of her knickers, and pressed herself against the table's edge. She wanted to sink against the shoulder beside her; she wanted her mother to protect her.

'Hello,' mouthed Sean from across the room.

Eleanor left Paula and joined him. 'Hello. Hello, Gary.'

Sean smiled and dropped his gaze. They fell into silence. Eleanor went to fetch him a drink. Tim was still stirring a punch watered down with his favourite hibiscus tea. One of the Totnes Centre workers had complained and poured half a bottle of vodka into it. Poppy was showily screaming at Tim and drinking mugfuls of punch.

Eleanor gulped her drink. 'It's nice to see you again,' said Sean. He drew on a roll-up and flicked the ash into the fire.

'Hi there,' said Rolf, who was sitting in a darkened corner beside the fireplace, eating magic mushrooms with his friends.

'When are we going to the cemetery again, then?' said Sean.

'Oh, I don't know,' said Eleanor. 'Soon. We can take some drink up there.'

'The swot's turning rebellious.'

'Shut up.'

His comparative fairness, his bone structure, were a source of fascination to her. She saw Paula looking at her; their gazes caught in a clash of understanding.

'Oh God, come over here,' said Eleanor.

'Why?'

Paula had returned to the kitchen. 'It's just my mother, she's so nosy.'

Eleanor and Poppy had a joke about Paula that had sprung from a moment of empathy and was now furnished with absurdities. It concerned Paula's 'contraceptive trained eyes', as Poppy had labelled their mother's intrusive perspicacity. Paula had prophesied Eleanor's menarche with motherly greed since she was an underdeveloped ten-year-old; now Poppy was inspiring that same tilt of the head with every mention of a stomach ache. In their imagination Paula had menstruation graphs tacked to her wardrobe door; she had bought X-ray glasses to spot tampons in sock drawers and tubes of spermicide hidden in dark recesses. Her dream was for Eleanor, her best friend, to embrace her and declare, 'I have now experienced sexual intercourse, mother,' so that she could tell her friends, an anxious expression masking secret pride, of her daughter's lost virginity.

Sean and Eleanor fiddled in a nervous limbo. The opposing pull of small talk and resolution kept them immobile. Eleanor felt faintly nauseated. The wetness pooled coldly against her vulva. Her vagina ached with wanting him, but images flapped sickly against desire: knobbly male feet, a tongue thrusting beerily.

'What shall we – ?' said Sean.

'Mmm?' said Eleanor.

'I don't know,' said Sean Kenny awkwardly. He put his hands in his pockets and wrapped his feet around each other.

They were silent. 'Look at your sister!' said Sean.

'Where?'

'She's putting lit fags in her plastic horses' mouths. She'll start a fire!'

He leaned against the staircase. 'Come on,' he muttered, gesturing with his head, and Eleanor followed. They walked up the stairs. Paula and Tim's taste had developed only minimally over the years: the same brown walls as the Somerset house, or bottle green or white with scarab skirting boards, a preponderance of pine, dusty tin toys and local pottery. M. Hulot and Troubadour Coffee House posters alternated with hangings bought in Delhi or Teheran. As they walked along the passage, Eleanor imagined Paula probing telepathically to register their every creak.

In Eleanor's bedroom, old bottles, heaps of black clothes, *Brodie's Notes* were lumped against furniture. The party thumped through the floor, distant then swelling with the clarity of individual voices.

They had had sex together twice before, yet Sean was still shocking to Eleanor in the unfamiliarity of his body. She wasn't sure that she wanted sex at all. It was terrifying. She wanted to have had the experience, not to have it, virginity being the worst stigma. She preferred to touch her vulva idly as she read Victorian novels of great love, or muse over Mr Lennock the English teacher from a safe and stultifying distance.

They kissed. The stubble, the hardness of his hips behind jeans, propelled her into an excitement beyond herself. The repulsion that edged her lust made her want to bolt to safety, but it filled her with a masochistic elation, as if succumbing to duty and pleasing him gave her power and secret sexual pleasure.

He stroked her breasts and pulled her hair back from her forehead so that the shape of her eyes changed and she looked up at him with a different face. He kissed the hollow of her neck; she soothed his taut back under his shirt.

They kissed for a long time, and she parted his hair as his head fell to her shoulder, and ran her fingers through its roots where the fair was a dull mouse. They edged together clumsily. Suddenly it was all hardness, hip bones and legs, the hard seams of jeans, and their weight combined on the bed. Eleanor arched her back. Impatient. She wanted him inside her. Now, fast. Smooth, resisting at the entrance, and then he was inside her, and the shock of fulfilment made her hazy. It filled her, the feeling huge and illicit. The idea that his penis was inside her was supremely exciting. But temporary. Then boredom, the familiar disappointment of repetition. The party was distant. His breath by her neck. An Arthur Rackham fairy tree loomed over her, swung, swam into sharp focus again. His fingers circled her clitoris with urgent pressure. She winced.

Sean's thighs tightened; he glimpsed her through windows of pleasure, and was fleetingly aware of the ridiculousness of his buttocks as they rose and fell in all their whiteness in the home of her parents. His face contorted in a rictus of animal emotion, and she watched cool and objective, and saw his lips crumple and the sweat break out on his back. They hugged in a film of sweat, and, unsatisfied, Eleanor wanted to be full of him again. Voices echoed with horrible proximity beneath the pillow. They looked at each other.

Poppy was semi-inebriated. Paula suggested bed and Poppy laughed at her incredulously. Paula held in her stomach and tilted her head to disguise her slack chin. She was having a fat day: she yielded miserably to the fact. She listened for the door as she talked and filled glasses. Forlorn spurts of hope erupted beneath her disappointment. Poppy lurched round the kitchen in her Christmas glittery socks and attempted to elicit reprimands to which she could respond with loud indignation. Paula was immune to her ploys, so Poppy amplified them.

Poppy was branded by her decade in name and attitude alongside all the Saffrons and Hollys and tamer Lukes. The hippy dream had touched Paula and Tim only with vague longings as they brought up two babies on a small income during its heyday, but they had embraced its after-effects as Tim's burgeoning photographic equipment business financed their numerous explorations. By the time Poppy was born, they were equally absorbed by sisal and the Maharishi. Poppy the foetus was variously Dillon, Ishbel and Lola.

Poppy, the youngest, enjoyed an extravagant freedom full of imperious demands that would have been checked in Eleanor and Rolf. She practised her neighing. She dragged Louisa, Selma's daughter, under the table and demonstrated the exact trumpeting of the lips and inanely rolling eyes. Their screams barely dented the boom of music and talk. They neighed louder until they strained their voices, but Paula placidly lifted more potatoes from the oven.

'I'm going to stay up all night.' Poppy's voice was a reedy shout from under the table.

'All right,' said Paula.

'But *Paul*– What?' Left with nothing to rebel against, the foundations of her act crumbled.

'Shall I bring down Owlet and your tape recorder for you?' said Paula.

Poppy ignored her and waited for a lead from Louisa, whose more devious brand of mutiny she admired.

Paula slipped from the room. She yanked down an anorak from its hook in the hall and wore it like a cape over her party dress as she opened the front door to a slap of cold spring air beyond the porch. The house thudded mutely mere feet away; the outbuildings moved like shadows, cats, in the dark as she focused on the distance. Cars were piled up outside the house, mounting the bank of the road, reversed into a muddy section beside Poppy's pony's field. Paula wove her way through them, gripping mirrors and bonnets so she wouldn't trip in the dark, but the row of vehicles trailed disjointedly up the lane, and there was no engine sound in the distance, no David Harpur slamming a Honda door. A couple came out of the house; Paula ducked behind a car and crouched on the ground, their hushed chirruping reaching her through the stillness, and she sat crouched there long after they had left, the hem of her dress dampening on the ground, and wondered whether she should stay there like that all night, when Tim would notice, whether she should shit into the leaves and grass, crapping out her fatness in one go.

She shivered and returned to the house, and Selma Healy saw her in the corner of the room and instinctively knew to sympathise, touching her and silently handing her a cheese pie and a napkin.

Selma's hair was pulled tightly from her face, so it formed smooth sections over skin that was less smooth than the hair. She looked somewhat careworn and artificial that evening, her exhaustion from the week's work and from seeing Louisa through a school crisis visible on her face through the attempted disguise of make-up. The face was a palette of extremes: pale skin, red lipstick, but she emanated a gentleness that made Paula want to touch in return, because she seemed so tactile and assured. They stood in the corner and talked, Paula blank with alternate disappointment and anticipation.

Selma looked over at Eleanor, but Eleanor, caught by shyness, pretended not to see her and looked away. Selma was aware that these children of Paula and Tim's had insecurities that broke through their life of wall painting on barns and musical instruments. The younger two were more affected by the progressive school ethos; the oldest was an upstart who thought she was clever, but she betrayed something else.

'So was it a good fuck?'

Selma Healy laughed hot breath into Eleanor's ear.

Eleanor stopped still. Her face flooded. She looked at Selma questioningly. Selma laughed.

'Could you – ?'

'No I couldn't. What, with this racket going on?'

Sean slipped down the staircase. He cast a glance at Tim.

'How do you know – ?'

'I am a woman of this world,' she said lightly.

Eleanor looked blank.

'You disappear for forty minutes with a bloke, you come back reeking of self-consciousness. And your hair's brushed.'

'Look at them all,' said Eleanor, sweeping her hand around in a rushed attempt to change the subject. 'How can they all accept being so ordinary without loathing themselves? Without being embarrassed that they're not famous? Or they haven't done something special in their lives?'

'A mystery, eh?' replied Selma.

'I don't want to be like that, *ever*,' said Eleanor, panic in her voice. 'It frightens me. Look, they're *thirty* or *forty* and they haven't done anything, just got children.'

Selma was silent.

'Is it true you wrote a book?' said Eleanor, emboldened by Poppy's claim that she had seen Louisa's mother in a magazine.

'Well I've written three books, but people only seem to know about one of them,' she said.

'Oh,' said Eleanor.

She pictured the collapsed condom in her waste paper basket and the tang of warm rubber hanging in the air like an accusation, imagining its aroma clinging to her.

Selma laughed at Eleanor again, and made her blush. She was teasing, affectionate. Eleanor suddenly felt part of a conspiracy in which they shared knowledge exclusive to women. This woman, too, had pleasured men. She would have challenged them, honoured them in allowing them access to her, firm and rhythmic. She had taken men – how many men? – inside her and knew, like Eleanor, that ache and fullness. Eleanor contracted her muscles to test out the slight soreness she felt. She looked up at Selma and felt somehow favoured, a sensation which had no precursor amongst Paula's friends, who were indifferent or perceived her only in the context of her youth.

The music was vibrating through the floor. Rolf reached out to turn off a light. Selma appeared grainy beside Eleanor, half shot with dark.

Eleanor was vaguely discomfited, but she was weighted to the sofa. Selma looked her straight in the eye, older, glittering; it seemed to Eleanor as though she were plunging into her. She caught the edge of Selma's breath, a muted unpleasantness of garlic and an older digestion system. Its aftertaste combined with the dregs of her perfume and was somehow jaded and exciting. The skin on Selma's neck was paler but fascinatingly rougher than Eleanor's. Eleanor imagined the layer of warmth at the neck where Selma's dress met her skin, and wanted to dip into the warmth.

'Why are you called that?' said Eleanor.

'Selma? It's terrible, like a fat Swedish grandmother, isn't it? It's from some far back relatives of my mother's.'

'I like it – it's pretty, it's strange.'

David Harpur turned up at half past eleven. Paula exhaled tension like gas. She found him a place by the fire, near Rolf and his crowd who were slumped in a magic mushroom-induced torpor. David Harpur leant forward with his hands pressed between his knees, the only man in the room wearing a suit. Its dark angles set off his strawberry blondness. To Paula, an oasis of peace grew by the fire. She sailed over to Tim, and realised that she no longer felt excluded from her own party, a realisation that touched her with sadness. Tim finally left his pan on the Aga, caught sight of David and hesitated. David rose, and Tim threw his arms round him and hugged him close.

Eleanor looked askance at Sean and wondered if he was noticing her quarter profile. His hands were in his pockets, and he leaned against a doorpost deep in conversation with her friend Karen and a couple of men. She wanted to press her lips against his and feel the wet probe of his tongue again.

By mutual consent, they had ignored one another since returning downstairs. Eleanor watched him jerk his head in laughter at a comment of Karen's and resented him for reverting to normality after having had sex with her. She looked at his groin and could scarcely comprehend that his hips had been flailing, pumping, minutes or hours ago. He had thrust into her and taken his pleasure. She had pleasured him. That same penis now nestled limp and satisfied in his underpants while his mind was elsewhere. He had been erect in excitement at her, inspired by *her*, hard and pink-grey rubber sheathed. Then he looked over at her and she smiled inwardly at the memory of clandestine shared pleasure.

'Oh, hello Paula,' said Selma suddenly.

'How's things?' said Paula. She glowed.

'Paula, this is lovely. Just lovely,' said Selma.

'Paula!' bellowed Rolf.

'Oh,' said Paula. 'Selma, there's someone I'd love you to meet. Excuse me a minute.'

Selma laid her head on the back of the sofa so that her eyes were level with Eleanor's and talked, and Eleanor strained to catch her sentences, carried as they were only by a faint swell of intonation. Her voice was so measured and lacking in emotion that Eleanor floated on its surface until she was barely listening. She clenched her muscles against the ache inside her. She thought she had been wrung dry, but wetness clung, and irritated her soreness.

She wondered who the guest by the fire was, and why Paula was now so animated. Without recognising him, his face troubled her as though there was something phoney in that aura of sweet serenity. She was unreasonably indignant with Paula for merely speaking to a man, though Tim sat beside her. The face swam in front of her, the distinct blue of his eyes in all their persuasive goodness now placed in an older and fleshier set of features which re-arranged themselves in a sickening configuration before reverting, the image slipping her grasp. She talked to Sean's friend Gary, then looked again and, catching him full face, knew who he was. David Harpur was sitting by the fire. Eleanor stared at Paula until she turned, and raised her brows questioningly. Paula nodded, smiling assent, and beckoned her.

Eleanor watched Paula, plump in her animation, and remembered how she was in the mornings when Eleanor would take her breakfast into the sitting room to avoid hearing her eat. The dressing gown. Coffee. The small, frank slurps. She had a disembodied memory of the strong bone of the bridge of David Harpur's nose. She despised herself. She wanted to run into the arms of someone who would save her from her failures.

Her attention balked. Thoughts fell into fragments. She sat perched by the sofa arm and swung her leg.

All that Eleanor was able to focus on was Sean, who was still avoiding her, though their tacit agreement had by now clearly expired. The notion of masculinity filled her with another wave of

40

nausea: the rubbery smell, David, Sean with his nervous thinness and thrusting buttocks merged. She had provided him with gratification, and the entrance to her vagina still hurt. How dare he? Those fingers, predictably fiddling with a reefer, had traced patterns of pleasure over her breasts, and they had forgotten already. She wanted to shriek at him. She turned round and faced David. Equally cruel. His hair, now flecked with grey, adding to the ashen softness of his face. The clear kind eyes of the guru. His teeth were too white when he talked.

Paula and David Harpur were ruminating over old times by the fire. Paula let guests fend for themselves and sat smiling with her chin propped on her hand. Tim organised a game for the children in the corner, stocky toddlers jumping in their dungarees, hurtling themselves into the centre of the room.

David Harpur had arrived in their lives a whole decade previously. Taunton by way of the Coromandel Coast, where he had studied under his spiritual master for some months after migrating from continent to continent. Tim met him one day in the Riverside Café in Taunton, and they talked at such length that Tim was late for his afternoon conference, and he casually invited David to stay when he was supervising his first meetings and meditation sessions in the area. So while David Harpur started disseminating the message of his master, Nirhanjan, in the West Country, he made his base at Tim and Paula's, where it seemed to the children that their lives were guided by spiritual mentors, or people with specific dietary advice, people whose particular vision Paula and Tim easily absorbed.

The children nervously anticipated the effects of newcomers on Paula, because with each new phase of her spiritual life the household routine was irredeemably altered; Paula's absences increased; it was assumed the children would participate in the flux and flow of each spiritual shift. When David Harpur arrived,

Paula changed once again.

Now Paula hadn't seen David for years. He had only returned to England in recent months, and eventually she had heard about it on the grapevine.

'They're simple, fat great failures,' spat out Eleanor, to herself or to Selma who was sitting near her. 'All these people who follow stupid gurus. They just haven't got successful careers so they follow someone else like bleating sheep. They've got a kind of blankness underneath it all, a uniform wall you hit when you talk to them. Do you know what I mean?'

Selma Healy had shifted guises. Now tinged with earth mother, seeming to embrace Eleanor though she only rested against her shoulder. Eleanor felt the warmth of Selma's skin beneath the cloth of her dress and Selma's breast against her shoulder, too frank in its curves. She saw her for the first time as the mother of a child: it was not an identity that fitted her easily. She drifted against her. Eleanor's eyes throbbing drunken purple against their lids, she imagined Selma lying in fields, the grass around the Glastonbury Tor of her own childhood outings, Selma's breasts facing the sky and women and children draped around her. Eleanor felt she knew how the fleshy nub of Selma's nipple would taste in her mouth, then surfaced to the present in a rush. She wanted Selma to go, because she suddenly dreaded her going.

Paula, David and Tim were deep in conversation. Tim ran his beard through his fingers and let Paula, as was customary, do the talking. Paula bloomed. This man laid a sense of well-being upon her like a gift wreath at her feet. He emanated approval; the vaguely sexual nuance of his smile iced her self-containment. She marvelled at her composure in the face of it. The shreds of nerves had tailed away with his arrival. The thighs that had been folded and stony beneath large knickers, the ballooning of her stomach, were desirable, a paradigm of womanliness.

Tim relaxed. He laughed. 'David! I just can't believe you're here. You know . . . it's so great to see you. It's unbelievable.'

'Thanks, Tim,' said David.

Eleanor leant her head against the back of the chair and talked to Selma.

'Because I was – difficult – it made things worse for Paula when David Harpur was around because he was, like, their guru, and Paula was humiliated when I didn't behave, and so everything at home got a lot worse when he was there. I just couldn't seem to do anything right at all.'

'In what way?'

'Well – I was just this difficult child. I was naughty and they said I spoilt the atmosphere when David was in the house, so then I hated him being there, and then Paula got more upset.'

'You probably weren't, you know,' said Selma.

'Weren't what?'

'Naughty.'

'Oh I was.'

'What did you do?'

'I . . . I'm not sure.'

'Did you break things on purpose, or hurt anyone, or burn the house down?'

'No!'

'You probably weren't *naughty* at all. What does naughty mean anyway?'

'It was more I was *difficult* to deal with. Rude, or whatever.'

'I doubt it. What does that mean? All children are "difficult" sometimes in their parents' eyes. Louisa's a lovely child, but sometimes I'd like to shove her into a reform school. It's just an adult label conveniently slapped on you at the time that you've swallowed and accepted ever since. You were probably just a normal, nice little kid. Anyway, who wouldn't react against some strange man being in the house?'

'Oh,' said Eleanor. 'I never thought of that. How strange.'

'Sweet silly girl,' said Selma.

'It can't be,' said David, coming over. 'This cannot be little Eleanor Strachan!' He laughed in genuine astonishment. 'It's so hard to imagine . . .' Eleanor looked up. He leant over to hug her or take her by the hand.

'Could you leave us, please?' said Selma.

Eleanor dreamt as she fell asleep. A drunken, banging headache sleep. She was following a tall dream figure, Selma, calling after her. Through the crowds the figure didn't hear her; Eleanor ran to catch up. She could never see the figure clearly: she shifted between dream frames, disappeared then became visible again. Eventually the woman stopped and turned round. As Eleanor reached her at last, they hugged, the touch solid and real after fluid images, and it was Paula's thighs smooth against hers, and she felt, in horror, the scratchiness of her pubic hair. She drifted in and out of sleep, and woke with the aftertaste of a dream memory of freckle-rimmed eyes and a quilted stomach.

THREE

THEY WERE NOT A PROPER FAMILY, THOUGHT ELEANOR. They pretended. There was an indefinable cohesion lacking. The laughter at meal times, the swearing laissez-faire, hovered over a void of which Eleanor, and sometimes Paula, was uneasily aware. Eleanor nervously anticipated boredom when they were together, as if the responsibility for failure were hers. The comforting weave of traditions – teasing Tim, pulling horse faces at Poppy, abbreviated reference points – cemented the illusion, but when it was shaken they were dispersed and somehow unconnected.

For some years, Paula had watched Eleanor and marvelled that she had given birth to this separate, beautiful, disdainful being. Since Eleanor had become aware of incipient power at the age of fifteen, Paula had seen her drift away into her own world of achievement and contempt. She herself was only the begetter of such a glorious being, a tired old hag.

Then Eleanor would stumble self-consciously over a phrase she had stolen from Hardy, make a mistake with her lipstick and parade it defiantly, uncertainly, and she was Paula's transparently clumsy child again. Paula knew all her tricks. But then Paula would stop in awe to remind herself that those very same lips had

45

suckled her, desperate for life, that she had scraped shit from nappies covering that very body that hovered so disdainfully, independently, by the table. She who had covered her hands in excrement was now an object of embarrassment.

Eleanor's metamorphosis from prickly child to young woman relieved Paula. Paula no longer had to kick so hard against her daughter's inadequacies. Her children had blossomed in the climate of liberal ease she had created, rich with the fruits of her new-found knowledge, but they repaid her by showing her no respect. They didn't seem to love her. Even Rolf, Paula reflected, had withdrawn from her. She had instilled such confidence and freedom in them that Eleanor had never assumed she must get married or defer to her parents or keep from speaking her mind, and took it all for granted. No gratitude. No idea that anything might have been different. The world was Eleanor Strachan's oyster, and her friends', all those privileged beings she brought back to the house, and Paula's pride was marred.

They would thunder through the house shouting casual greetings at Paula. Part of the show Eleanor laid on for visiting friends was a demonstration of how insulting she was allowed to be to her parents. Singing in the kitchen with Sean and his guitar and Rolf's friends loping through in socks for more tea, the bags left on the oven, and Eleanor showering the bounties of the Strachan household upon her friends, getting up on the table to dance and calling out for Tim to bring her more tapes. Effortless clothes. Sniggers. Smiles that would let Paula know she hadn't made it. Eleanor was a different class, a different race. The room prickled with mockery.

'I feel I'm really not appreciated,' said Paula.

Selma and Paula sat on the front lawn at Webburn House and, a recent innovation by Paula who was aspiring to the sophistication Eleanor hinted that she lacked, drank spritzers. Paula had been lying on her bed that hot morning looking down on the roof of the barn opposite, the saplings beyond it that had shot up along the river. Sun motes drifted across the carpet illuminating a shorn expanse of vacuumed regularity, to her pleasure. When the carpet was dirty, her eye would return to its clumps of wool, its inexplicable oily specks, like someone obsessed, even though the dirt itself did not trouble her. She would stare at the loose fluff and imagine gagging on it like a cat choking on hair balls. She would circle the room, then gravitate towards it again as if demented.

That morning she watched the haze of sunlight and felt the thick hot weave of her bedspread beneath her and stroked thoughts of David Harpur across her skin. Across her breasts. The hairs on his legs would be golden if he stood by the window. She conjured him up, and he seemed almost to appear, bleach-white, like Michelangelo's David himself, the two images fused in the slanting glare. Age had not withered him, she mused. His legs would be firm still, he would stand there, and she could smell the skin of his chest, of his chest hair and nipples, aroused by the warmth. Just the fleeting damp kiss of his erection touching her thigh as she leant over to hold his chest to her face.

She got up and drew the curtains near her bed, so half the room was shaded, and David could climb out of the blinding haze at the end of the room and into the shadow of her bed. She rubbed her thighs and kissed him in her mind so forcefully that she felt her lips loosen with longing, with the imagined sudden cool of wetness as he ran his tongue inside her lips, then her hand edged down her stomach and lifted her skirt and worried that the expensive bedspread might stain. But it never did. Images of her lugging it to the dry cleaners on Fore Street in Totnes, the weight in a laundry bag, paying the woman, interspersed with visions that were now fragmented, the golden man's face breaking into cubist shadows, and as she came she was thinking of the builder working on the house down by the Splash pumping into his girlfriend, and wondered why it was that she could never orgasm thinking of those she desired.

Selma stretched out on the cloth on the grass and eased into this respite from work. It was so warm, Paula and Selma had both decided to let Jude the shoemaker's sister look after the bookshop while they spent the afternoon on the moor. They lay about in the garden.

'Why do you suppose he takes you for granted?' said Selma. 'Though in my experience, I have to say, it's quite standard. Aren't they dumb idiots. If I were Tim, *I'd* appreciate you.'

'Perhaps one of these days I'll go out there and pick up a toy boy!' Hurt behind the bright tones. A vision of David floated across the image of fair skinned youth.

'Paula Strachan, you're worthy of better things. Tim absolutely adores you, I'm sure, but men are thoughtless to say the least. Possibly it never occurs to him that his feelings for you need to be overtly manifested from time to time. He's been married too long. Like my dear husband.'

'Actually, he was always more or less the same. I don't seem to interest him . . . he doesn't – desire me in any way. What am I supposed to do? I can't force the man if it's not there. When we *do*, it's very good, but honestly at the moment – well, he's entirely uninterested in sex, really.'

'You –'

'Once I told him, in Somerset, I was just going to have to go out and pick up some farmer, and that roused him into action, but it was short lived.'

Her voice was plaintive. She continued, then stopped short. Selma was gazing at an aeroplane above them.

'How's Louisa?' said Paula.

'Louisa's fine. I'm very proud of her progress this year. I think Louisa Mecklen will grow up to be a formidable woman. But we're talking about *you*, Paula.'

Paula swallowed the inevitable tears. 'The thing is, I don't know how to say this, I know I shouldn't care, but what if it's not just that he's not especially sexually motivated?' Paula knew as the words tumbled that she spoke of David Harpur too: the poignancy, the sharp edge, were all for him; he compounded her dilemma. Her voice lowered to a whine of honesty. 'Selma, I feel past it! I see the way Tim admires Eleanor – her slimness and clothes – and I just feel past it. I mean, who's to say he doesn't fancy all her friends? He doesn't know he's doing it, he could be attracted to all sorts of other girls her age – my *daughter*'s age – and how can I compete with that? I can't even begin, you know. It's so hurtful and degrading to feel undesired like this. You wouldn't know. Even if there was someone else, I think I've lost confidence.'

Paula felt, when Selma left, that she had trampled over their friendship with her pitiful confessions. Selma had comforted her, but she seemed absent, merely fulfilling an appointed role. Even as she hugged Paula and assured her of her desirability and strength, all that she had achieved as a woman and mother, her gaze swivelled disconcertingly round the garden and her words lacked spontaneity. Selma Healy, with her rarefied style and her formidable child, could sail into her garden and shower her with strength and support, and then swan off again. Paula went inside and put her head on the table and cried and cursed David.

Rolf walked past with a sandwich.

'Make us one,' said Paula.

He presented her with two wedges of unbuttered bread and a toppling pile of salad and cheese, then returned to his room. He spent large parts of his day smoking, looking out of his bedroom window. If he was downstairs, he maintained a silent sneer. He had been suspended during the summer term at Dartington, and hadn't bothered to return.

Paula sat at the table balancing her sandwich. It was dry and bulky, but she stuffed her mouth as if mothering a sore, swallowing lumps with tea. Eleanor had been in bed. She came downstairs, and her head spun with lethargy. She fought through the film of sleep residue. The sight of Paula at the table in her Laura Ashley dress copied from her friend Margy made her want to bellow in frustration, to bolt to a place where achievement and intellect and expensive jewellery reigned.

Paula looked down as she spoke and Eleanor caught the edge of a tear on her old eyelashes and in her mind she kissed her, kissed the tear that streaked beneath the lid, but in reality she couldn't bear to touch her beyond a perfunctory hug of greeting.

The thought of Paula having emotions hit her. What went on in her mind? Perhaps she needed a fuck. Eleanor nearly giggled. The idea that her overweight mother could be randy was ridiculous. Solid thighs wet with lust. Hips thrusting out of control against a man's. Sidling up to some neighbour, glance suggestive under those freckled lids, asking him to fuck her. Her breath was always thick with coffee; she spoke hesitantly under the guise of assertiveness; her earlobes sagged.

Then perhaps, thought Eleanor, as a human, another human, she had thoughts like her own. Paula had a mind through which darted fears, hopes, little imaginings. Eleanor had always perceived her as too insensitive for such emotions, the terrifying critic of earlier years. Now she had an image of her high up on the back garden, taking a coffee break, drinking her Blend 37 alone while her Centre friends, younger and relaxed, drank Barley Cup at each other's flats in Totnes. What did she think about up there for hours at a time? She had such pride in her plants, but her family weren't interested and mimicked her eulogies, so she showed guests around unobtrusively. Did they hurt her, wondered Eleanor? Her hours of dedication to those creepers and vegetables that all looked the same, and they ate her potatoes and were irritated that she wanted them to comment. She worked, and she was not noticed or praised. Eleanor suddenly remembered finding a calorie book hidden in the pile of tea towels in the dresser drawer: despite the truisms learnt from the Totnes Centre feminists, Paula secretly struggled. Overweight, more sparsely educated than her children – her faulty memory was a favourite joke – perhaps she cried in bed and had wild dreams up in the garden.

It was the remoteness that exacerbated things. That western fork of land that branched away from the body of the country, connected to a larger life only by the M5; beyond that, Cornwall and the sea. It had its own slower rhythms and watered-down customs.

Dartmoor was high deserted moorland, vast tracts of granite, bog and gorse growth. In its dips were rivered valleys where the houses were built, the valleys so green and water fed, like lettuce, green splashing the larger tracts. In summer the moor framed postcard vistas: rocky outcrops, ponies, high blue skies. 'Oh, how beautiful to live here,' said visitors. Eleanor wanted to get in such careless admirers' cars and drive back with them to London. Streams lined lanes and fattened over doorsteps in the winter; baked cottages stood flush by breezeblock bungalows built by the sons of established farming families who had tacit influence over the council, while newcomers were refused planning permission for minor conversions in local granite. Bearded men in khaki jerseys cruised the lanes in trucks for the Forestry Commission.

The military held its target practice on the higher reaches.

Around Webburn, the villages were barely villages, rather clusters or hamlets oozing mud, leading from lanes bordered by dry stone walling. New evergreen forests were changing the landscape. Muddy pine-lined tracks led to B & Bs and cream teas with views of the tors. Hamlets were frequently marooned under snow, the snow plough reaching only the larger roads; traffic was delayed by free-grazing animals. Buzzards and military aeroplanes wheeled and shot overhead, and rain clouds flooded the light skies, staining grass and windows with sudden dullness.

The moor was rife with rumours: a man who ate grass and wore Lederhosen; incest between twins who lived in a converted church; but mostly it was rife with monotony, sedimented layers of prejudice, the despair of mud on new shoes, and slow dialect, ignorance; and fields, fields meeting the sky, no sound but the buzzing of electric fencing; the knowledge that you could look out of a window and absolutely nothing would be happening, only trees stirring, and nothing happening later, fewer birds on the telegraph line; and television aerials always going wrong, and farm machinery jamming the roads, and stifling bleak beauty everywhere.

Eleanor thought that if she made herself thin and clever she would escape. That people were happy to work at the Unigate Dairy or Harris's Bacon Factory or selling regional crafts at the Cider Press Centre made her almost rigid with panic in case she were trapped in the same destiny. She was slack-mouthed with a mixture of scorn and fear. She begged lifts to London on Tim's occasional business trips, but that meant missing school, and good marks were the key to escape. That people could pronounce local names with all the gravitas of proper towns, capital cities – 'Going up Newton way,' they said, 'A day out down Plymouth for the shopping centre' – cemented her determination.

There was a girl at school, her mother had been painted by Picasso. She had been his model, a young French girl with a high blonde ponytail. And such things gave Eleanor hope, because there were these people in the world beyond reading about them; in her world even, someone at school.

Selma Healy knew that the West Country would slowly hem her in. She had half known it before her retreat there. She planned to live there for a year or more, sort out her marriage, complete her book. But she found she couldn't bear to think about her marriage: she wanted to leave it on one side, like a painful sore, in a corner of her mind. The longer she was separated from that arrogant husband, the more industrious she became. Then she'd probe the sores and they'd throw up this grief or that cause for amazement or a certain never resolved argument, and she knew that she would stay on in this place because she couldn't return to London. But the flavour of her was wrong here: she clashed with the ethos.

Eleanor had seen her from the window, lying on the lawn with Paula that afternoon, like cut-outs in the sun, Paula in one of her large dresses, Selma pale haired and restless. The hard light illuminated the lines on her face and the individual hairs that drifted around her head. Eleanor remembered Selma's scent and she could almost smell it rising to her bedroom in the sun. She was Paula's yet not like Paula. She was rude and distracted and very charming. She waved at Eleanor from the garden then turned back to Paula.

Eleanor felt personally affronted, though she knew she had no grounds. She wanted to clutch at some indefinable quality Selma possessed. She lay in the shadows of her bedroom and pulled off her clothes. Her nipples were a light brown. Her pubic bone was raised, the mound dark and stark in contrast to her skin. The bedroom was all in shadow, the window so small and deep set.

The sun was crazed through its smears and irregularities. Light patterns shivered on the ceiling above her, throwing gleams and shadows on her skin. She stretched and pulled in her stomach so that her hip bones rose as ridges, her pubic bone arched higher. She kissed her own arm, dragging her mouth along it. It smelled of the Totnes swimming pool.

She imagined Sean's penis penetrating her below her pubis, and the thought excited her, as it did when she lay down in the back of the car and the engine's vibrations bred such fantasies that by the end of the journey her breathing had changed. But when she saw him, with his leather jacket and Adam's apple and smell of alcohol, she was afraid.

Eleanor lay there, and nothing moved, nothing changed. Light on the ceiling, the river, nothing. The house was cool. Nothing moved, but there was that woman outside. She got up and wrapped herself in a sheet and looked out of her window at the garden. She hid behind her curtain so she was concealed. Selma Healy was lying on the lawn apparently talking to the sky, while Paula anxiously addressed her profile. Eleanor felt a strange muted desperation at being excluded, though she would not join the conversation for fear of Paula's judgement.

Lying on the lawn, Selma looked like a forties screen extra. An ageing actress. Eleanor thought of training her telephoto lens on her from behind the window, as she and her friends had done to their English teacher at school, then wondered why. Breezes edged and drifted; there was bird song; she felt agitated.

Later, Paula returned to the house and sorted through a sheaf of forms from the DHSS. She filled in sections concerning Rolf's availability for work, what kind of jobs he'd ideally like to do. 'Music. Work in a recording studio. Anything artistic,' she ventured. She looked down at what she'd written and felt a wave of anxiety about Rolf. She could hear a monotonous drum beat emitting from the stereo in his room. She realised how hurt he must be, somehow, for being suspended and unqualified, and wanted to hug him for his gruff manner and his sweat, all his shortcomings. When he finally emerged, she saw the spots under his stubble and wondered if she could help with them, perhaps try out some new antiseptic lotion from the doctor, and give him a bit of money to buy new clothes. Poor Rolf. She had responded to his hostility and neglected him.

'"Artistic"!' exclaimed Eleanor, swooping round the corner. '"*Artistic*"! Oh yes. The Job Centre's got hundreds of jobs for fresco painters. Packer in Unigate is what he'll get, more like.'

Rolf turned round, unaware.

'What?' he said.

'Paula thinks you'll get a job as a pop star if you go up the Dole! Why can't he fill in the form himself? Honestly, they'll crack up laughing when they see this! I don't mean to be . . . but with half a CSE . . .'

Rolf had rattled Eleanor's chest against walls. He had thumped her seven-year-old body, her seven-year-old verbal weapons against his five-year-old kicking legs. She was a punch bag. She read her big girl books in her rapid, high voice, skimming and pouting over long words while he struggled with individual letters. He thumped her ribs, he thumped and thumped, a little bull, winding her, jolts behind the sternum, and more and more, like the satisfaction of scratching an itchy sore, pounding her like a drum between her ribs behind her dress, Miss Clever-Clever.

'That's pretty bitchy,' said Paula. 'Rolf could get something in the music line. You never know. And it's a shame to waste his talent.'

'Yes, Paula,' said Eleanor. 'Why are you filling it in for him, though?'

'Why are you asking questions?' said Paula. 'Eleanor, I . . .' she said. She closed her mouth. Eleanor began to tick inside with nerves.

Like a cat in the house, her long nails, thought Paula. Rolf a long-tongued dog. Eleanor a cat.

Eleanor escaped into the garden. The afternoon was cooling into spring thinness. She saw that woman walking down the lane, once more cut out in the sharpness of light.

Selma called to her. 'I wanted to walk about the fields before I go. It's such a lovely day.'

She was milky and full. She wore a wedding ring. The hardness she gave off was in her perfume and her face powder, which appeared incongruous under the glare of the sky.

They met by the gate. They hugged slightly, involuntarily. 'Let's walk this way,' said Eleanor urgently. 'I've got to get out of the house.'

'OK, let's walk this way,' said Selma, 'but I've got to go, and really, I really can't sort out your problems with your mother. You'll have to do it yourself.'

'Oh. Well yes, I will,' said Eleanor defensively. She glanced at Selma.

'Everything is so beautiful, so utterly gorgeous,' said Selma. 'Look at the way the stream fans out over this rock, it's so even, like a woman's hair. Look at that moss on the wall, it's almost fluorescent.'

'Yes, and look at the horse shit in the middle of the road – so beautiful!' said Eleanor.

'Oh, horse shit's quite beautiful really,' said Selma. 'Look how spherical and dun coloured it is. It's only grass, it's not repulsive like the dog shit all over the streets in London.'

'Oh oh, look at that military plane, magnificent, like a golden eagle poised over the valley,' Eleanor mocked, as a low flying plane thundered over the fields to the left of them.

'But it *is* all beautiful,' Selma said. 'The moors are so wild, there's a purity in that wildness, you don't get it anywhere else.'

'You only say that because you can escape,' said Eleanor.

'I can't, I'm going to stay,' said Selma.

They paused on the road. Their feet scraped stones as they walked up the hill, their breath synchronised. Eleanor's complexion became ruddy; her arms were goose pimpled, and then she began to sweat. Selma remained pale, but she was breathless.

'But you have that as your – your context,' said Eleanor. 'You have a mental escape, whereas I just panic.'

'But you can leave home soon, and then you can go where you like.'

'I know, I know,' said Eleanor. 'I just have to get my exams, and I need money too. But I'm still stuck here *now*, *now*, and that's what counts. And I love it in literature, and I love to photograph it. I read *Wuthering Heights* or *Tess of the d'Urbervilles*, and then all I want to be is living in the wildness of the country, the wilder the better, and I dream, and it's all wild and wind whipped and kind of springy or balmy in my head, and then I put down the book, and there I am, I *am* there, but to get up on the moor you have to edge past these wet dustbins that leave fungusy gunge on your clothes as you pass them, and everything out there smells of damp coal, dogs, soaking moss, and then some car with a wide-faced neighbour comes trundling down the lane as you're climbing to the Wuthering Heights bit, and you have to have a conversation and you go all shy and they think you're stupid, and then when you get up on the high land, and avoid the ice-cream van parked by a tor, there's the riding school out there, all hearty and horsey in a line, and they lean down from their great heights to patronise you. And then there's all this wind and sky that hurts your

57

throat. But it's quite exciting. But then your shoes that you want to wear in town start sinking in the swampy bits, and then you run along and jump gorse bushes for a while, and probably some tourist in a car thinks there's a madwoman set loose on the moors, or someone escaped from the Prison. And then you come back and someone needs you to help push a car down the hump before the lane goes uphill, because car engines never start here in the mornings. See?'

'Yes, I see,' said Selma.

'It's like when I went to Rouen, and somewhere in my head I must have thought I'd see a Madame Bovary, or thought I *was* Madame Bovary, because somehow I was disappointed. I only want to live here if I can be filmed living here, or be in a book.'

'That's because you're such a little "Oh, the wind in my hair", long-haired little Kate Bush kind of Emily Brontë girl, and you have a romantic ideal of yourself. Me, I'm all functional and practical with just a bit of romance thrown in, so when I go to Finland, I don't expect Sibelius' violin concerto to be transmitted magically from the mountains. But maybe I'd take a tape of it. Duck, there's a wide-faced neighbour coming towards us in his car!'

Selma grabbed Eleanor and hid her behind her back. Eleanor almost fell over. She screamed. 'Don't!' She scrabbled away from Selma and giggled. 'It's the man from the farm up the road, he hates us, he'll think I'm a lunatic.'

The driver slowly cruised past, nodding at them.

'Oh God,' said Eleanor, giggling, 'he's the one whose wife thinks Paula's a witch because she caught her picking nettles after she'd bought *Food For Free* and decided we all had to eat nettle soup. It was disgusting.'

Selma looked down at Eleanor. 'Sweetheart,' she said, 'I have to leave you. Go back and read *Cold Comfort Farm*,' she said as she opened her car door. 'I'm only mouthing stuffy fogey platitudes by rote. You can come to London with me next time I drive up.'

'Can I?'

'Of course.' Selma shrugged.

Eleanor stared at the car as it left. It drove away in a scraping of gravel, and disappeared, and she saw it small in the distance on the Corndon route, and then it was gone. She was alone. The cows were shifting behind the trees. A trail of smoke rose from the valley. She ran frantically back home, and she *was* Tess, she *was* Bathsheba. She rounded the corner, and there on the back lawn was Paula with David Harpur.

The back garden rose behind the house, greener, wetter, than the lumpy front lawn. It was an evening sun trap, facing the hillier horizon to the west. The washing line rotated idly there with faint squeaks. A gate, a wall and the dustbins sealed it from the road, and Eleanor could only see it through a gap between the gate post and the wall.

David Harpur's occasional appearance was accepted as a fact by Rolf, unquestioning as he always was. In Eleanor, Paula knew, it would cause instant suspicion. Though banned by Poppy and Eleanor from questioning any aspect of their lives – she was '*incredibly* nosy' – they would bombard her with a barrage of questions, assumptions, inferences, when anything disturbed the normal flow of life.

Eleanor walked round to the front of the house to let herself in. She went up to the bathroom and craned her head carefully round the window. She saw David's bullet head from the back. His good looks were a cliché against the green green grass. Nature clashed with him: he belonged to a television screen or a dinner party.

Paula glimpsed Eleanor like a ghost at the window. 'Eleanor!' she called, but Eleanor had disappeared.

Powerless. She sat pinned back against the wall and the minutes ticked, and she hoped she was not ludicrously on show like trapped vermin.

She remembered feeling hopeless, picked upon, in the face of those two as a child. Her awkwardness was spiny, overt, like a piece of fringe that curves up and bounces out of line, so that people are irritated and pitying at once, all attempts to plaster it down to conformity having publicly failed.

Paula had been exhausted by the round of washing, feeding, cleaning; by going to Weight Watchers with Penny from the farm and bingeing in a field on the way back, the two of them laughing like hysterical school girls verging on tears; by her search for spiritual solace. There were times when Eleanor was too much for her. Rolf gambolled in, demanding, uncomplicated; Eleanor was a gawky package of complexities. Then Paula wanted to grab her and shake her until her ribs rattled against her cotton dress. Her plain looks, her very presence, grated upon her. Even her happiness. That she could be so thick-skinned. Then Eleanor, overstretched, would let her defences flop, drop her gaze and demand nothing, which drove Paula to paroxysms of irritation, lashing out because Eleanor stood there inviting it. Eleanor would come into the sitting room just as her favourite programme was ending, perfectly timed, and Paula would say, 'Didn't you want to watch Dr Who, Eleanor?' And Eleanor would answer, eyes unfocused and hesitating by the doorway, 'I didn't think I was allowed,' and Paula would bite her lip, and it was all she could do not to hit her, run to her, lift that skinny body up and thump it onto a chair and shriek, 'Of *course* you're *allowed*, you stupid fool.' Paula would roar inside, the act so obvious she wanted to hit her in the face with it. Poor little martyr, poor suffering bloody deprived orphan.

Eleanor would wait to run to the haven of her room where she could, oh delicious, cry all alone, make herself choke with crying at the image of Rolf tucking into his yoghurt and bananas and Paula and Tim talking to him, and no one noticing she had gone because of course she did not deserve to be there, there was not even a question of it.

Eleanor had wanted, one summer holiday, to be a nun. She decided it was her vocation after she had watched *The Nun's Story*. She knew. She plotted to run away to France and give herself up to a kind austere nun, in a place where they walked past smiling all day in couples, their veils flapping behind them, looking for little girls to save. She would submit to her calling with trembling obedience, give up her possessions, renounce her contact with her family while secretly nursing the thorn of knowledge that they would not visit her anyway, and somehow manage to keep her fantasy long hair, her long long tresses bound but intact beneath her headdress. She would grow thin and pale on gruel, the ecstasy of her ribs showing through her skin, fainting in the cloister; a life of dedication. She was an *orpheline. n petit ange.*

One evening she threw herself into a bush and tried to have visions. She willed herself, the pain of twigs spiking the flesh of her face and birds screaming overhead, and saw nuns and white robes and flickering images intensified by the pressure on her cheek, and half persuaded herself she had seen visions, like Bernadette Soubirous. She ran down the lane, sinking inside with shame at the thought of Paula's response, but after tea and *Captain Pugwash* she was less certain.

First she had to go to church. The village church squatted brown and homely under the horse chestnut trees, its spire leading her home from outlying fields. She had been there only once, to a school Christmas service. She cast her eyes up at the spire from the end of the garden, rooks wheeling round and clattering at her, confusing her. She longed for parents who would take her to church, to be like the other children in her class. She would wear a pinafore and white socks, and hold her Bible with her hands clasped together, head slightly bowed, and Paula would tell her not to scuff her patent leather shoes with straps. The longed-for clothes as wonderful as the hallowed cool of the church.

Paula and Tim were easing out of their year of macrobiotics: the children had grown pale, and the choices that they had embraced with such fervour had dulled with the passage of time. The Maharishi had come in and out of their lives. Tim meditated before work, Paula before her coffee break; the children were less disciplined. As Eleanor and Rolf ran to school along the lanes with their anoraks attached by the hood and caping out behind them like Batman, Eleanor recited her mantra in her head, drummed it in time to her feet slapping the tarmac until she felt she could fly. But at weekends her mind drifted, and she grew scared that people might die if she neglected her meditation. Rolf shouted out his private mantra to everyone in a momentary fit of rebellion, and its effect was tarnished.

EST was to take over later, but for the moment Paula and Tim desultorily attended workshops and watched their lives ease out of insolvency. Paula could not name her dissatisfaction. Then the rumours surrounding David Harpur began to filter through.

Eleanor crept up onto Paula's lap. People were draped over the lawn. They had come to hear David speak, and were staying with Paula and Tim, some of them in tents in the garden. Children ran across the grass; Tim stoked a barbecue fire; a group were singing and laughing by the apple tree. The spire pointed to God in the haze a couple of fields away. Paula stroked Eleanor's hair and laughed with her friend, and Eleanor nestled in her lap and sipped the wine Paula held to her lips. She had rehearsed her request at the top of the garden, hot with nerves in anticipation of Paula's response. But Paula was holding her and showing her off, her pretty-girl.

'Paula,' said Eleanor. 'Can I go to the church?'

'Of course you can, darling, if it's open.'

Eleanor hid her head in Paula's neck. 'No, I mean, I mean can I go to the church on Sundays?'

Paula hooted with laughter then she tried to suppress it. 'Whatever *for*? Cally, my daughter wishes to become a church-goer. Wherever did I – ?' Surprised amusement. Laughter from her friends, cross-legged on the lawn. Affectionate jokes.

'Why don't you come to Family Satsang?' said David gently, silently appearing.

'Eleanor,' said Paula, 'is going to spoil it for all of us, because she says she doesn't want to come. So I'm afraid we won't be able to come as a family.'

'I will go,' said Eleanor.

'Ah, you've changed your mind now, have you?' said Paula. 'But that's no good, because you don't *believe* in David, do you?'

Paula's thighs were stiff as dead flesh. Eleanor jumped down and ran off to hide behind her tree. She watched David speaking solemnly to Rolf. All she could see, as David spoke to his new followers in the garden that day, was Paula's wide back turned against her, and she held her head hard against the stone wall as she hid, till it hurt.

FOUR

TRUCKS WHINED PAST THE OLD FOUR-STOREY BUILDING
which housed the Totnes Centre. With every clap of wind on the
door to the ground floor bookshop, Paula jumped, but it was
merely the thud of the lorries' wake and no one entered.

The Totnes Centre was at the bottom of town, in The Plains,
that flat area where the coaches parked and river pubs alternated
with tall houses, giving it a flavour of Holland, of waterways and
liberal calm. Only women ran businesses there, its four storeys
and its annexe running to a warren of rooms overlooking a
geranium and cat sprayed courtyard. The women held monthly
Centre meetings to air their grievances and sort out any tensions,
and secondly to discuss business matters, group advertising,
electricity meters, the lavatories.

The Centre and its attendant crowd had been Paula's love for a
couple of years. It was an escape from eating biscuits at home. It
was an alternative, thought Eleanor, to spiritual gurus, diets,
meditation. Laid-back voices sang between rooms; the shoemakers' machinery thumped throughout the day, turning out the
bulbous boots on a sandwich of crêpe that were a town
trademark. The reflexologist was booked until summer.

Paula suspected David Harpur would visit her that day, and imbued every stranger in a suit with hope. She and David were tetchy, cross with not knowing. They edged around one another. When he had arrived in her life, his simple presence had been enough to fill her with a kind of happiness. Now that he was a mortal who made money and wore suits, no longer the serene teacher with the magnetic gaze, human emotions were there for the sampling. It was all forbidden, but she liked to toy with the emotions, playing with them behind her bookshop desk until she was blank on the outside with desire.

Paula sat waiting for David, and reflected on his coldness, all English blue and reserved charm, could transform itself. The humourless set of his jaw moved; the skin around his eyes fell into sudden laughter lines, and she saw him as merely a man. A man with solid thighs and questionable taste in after- shave. The spiritual teacher gone conservative. When she was alone with only the drone of the shoemakers' machines above her, and teenagers and road workers milling outside the window, the thought of him was like ice inside her. The hard edges, the inescapable charisma. He would arrive in seconds.

'Paula!' The door swung open; Paula was jolted from her abstractions.

And Tim arrived, a vision of brown, like a wood cutter returned from work expecting only homely pleasures and a bowl of warm soup.

'Tim!'

'Hello, mine bean. It's quiet in here. Would you like lunch?'

'What are you doing down here, darling?'

Tim stood there in his old khaki cords and Professor Calculus jersey. Paula looked at him with loving hating despair, and willed him gone before the other, harder one turned up. But David never arrived, and Paula was left to watch her husband masticating a fibrous salad with a napkin tucked beneath his beard like a bib, and his slow sweet conversation.

Selma, sitting at a word processor upstairs, was listless, yet panicky. It was still warm for spring; a holiday atmosphere invaded the offices, the women who made the shoes, whose names she could never remember, running in and out and taking food to the park benches near the river. She was beginning to agree with Eleanor Strachan, to despise them. She stopped herself.

She and her researcher, Janine, keyed data into the word processor and categorised and sub-categorised it. Selma wrote weighty yet populist historical studies with a feminist perspective. Her last had been markedly less popular than her first, and in London she had become too absorbed by spin-off projects, the paraphernalia that trickles down from earlier successes, mini investigations, newspaper features. She was glad to escape to focus purely on her book; but then she found on long afternoons she was lacking inspiration; the bustle outside the window was small town business, not the banking of sirens and traffic jams she was accustomed to.

Eleanor and her friends straggled into town in their lunch hour. They rarely visited the Centre, keeping to the top end of town near the market and the cafés. Occasionally they would march down to the Plains to visit Paula, who was always gentler with Eleanor in the bookshop than at home, pleased to see her; they showed off in their hoity-toity voices, thinking up laboured witticisms about the book titles that sometimes made Paula laugh, and she'd give them money for snacks next door, and take an interest in them; and somehow, Eleanor was proud of Paula, for sitting behind a leaflet-strewn counter and smiling at her friends, appearing more relaxed than their own mothers, un-shockable. Even her friends could tease her.

Eleanor arrived there that evening on her own. The Centre was crowded. She found herself looking forward to seeing Paula, the welcome, stretching out on a chair and lording it over the workers. Paula was shiny-faced and happy behind the counter. To Eleanor, the people who were mingling and talking but seldom, it seemed, buying, were virtually indistinguishable from her parents' Somerset friends, or from the crowd which had followed David more than a decade previously. Even their children talked the same language. Their ponderous spacey tones, the vague and laid-back edge of Cockney was the same wherever they went.

Eleanor recoiled at the smell of body odour that eased from a woman in the corner. Another woman tucked her child under an arm and leant over and kissed Paula.

'See you soon, Paula.'

'Yes, bye Jeannie. Send my love to Yoshka. Bye-bye Shudy.' She shook her head at the child.

She looked up, smiling at the next customer. How could she? Eleanor thought. How could she say names like 'Yoshka' and 'Shudy' without cringing, without encasing them in smirking inverted commas, without being sickened by the mediocrity of those who bore them?

'Eleanor! Hello darling. I didn't see you.'

'Hello,' said Eleanor. She felt her new dress drift about her and surveyed the room with her nose slightly wrinkled. She always imagined they would be surprised to find that Paula had a slick daughter who was slim and clever. Centre workers popped their heads round the back door with requests, snippets of gossip; they didn't appear to recognise Eleanor, but smiled beatifically in all directions.

'Hi, Tasha,' said Paula. 'I'm doing a tea round. Would you like one?'

'Why do they all have these ridiculous names?' said Eleanor under her breath.

'What?' said Paula, smiling, distracted, but Eleanor could not hurt the shiny face.

'What have you been up to?'

'Oh, not much.'

'How's Sean?'

'He's fine. He said to tell you thanks for that book you sent.'

Paula smiled. 'Are you going to sign on instead of working in the café over Easter?'

Eleanor shook her head. 'It's not worth it.'

Paula paused. 'Have the school got you any Work Experience?'

'Yes,' said Eleanor.

Paula knew not to push.

'Well. What happened?' she said eventually. 'What are you doing?'

'Oh, it's at the library, and I do all this boring stuff. I have to reshelve books, and type letters, and tidy shelves, and things like that.'

Eleanor cringed as she waited for Paula's reaction.

'It doesn't sound like much,' Paula commented guardedly.

'I *know*. But I bloody need money, don't I? Anyway, it's only holiday work.'

Eleanor stared at a split end with steady concentration. 'How's Rolf doing at that burger stall, whatever it is?'

'He's been sacked.'

Eleanor snorted. Paula shot her a look of amused disapproval. 'On his second day?' said Eleanor. 'Rolf and his brilliant career.'

A man arrived, tall and stooping in a baggy jerkin over a sweat shirt.

'Dick, hi,' said Paula. 'How was Holland?'

'It was great,' he said slowly, 'fantastic, but I'm feeling a bit out of it.'

'Yes?'

'Yeah, you know like they say that if you fly you leave your soul behind. Your body travels, but your soul takes another day to catch up, so I guess I'm just –' he laughed, 'feeling a bit soulless.'

Eleanor kept her eyes to the ground. Had Poppy been there, they would have cast knowing looks at one another and even giggled audibly. They had regular and scathing discussions about the people they called the 'hey-nonny-no-hopers' who attached themselves to Tim and Paula. They were gentle and friendly, these people: Eleanor's disdain tangled with guilt.

'Can I get you a tea or a Barley Cup? The kettle's in the back.'

'Oh. Cheers, Paula.'

Eleanor felt claustrophobic. She wished she could see Selma's office, she thought suddenly, another world. It would be the antithesis of this one with its red paint and notice boards and Paula quite inexplicably happy with her lot.

She waited around for Sean until Paula was ready, trying his favourite haunts, the market steps, the Castle pub. She waited in cafés and on benches, hunched in case the trendy gang from school saw her on her own. She wondered if Sean was a proper boyfriend, like other people had, or, more to the point, whether she was a normal girlfriend. She had uncomfortable suspicions on the subject: she dreamed about him in the car, and then she spent considerable efforts avoiding him so she could be alone with her friends. She was sickened, fearful of the thought of sex with him for weeks at a time, buried herself at home, was nervous of the phone; the notion of him on the end of the line waiting for sex with her revolted her and panicked her; then suddenly she

wanted vigorous penetration, every day, for a week, day-
dreaming about it.

They were so close, she thought she knew exactly what he was
thinking at a given moment, and loved him for it, then couldn't
think of anything to say to him. He would look at her sometimes
as if he was wondering what went on behind her efforts at chatter,
as if he had discovered only blankness there. She watched other
people, other couples, and they seemed normal, normal people
unlike her, who could conduct proper relationships, had that
ability, not her oddities, her strained silences. She pulled at the
dry skin on her hand, and couldn't find him, and returned to catch
a lift with Paula.

'I just tell her to fuck off,' said Poppy, sitting in her bedroom.
'You don't,' said Eleanor. 'You don't actually say "fuck off".'
'Yeah I do.'
'Yeah, but joking.'
Poppy was scornful. 'You know how easy it is to get round
Paula – she pretends to be strict then gives in if you batter her. If
she tries to get me to do something, I just say fuck off.'
Eleanor was impressed. 'God.'
Poppy took a cigarette out of her model stable and began to
smoke it inexpertly. Eleanor shifted to find a comfortable spot
amongst the clothes and toys that were trampled into a solid layer
over Poppy's floor. The room was sordid in the mid-day light;
later it became mellow.
'I just wouldn't dare,' said Eleanor. 'She gets so . . . I don't
know, I don't do it. I hate it when she has that trembly, angry sort
of . . .'
'You're scared of Paula, aren't you?' said Poppy.
'No, not really. But she used to be stricter with me and Rolf
than she is with you.'

'Getting old. You *are* scared, you always get guilty and things. But she's so – impressible – is that a word? You can tell her what to do. I just tell her that I don't want to do the garden because it's not fair because it's not *my* stupid hobby and she argues for a minute, then says OK.' Poppy stubbed out her cigarette, half-smoked. 'She even thinks *my* ideas are interesting and clever. You know what she's like – look when that revolting fat Melly – "Melly's wise and very knowledgeable about animals and people", whatever the fuck that means – fed her dog on that vegetarian food. Of course Paula put poor Gandalf on it *immediately*, and poor poor Gandy got all thin and manky, but she took no notice until I shouted in the supermarket and embarrassed her and just put a big tin of Chum in the trolley and made her buy it. And she raves on about all her new friends all the time and tries to be like them for about a month and then it all changes. Fuck that! I just tell her to stop being mongy when she's got a new idea about me.'

'She simply acts as the mouthpiece of whoever for a few months,' said Eleanor. 'She just swallows their line.'

'Yeah, she's got that woman she works with, hasn't she? And there's this spazzy guy she's always quoting.'

'Yeah, well, Paula's a bit easily led.'

Eleanor was impressed by Poppy's easy rebellion. She was prickly and bold. At ten, she was still short and looked like a boy with her pudding bowl of hair and country red complexion. She was compact in her dungarees and bumble bee jersey: she wore odd socks as a matter of habit. She sucked her thumb clutching an old silk rag, pulling it out for puffs of cigarette. Eleanor wanted to kiss the small wet thumb.

'Old Paula would collapse if she really knew what we did,' said Poppy calmly.

'She wouldn't – she'd just be a bit amazed, even though she's so nosy and thinks she knows everything.'

'She's so proud when she uses her contraceptive-trained eyes and says, "Yes, Eleanor's seeing her boyfriend this evening." She loves it that you're *seeing* your boyfriend so –'

'So she can let her pals know she knows I'm fucking Sean and she doesn't mind.'

'Yeah.'

Eleanor paused. 'Fancy anyone, Poppy?'

'No,' said Poppy. She shrugged, and her eyes took on the hard glaze she adopted when Paula embarrassed her with intimacies.

'Snogged anyone yet?' Eleanor persisted.

A wave of self-consciousness twisted Poppy's mouth. 'Snore,' she said.

'Got any good gear?' asked Poppy, changing the subject.

Eleanor was taken aback despite herself. 'Er, now what exactly do you mean by that, Miss Strachan?' she said.

Poppy giggled and blushed. 'Me and Alice had some good stuff, but we sold most of it at the junior school.'

'*God*, Poppy, you'll get yourself expelled, you great burk.'

'No,' said Poppy casually. 'They're so desperate for it, they'll buy it off anyone and you can rip them off. I just sold a few sixteenths and undercut them a bit. Everyone used to undercut in the junior school, so it's perfectly fair.'

'Blimey, Paula would be shocked, yes.'

'Tim would probably just smile, stroke his beard, and say, "But is it good for you?"'

Eleanor cast her mind back to her own existence at Poppy's age, and felt as naïve as Paula herself.

'Let's go down and get some crisps,' said Poppy. 'There's a stash of egg flip they don't know I've raided.'

'OK, Poppy, OK,' said Eleanor.

'What?'

'Nothing,' said Eleanor and double-stepped the stairs singing loudly.

'Paula knows what that is, don't you?' said Poppy.

'What?' said Paula, appearing at the door.

'That song.'

'No.'

'But it's by the *Police*, your favourite band.'

'Yes,' Eleanor laughed. 'Paula knows all about the pop scene. After all, she knows who the lead singer of the Police is.'

'And Paula's an expert on *Rowan Atkinson*, her favourite.'

Paula gathered her wits, and laughed. 'That's right. I'm well up on Sting, aren't I? I even know a bit about Stewart Copeland.'

'*Paula*! You *know* Stewart Copeland's name! My God, did you hear that? Paula'll soon be telling us again about the "hottest new act on the clubland scene".'

'I never actually said that, you know,' said Paula.

'Oh, but didn't you know, the hottest-new-act-on-the-club-land-scene is a group called the Police, led by — I'll just toss the name off here — Mr Sting.'

'What exactly *do* you two want?'

'Hey, Paulie babes! We want nothing but the fruits of your intimate knowledge. It's New Wave now, isn't it, Poppy? Oh no, Rock And Roll. Or is it, er, punk? There's this jolly good young act called The Beatles.'

Paula raised her eyes tolerantly. 'Pack it.'

Poppy and Eleanor snorted with laughter. 'What's In for the autumn season, Paula?'

'Yeah, got any hot tips?'

'Patchwork loon pants and sacking bags, perhaps?'

'No! Those — what are they called? Things. Afghan dresses! Maybe you could parade your new buys for us, so we could pick up a look? I'll turn the dough vat into a catwalk.'

Eleanor's and Poppy's slim torsos trembled with laughter. Paula breathed in and her breasts rose to bulges above the edging of her bra. 'You two are relentless. Honestly. It's just about funny coming from Poppy, but it's painfully puerile coming from you, Eleanor.'

'*Puerile*,' said Eleanor in an upper-class drone. 'Paula knows a new word! God, I'm so impressed.' A tremble of Paula's small mouth. Poppy and Eleanor dived into the larder shrieking and mimicking, and Eleanor was light-headed with laughter and guilt.

She should be glad her children felt free to express themselves, thought Paula. But she knew there was more to life than applauding Eleanor's supposedly glorious existence, and a spoilt younger daughter being rude to her, and a son who sat around at home all day.

There must be more to life, she had once thought, than bringing up two small children in an obscure West Country village, and a husband who was gentle and good to her. Her children were oddly uninteresting, she thought at times. They were tetchy and petty; they came home from school demanding chocolate digestives like any other children. She tried to take them to kids' creative weekends at a nearby farm workshop, but they didn't want to go. They wanted to stay at home in front of the telly on bright evenings and squabble about their sweet allowance.

David Harpur had appeared at that time as in the lights of a circus ring, the mystical, floating light that transforms the tawdry and owes its effects to unashamed artifice. Initially in Glastonbury Town Hall, and then front room gatherings, and then Centres in Taunton and Bristol, and the later venues had lost some of the essence of those first tentative miracles.

This is my life, thought Paula. I am not so old, I have only restricted myself. She took to wearing hats, her chin set in uncertain defiance. The children sniggered and squirmed. She turned up at their school's Open Day and argued volubly with the headmaster. She bared her freckly arms to the sun, and knew that what she sought shimmered all around her in the grass, and in David, and in her own lovely soul, just within reach.

By the time Rolf was six, he was stronger than Eleanor, and wet himself at school. She took her duties as an older sister seriously. She was spiteful, clever and bossy. She thought of his little willy hanging in his shorts, and how it wet itself; she thought of his tears of panic when the rules of the most rudimentary game were explained; she thought of his rough, glossy head of hair and how he stood and played with his trolls looking up at Paula in the certainty that he charmed; and Eleanor pestered him with questions whose very innocence contained barbs. He winded her and pinned her down with his thighs. Paula saw him baited and confused like a baby bull, and when Eleanor interrogated Paula in later years with such clumsy efficiency, she was reminded of little Rolf, and how he had to hit.

Beautiful boydom. A creature so alien, Paula was in awe of him at times. How did a little boy's mind work? Boys were a mystery of autonomy. Eleanors were an everyday phenomenon: they kept notebooks with flowers and horses in the margin; they believed themselves the girl heroines of novels, sticky with contrivances and imaginings. Theirs was a secret, calculating existence. Eleanor and Tim inhabited a woodcutter's kingdom, the forest of fathers and little girls.

Poor sweet Rolf, thought Paula, with his reading difficulties and big buckled sandals. She kept an eye on things. He needed protection from the clever one.

Eleanor dreamed: she wanted to be blind and good like Mary in *Little House On The Prairie*. Or good with a touch of scarlet fever, like Beth in *Little Women*. Or a singing nun. The glamour of correction: she dreamt of a plaster cast, NHS glasses in pale blue, a brace. It was the attention, the submission to her fate – a snapping spectacles case a badge of individuality as worthy as an allergy to plasters or pierced ears from birth. She added callipers and hairnets to the picture, until she was trapped in a lattice work of corrective appendages. But denuded, she was the ugly older sister. She wasn't compact and six-years-old like Rolf. She was too tall, and too small, and lacking in bullying grace.

Paula was edgy with Eleanor after the latest bout of mockery. She didn't quite meet her eye. Eleanor was nervous about going down to the kitchen for breakfast, but she studiedly read the cereal packets, and washed up. In the evening, she was propelled by a need, for what she didn't know. She was apprehensive about going home with Paula, but she made her way through town to the Totnes Centre and let herself in through the back annexe, slipping past the communal kitchen. Fragments of Paula's speech were audible through the passage. Eleanor turned the corner and climbed the back staircase.

Paula waited. David Harpur could visit her there. He sometimes came to see her at the Centre, never making visits to the family up on the moor, only seeing her alone, yet nothing was said. Their minds loved and meshed, she thought, but perhaps as the former acolyte, the current admirer, she was deceiving herself. Perhaps he merely found her mundane. She waited. If the first book title she saw to the left of her had more 'a's in it than the first to her right, it meant he felt for her as she did for him. Suddenly she thought of Tim and was shocked to see how far her fantasies had gone, the idle desire now an established fact in her mind. She counted the 'a's, but she had forgotten which title she had first seen; then the phone rang, and it was Rolf saying he was out of

Ready Brek, and she cheerfully returned to normality.

Eleanor doubled back on herself beyond the annexe and walked up the narrow back staircase, now a fire escape, where the purple pipes and green paint tailed off to a thick scuffed cream, and it reminded her of school as it had been, or an idea of how school should be, before the specious freedom of the Sixth Form college, when she had been one throb in a grey mass moving through assembly halls suffused with the smell of canteen dinners and warm dust.

She walked aimlessly up and down the staircase, cupping the fire extinguishers as she passed them. She thought of the herb and grease fugged kitchen at home and Paula's sticky love for Rolf. A voice alerted recognition. Instinctively, she stopped and pressed herself against the wall, and then she saw her, along the corridor, looking like a raddled angel.

Selma walked beside a man, absorbed in conversation, her voice panning in and out of earshot as she went down the main staircase, like the receding babble you hear when fighting sleep. Her profile was imperious as she talked. Eleanor felt satisfied, as if she had been hungry and eaten food. The voice lulled and washed her hearing. She crouched down, and was then aware of the inappropriateness of her presence, and stayed crouched, embarrassed like a child.

In the evening, tension stained the air, the sound of the clock, the mundane interactions of daily life. They were guarded, Paula talking to Eleanor without looking at her, then staring her straight in the eye so that Eleanor flinched. Poppy battered through Paula's punishments by ignoring her back, or by increasing her demands, so Paula punished only Eleanor, who was punishable. Beyond that, Eleanor inspired emotions in her that the others did not, a bitterness or soreness, streaks of a brutality otherwise absent in her character; she was more alert to Eleanor's criticisms.

When they had first met, Paula had been entranced by Tim because alongside his oddities and the slow pace of his existence he possessed a youthful outrageousness. They had escaped their families and wandered through Italy living on nothing, talking of utopian lifestyles. Tim drove old bangers at frantic speed, veering off the road into fields to have picnics and sex.

Then, over the years, he seemed to become perpetually tired, perceived her less as sexual being than as sturdy friend. Eleanor was born, with her mazy gaze, her little tufted head, and she would lie still and solemn in Tim's arms gaping up at his face, and he stayed like that for great tracts of time, absorbing her as he never absorbed Paula any more. He never noticed Paula's new dresses or mood nuances. Eleanor lay naked on his chest, a little rosy body barely wriggling, and seemed to gulp sustenance from him. From Paula she took only the necessary substance of life, as if she were a cow. I am a cow, thought Paula, as she swelled with her second baby, her breasts drooping from the demands of the first, and it was Rolf who arrived, and he needed her, and loved her, he loved her.

And later, Eleanor wondered why Tim never defended her, he who alone offered her unconditional affection. He didn't notice Paula's twitches and blanketed bitterness, or how she cosseted Rolf and took his side as a matter of course. Or if he did notice, it was Paula he defended, with his steady unthinking loyalty towards her.

Eleanor went to the Centre through the back entrance again. The smell, or the essence, of Selma, lay somewhere behind the building's own smell, a barely perceptible suggestion threaded with strands of other smells, of reflexology oils and plaster. There was something of milk about Selma, in her calmness and her breasts and her skin. The air she gave off was one of tranquillity, yet she was volatile. Eleanor waited, and there was pleasure in simply waiting, as though collecting something: she wanted only to visit Selma and talk to her or just glimpse her, suck in her presence unnoticed even; it was like balm, the voice; but she couldn't, there was no excuse for it. The thought of Paula silently observing her, reserving her comments and then turning to Eleanor with that over-direct gaze, the gaze that heralded a weighty or censorious observation, made Eleanor contract inwardly with embarrassment.

Selma's office was on the third floor and overlooked the asphalt covered roof of the building's extension. There was a section on the fire escape from which the edge of her office was visible, her presence or absence surmised by a column of light visible from that corner.

The stairwell was chalky and barren, broken by fire extinguishers, the landings a thick scuffed cream. Old radiators banged there, large like cisterns ribbed with pipes. The scuffed paint, the metallic digestion of the radiators were again reminiscent of school, one she had never attended, not the modern paean to language labs and General Studies that hers represented, but an institution, like a nunnery, an academy, a conservatoire. Eleanor stood there in a slack faced reverie, her hair straggling, her jersey too short at the sleeves, her hand flexing and flicking in an echo of her thoughts.

Eleanor dreamed. She was fifteen in her mind. She had gone thin. She wore square necked muslin petticoats under her dresses. Her legs were kicky: she stumbled as she walked, and wondered what was happening to her. She was made to suffer, deny, work. Discipline. The banging radiators, the stringent standards. She was beautiful, the flesh liquid, but she must never show it. Selma was someone at the end of a corridor; she was the teacher who went whispering by, the authority figure in rebellion against the authorities; Fräulein Von Healy, Madame, Eleanor's childhood nun.

Selma never appeared; it was too early for lights to be switched on, so Eleanor was not certain whether she was in her office at all. She stood there for a while longer, and leaned her head against the wall, and unexpectedly she thought of Christmas.

Usually the dread started ticking inside Eleanor in September or October, autumns when Paula seemed to resent her, and then Eleanor would enjoy feeling sorry for herself, experimenting with the sensation with a feeling that was almost sexual, plunging through her, making her shiver with self-pity; but by November, when decorations were in the shops, she would cry, and try to fathom how it had all happened, wondering whether Karen or Georgia's families might want her, those families that seemed so bright and normal, a mum, a dad, some children, a bright clean house, rules. But she knew they wouldn't 'want' her – they might invite her and put up with her. She stood on the back staircase and worried now, in spring.

'I hate that man,' said Eleanor the next week.
'Yes, I know you do,' said Selma.
'He's just a disgusting, fat failure of a mountebank.'
Eleanor would fire repeated questions at Selma, sit there intelligently and responsively absorbing the answers, then throw her off course by unexpectedly challenging her; then Selma would snap. Eleanor would slacken, her anxiety visible beneath her animation, and Selma would want to protect her because she was

solemn and had that glow of youth, an alien property to Selma now, and was more vulnerable than she knew.

They walked up the hill to the car park at the top of the town where Selma's car was parked. She was driving Louisa out to Webburn to see Poppy. Eleanor had intentionally missed the bus, and wandered down to the Centre, as if by chance, where Selma was filling in Paula's afternoon off in the bookshop, her head bowed over her typescript while Louisa gorged urgently on crème patissière.

'Come and visit as well,' said Eleanor.

Selma twisted an earring and looked at her watch. 'I can't, I've got more work to do tonight,' she said automatically.

'"I've got work to do",' mimicked Louisa.

'Sorry, Louisa?' Selma raised an eyebrow.

'Nothing,' sang Louisa. Her hair was loose after her gymnastics. It framed the heaviness of her features. At the age of ten, she looked almost adolescent out of her school uniform. She was heavier-set than Selma, resembling her only in moments that disappeared before they were defined.

They dawdled on the street as if there was nothing else to do. Selma relaxed, suddenly placid.

'Come on,' said Eleanor. 'Just for a while. Paula'll love to see you.'

They paced up the High Street. Louisa strode ahead. Her hair hung down her back in a rough sheet, and she nosed the breeze and stared at buildings as if unaware of the company behind her. Their little group. Eleanor felt part of a family, the child Louisa alone in the distance while the adults lingered and talked.

'I'm sure that bastard's around again,' said Eleanor. 'What's he doing? Fucking my mother? Starting up another little money-spinning sect to keep him in his old age? He's a phoney. You should have seen him back then.' She laughed. 'A shaggy hippy man like a sheep, all droopy and weedy. Now look at him, he's got into this English gentleman number, like he's some hotshot businessman. It doesn't suit him at all. I just remember when he wore Indian shirts down to his knees over orange trousers – what a laugh!'

They walked on up the hill and turned off into the car park. There were few people about; the traffic had thinned into the lull of a warm evening, between muted cries from the tennis courts and the floating talk of people passing on their way to the pub. The ripe discordance of birdsong was sudden in their ears.

Paula and David followed one another about the house. He had come to see her at the Centre, he said, but when he had got there, there was only another woman, a stranger, behind the counter, so he had driven out, on impulse, to the moor. They talked in the kitchen; they stood in the sitting-room and looked out of the windows; they wandered into the garden. Tim was putting on his boots. He would walk up to Leusdon, he said, to see the sun before it set.

Then David had leant over and kissed Paula, only lightly, but she drew in her breath, and the chill of his saliva was on her mouth as the cool of the grass drove them back indoors. In the kitchen, alone, they were cosy with conspiracy, and laughed over silly things.

Eleanor and Selma walked in, followed by Louisa. For minutes, there was pandemonium in the hall. Poppy clumped down the stairs in a wig and Paula's shoes, feebly neighing in tribute to former customs, and Louisa resisted her before running over and neighing back.

Paula appeared muddled and radiant in the hallway. She was noticeably dopy, taking seconds to register Selma. She clung to her, hugging her, though they had only seen each other hours before. 'It's lovely to see you,' said Paula.

Eleanor watched them.

'I thought I'd come and see how you were doing,' said Selma, looking her straight in the eye and then embracing her again.

Paula shook herself as though her head was congested and laughed.

'David,' she said at last in a high voice, 'this is Selma Healy, a friend of mine who's a writer. A researcher and a writer.'

'Hello.' Selma held out her hand.

'She's also the mother of Louisa here,' said Paula. 'Where is she? She must be upstairs with Poppy. This is David Harpur, an — old friend of the family,' she smiled. 'And entrepreneur extraordinaire. David's been living in America.'

David strolled towards her. 'I know your name, I believe,' he said, shaking her hand. He looked at her with his unwavering blue gaze. 'And we may have met at some point? I know your face.'

There was a droopiness about him: a bagginess about his clothes, an insubstantial edge to the charm. Selma shook her head slightly.

'Your face is of a kind that has a particular meaning for me. It's the type of face I collect in my sort of internal gallery, my mind's gallery if you like.'

'What do you mean?' said Selma coldly.

Accustomed to charming, David hesitated. Paula led them through. Selma's senses were pleasurably assaulted as she entered the sitting room. The air was musty and sweet with dope; slow Joan Armatrading played; Rolf was there with an older friend, and they were gentle and indifferent. Back home, Eleanor regressed to showing-off mode and volleyed sarcastic comments up and down the stairs with Poppy before sweeping into the kitchen to raid the fridge for her guests. Paula followed to make tea.

Rolf and his friend had an extended conversation about the Civic Hall in Totnes, and which artists were on, and how to lig gigs; Selma sat and listened in silence, and they continued their enervated dialogue until Eleanor returned. Eleanor swung her feet up in a chair, pulled Poppy onto her lap and greeted David cursorily. Poppy squirmed; Louisa stood by the doorway and motioned to Poppy with exaggerated eye movements, but Poppy ignored her efforts and pulled Eleanor's hand onto her arm.

'Tickle and scratch,' she commanded.

Selma took off her shoes and drew her feet under her. She kneaded her ankle bone, the ageing dryness of the skin on her feet. The parental home infected Eleanor with a kind of proprietorial hysteria: if not cowed by Paula, she tended towards over-confidence. She spun round the room performing arabesques with Poppy as a continuation of one of their arcane childhood games, stampeded the kitchen offering up its contents, and conversed hectically. She talked blindly at Poppy.

'Look at this lamp Tim bought at the market,' Poppy said to Eleanor, and sniggered.

'If I may say so,' observed Selma in their direction when Paula was out of the room, 'you do have a rather amazing collection of lamp shades.'

'Why?' said Eleanor, who had not consciously noticed them for years.

'They're interesting,' she said, as Paula returned.

The sound of Rolf's guitar filtered through from his room; Paula cocked her head. The fire burned hotter, and Selma sank deeper into relaxtion.

'Look at this one!' hissed Eleanor in her ear, pointing. 'An ethnico fertility symbol or something, with a bulb at the top.' She looked around the room. 'I'd never noticed. Look at that one over there – hey man, dark yellow felt and wool stitching, and that one looks like it's just raffia wound round and round a frame.'

'Look!' said Poppy, grabbing a lamp off the dough vat. 'A bottle with a kaftan on top. Chills-ville, El?'

Paula raised her eyebrows but smiled tolerantly.

'A grass skirt!' said Eleanor, dashing over to another. 'And here we have what seems to be an old bit of rush matting or something mysteriously shading a bulb. Come on, Selma, I'll take you on a guided tour of the lamps of Webburn House, near Widecombe-in-the-Moor.'

Selma limply stretched out her hand, and Eleanor took it and pulled her up, and they went off to explore every room, Eleanor hectic and sarcastic, and Selma mildly, guiltily, amused.

Eleanor lolled against a chest in Paula and Tim's bedroom. She was flushed. She shook her hair back, and it hooked behind an ear as it fell, changing the shadow on her face, a face of large eyebrows, unremarkable nose, the lips full in their curve.

Selma stood, pale against the dark brown walls. 'We'd better get back down there,' she said.

'It's odd,' said Eleanor, making no attempt to move. 'Paula and I are getting on fine today. I mean, Poppy can usually get away with being rude about her – the lampshades – and stuff, just because she dares, but I can't. She seems so happy today.'

'Yes,' said Selma.

'I think something's going on. She seems . . .'

'Fulfilled?'

'I don't know.' Eleanor shrugged. Poppy and Louisa could be heard up the passage.

'We must go back down,' said Selma. 'Paula will be wondering where I am.'

'Oh just one minute,' urged Eleanor. 'I just wanted to say – do you think she's joined some awful cult again? I'm sure there's something. It gives me this – I can't explain – this feeling in the stomach, panic, as if she's into something again, like macrobiotics or some cult number. She's got that look. What do you think's been happening?'

'*I* don't know, sweet,' said Selma.

Paula and Tim walked into the room together. There was an awkwardness amongst them.

'We have now seen all things glorious and lampshadish,' sang Selma.

Later, when it was dark, and Tim had returned from his walk, he and David talked softly by the French windows, and then David disappeared and everyone was dispersed. Paula was unsure whether Selma was still in the house, but no one had come to say goodbye. She heard voices from the telly room.

A cold draft of night poured into the sitting-room. She stood a moment, then closed the windows and went to tell Tim about Selma and David, who had argued.

It was late. Rolf's music shuddered from the floors above; the girls were silent and probably asleep. Crossing the hallway to close the curtains for the night, Paula heard Selma's voice. She sounded tired, as if she were arched over the back of a chair, her speech emerging lazily.

'No no,' came Eleanor's voice in murmurs. '"The Philistines are upon us".' She laughed. 'Right, Selma, do you know who that's a quote from? Yes? It's Miss Jean Brodie.'

'Which only goes to show your ignorance. If it is, she is lifting from "Judges".'

'Oh.'

Curious, Paula stood in the space where the door was open to catch a glimpse of them.

Eleanor lay across the floor with her shoulders propped against the sofa. Selma was stretched out above her. Selma's head was solemn in profile, imperious, but there was a softness in her movements and the manner in which she lay curled on the sofa like a teenager. Her head was now thrown back, her mouth opened in relaxation, and the slight cast in her eyes intensified as her gaze hung blankly on the middle distance. She was almost looking in the direction of the door, and for a moment Paula thought Selma could see her, and raised her eyebrows at her to test it out, but it was too dark in the hallway; she was invisible. Eleanor's skin was soft in the half light, her eyes obscured by shadow, and she pulled her hair through her fingers, hanks of unbrushed hair with which she fiddled nervously for all her sleepy talk.

Paula forgot for a moment that this was her own familiar daughter. Selma and Eleanor seemed incongruous, Selma too old, too hard and self-contained, her rings expensive as she pulled her fingers through her hair, her aura of assurance intimidating. The girl was malleable and uncertain. But they were intimate together. Paula was suddenly confused by this friendship between her daughter and one of her friends. And then she remembered she had vaguely wondered about it before, in isolated incidents, but without formulating any conscious opinion. Eleanor had always been indifferent towards Paula's friends, viewing them as middle-aged and conventional, while secretly shy of them; or she scorned them, mere fodder for repetitive mockery with Poppy. Now she talked in long drifts of speech to Selma Healy, nearly twenty years her senior and infinitely more accomplished. Paula was somewhat surprised by how they were together, and didn't know why. She left them and climbed the stairs to her bedroom.

Selma's voice floated above Eleanor's head.

'I must go soon,' Selma kept saying, stretching without moving.

'Yes,' said Eleanor, gouging at the dry skin on her hand with her nails.

'Don't do that,' said Selma irritably, pulling at Eleanor's sleeve so she lifted her arm with it. She sandwiched the hand between her fingers. 'What a dear little hand. You'll pull it to pieces if you do that.'

'Selma?' said Eleanor.

'Yes, Eleanor?' said Selma.

'Yes, well do you, d'you think that there's such a thing as a true spiritual leader, or are they all con artists, like the fat bastard you met tonight?'

'Well . . .' said Selma. Her eyes travelled up to the ceiling. 'I think there are philosophers who've reached exalted heights, I mean, who've sorted out some kind of modus operandi that's superior to the one we've worked out. But not many. And then there are thousands and thousands of dream merchants with some measure of charisma. Or a lot of chutzpah. And a lot of them probably have real convictions; but the whole thing's open to exploitation. I think they tend to attract the same kind of people – lost souls. It's a dangerous notion to assume that someone is on a higher plane than someone else. What do you think?'

'I think that . . . I don't see why you can't address your own spiritual growth – you know, spiritual growth, man – while working at something more concrete and external. Paula thinks I'm spiritually lost – just because I'm ambitious. But I'm struggling with things all the time. I just want three A's while I do it!'

'And you don't have to have a ritualised, all-consuming focus to be spiritual,' said Selma. 'No. Anyway, they're all bloody sheep, aren't they? This place is crawling with them. Fields of sheep. Sheep in multi-coloured lace-up boots, eh?'

'Sheep with laid-back bleats. Why does she *respect* Mr Ex-guru so much? Did you see her when we came in? Why must she assume he's superior to everyone else, even now?'

'Women do tend to put their men before everyone else, I'm afraid.'

'He's not her lover though,' said Eleanor quickly.

'But he's a *man* and so he commands respect. A *man*, Eleanor. One of the great male race!'

'Do you think it's that? So, is that why, partly why, she puts Rolf first, perhaps? I've never actually thought – but it's got nothing to do with it; she just loves him and she doesn't love me.'

'It's the only boy who's favoured. Not a coincidence.'

'Yes, but what about Poppy? She doesn't *respect* and mollycoddle Poppy like she does Rolf, but I suppose Poppy doesn't set her off like I do.'

The house was quiet, only the background wash of the river, breezes pressing the window. A dog was barking in a distant field. Selma sank further back into the sofa. She extended her hand and looked at her nails, pulling at the cuticles. She stretched, flexing her fingers. Eleanor looked passively down.

'Why shouldn't family relationships, human relationships,' said Selma, 'be a microcosm of the outside world? Do you know what that –'

'Of course. I'm doing English, am I not?'

'Yes. Sorry. I forgot that you're the resident genius of the Sixth Form.'

'Oh shut up', said Eleanor.

'It does follow that the family situation echoes that of *society*. You've got to say that word in a sociology lecturer's – a *polytechnic* sociology lecturer's – drawl. Otherwise it's too terrible to use.'

Eleanor studied Selma, the defined nose and the angles of her face that were both harder and more blurred than her own, but Selma didn't see her. She focused slackly on the middle distance.

'But do you think,' said Eleanor, 'it's just Paula's training, whatever you'd like to call it; it's just that Rolf's male?'

'Yes.'

'*Really?*'

'Yes. Of course it's got a lot to do with it.'

'I wish that – basically she likes him better,' said Eleanor sadly.

'Maybe she does but I think it goes beyond that.'

'*Honestly?*'

'Yes!' snapped Selma. 'Come here,' she continued in matter of fact tones. 'You inspire something protective in me.' She stroked Eleanor's head as if she were a child, talking absently to her; then stroked perfunctorily, as though she were a pet, and then stopped.

'Isn't it funny,' said Eleanor, 'how comforting it is to find you fit into a larger pattern, a scheme of things, even if it means you're not a unique little being after all?'

Eleanor fell silent; she examined sections of her hair. The low light made an orange glitter through it.

'If you were a mother –'

'I am a mother.'

'Oh yes. Yes, it would be nice to be your daughter!' said Eleanor playfully. 'Would you like me to be your daughter?'

'You are like a daughter,' said Selma. 'A beautiful brown-haired daughter who's highly demanding and fails to confer upon Selma Healy the respect her age demands.'

Eleanor blushed, but unseen, into the pool of orange light.

'I'm not old enough to be your mother. Oh God,' Selma paused. 'I suppose I am.'

She was silent. Eleanor turned to her and smiled. She lay her head on the edge of the sofa, in the warm pocket in front of Selma, and they sat in silence.

'I enjoy talking to you but I must go,' said Selma.

Eleanor was silent.

'Don't go,' she said.

'Why?'

'I want you here with me.'

'Do you? Thankyou,' said Selma, 'but I must go.' She heaved herself from the sofa, disturbing rumples and patches of warm air, and leant over Eleanor, who still lay with her face on the cushions, and kissed her cheek. Eleanor closed her eyes.

'You know I don't want to leave,' said Selma as she stood by the door. 'It's so warm and comfortable in here.'

'I was meant to see Sean this evening. I stood him up,' said Eleanor.

'Who's Sean?'

'You *know*,' said Eleanor.

'Oh yes, the boy – sorry, the *man* – who causes you to brush your hair at inappropriate moments.'

'Well yes.'

'And I'm better company?'

'He'll be really angry with me.'

'Come on. I'll give you a lift into town.'

'What, now?'

'Then you can stay with him.'

'I suppose so. It's so late.'

Selma stood patiently. She said nothing.

'You don't mind giving me a lift?' said Eleanor.

'Why should I when I'm going anyway? We can talk on the way.'

They closed the front door quietly, a plume of woodsmoke following them out into the stillness. They drove through the lanes, the moor black, barely lit. Sheep were wall-eyed in the dark, luminous spheres catching the headlights. Selma turned up the heater and drove in silence. Her mood was large and impenetrable. Eleanor threw comments into the silence, making observations in a low voice, but Selma was now incommunicative, her mood altered; she barely answered.

Outside Sean's, Eleanor awkwardly kissed Selma goodnight. The lights were still on in the house. She clamped her teeth together, muttering in half-formed exclamations of embarrassment as she walked round to the garden entrance, recalling her own comments, her self-consciousness chirping into the silence.

Sean lived in a house largely inhabited by young people. It was owned by a confirmed Salcombe resident gone downmarket. Joyce Cochrane, long divorced and bordering on alcoholism, charged rents that students could afford and opened up her own rooms to her lodgers, who were to be found, on many an afternoon, consuming her wine and giving her half an hour of their easy company. Her wine glasses found their way to everyone else's rooms and got broken; her milk was borrowed until she rarely saw a drop of it; rent payments lagged behind.

Radios buzzed in the street all day in that top section of the town. People sat in windows and held inconsequential conversations with passers-by; groups lurked and stared on the estates; at night, a crowd Eleanor's age, many of whom she knew from school, spilled out of the pubs onto the pavements; an uneasy carnival atmosphere prevailed. The nearby market haunted her: she could hear its reverberations from the end of the street when she wanted to hide. She had no enthusiasm for seeking out bargain jazz records and old clothes. People looked down on her from the Bagel Café as she shopped; no one seemed to work and yet they were busy, preoccupied with life. Moody and remote, Webburn House, her parents' home, was more akin to her current mood.

Sean had waited up. He was angry with Eleanor for failing to appear. The blankness between them had grown worse. He plunked at his guitar in the kitchen, intentionally discordant, until people objected. He felt stirred by the sight of Eleanor, who had been distant lately. She was glowing, but lit from another source, a glow that she brought in from outside. She took her place on the bench and made marks on sodden tea leaves with a teaspoon.

Joyce was overblown on the table bench.

'Here's Fart-face,' said Don, a lodger, massaging Joyce's shoulder with one hand and smoking with the other.

'Hello, Fart-breath,' replied Eleanor unimaginatively. She was weary of being the only female other than Joyce at these gatherings, since the two girl lodgers rarely convened in the kitchen. She and Joyce were bound by a reluctant affinity.

Joyce was noble in her drunkenness. She had good cheek bones under the fat. She wore a dated expensive smock over women's slacks, her voice a well-bred whine. 'Eleanor will come to my aid, won't you Ellie?' she said.

'Mm?' said Eleanor, barely listening. The directionless conviviality touched a part of her that she wanted to leave hidden.

'Get the mandolin and play, Ellie?' said Joyce without enthusiasm.

'Nope.'

'Gerrit,' said Don.

'I'm knackered.'

Sean waited.

'Where have you been?' he said.

'Webburn.'

'Who was there?'

'Usual. David creep. Selma and Louisa.'

Marty, Sean's best friend, tinkered with the end of Sean's guitar. Sean was invariably either silent or speedy. Tonight he jabbed at Eleanor, questions and comments, low against the background. Eleanor smiled absently, sallow with tiredness. Sean was angry suddenly. She was transparent: she made no effort.

'Let's go to bed,' he said. They gathered up the guitar and went together down to the basement, cigarette smoke preserved in the cold.

'So,' he said. 'Did you have a nice time?'

'Where?'

'What do you mean, where? Webburn.'

'Oh yes.' She smiled. 'Selma turned on David a bit. It was –'

'You're obsessed with this bloody woman.'

Eleanor hissed with laughter. 'Of course I'm not.'

'I knew her name would come up.'

Eleanor ignored him and changed a pillow case.

'So?' she said.

'Who is she anyway? Another crackpot friend of your mother's?'

'She writes books, they're –'

'She says clever things to nice little Totnes Centre girls whose Mummies she knows.'

'No.'

'She'll pull strings for you.'

'Bollocks.'

'If we're talking of nepotism,' Eleanor flared. 'Who's tied to his father's apron strings? Who runs around all day on little missions for *Daddy*? Pathetic.'

'Crap off.'

Eleanor had rarely wanted to fuck him so much. His chest was white and drawn as he undressed. She glanced at the compact shape of his penis in his underpants, and wanted to have him full inside her and be powerless and powerful simultaneously. She needed to fuck the other image out of her mind.

FIVE

LIVING AT WEBBURN HOUSE, WHERE THERE WAS NOTHING
to do except let the imagination sprout wings or grow freakish
limbs, Eleanor read novels that bore little relevance to her
syllabus, and photographed Poppy posing in make-up and hats.
Rolf got up late and experimented with harmonies but didn't
bother with chords. The river levels dropped. Eleanor and Poppy
shared heated intimacies.

Paula was dark and edgy, yet there was a febrile excitement to
her. How were you supposed to stay contented in marriage, she
wondered, when a husband never changed? This was the slower
version of the man she had married twenty-five years ago. A
gentle man who quietly got his own way. He was passive, made
few demands, but his desires were a wall; his will was a thick
invisible wall. 'He's a typical passive-aggressive,' said Selma, a
judgement which annoyed Paula before she saw the truth of it. He
was like muesli, some well meaning substance to be digested
slowly. Paula didn't even know if she was bored. All she knew
was that her life had been kicked in a different direction.

A cascade of giggles. 'Paula's going ga-ga,' Poppy informed

Eleanor.

They sat in Poppy's room at the top of the house. Its opium den decor was mellow. Eleanor demonstrated notes on the mandolin.

'Her memory's gone even more crap than usual,' said Poppy.

'Is this possible?'

'I think she suddenly thinks she's a real townie sophisticated woman. A *real* one!' said Poppy giggling. 'She just loves rolling into NSS and ordering the *Observer* in a posh voice.'

'With her chin jutting.'

'Yes, her chin jutting,' said Poppy. 'Defiant Paula the Extremely Sophisticated Woman.'

They laughed some more. 'I tell you though, she's going really bonkers,' said Poppy, looking concerned. 'It's not just her crap memory. She's gone all vague. She lets me do even more exactly what I want, and then suddenly she's strict – chin juts – because she's gone all assertive. She's sort of suddenly confident. Do you think she's on something?'

'Yeah, Paula toking!'

'Paulie-babes the coke head!'

'Maybe it's that thing – when ladies stop having their periods.' Poppy blushed slightly.

'Started yours yet, Pop?' said Eleanor flippantly.

Poppy assumed her blank expression.

'The menopause,' said Eleanor.

Poppy picked at the mandolin. The moon appeared in the trees at the bottom of the neighbours' garden. 'Well what then?' she said. 'Maybe she's having an affair!'

'*Paula*! Who'd – ?'

'Who'd want to fuck her?' Poppy snorted.

Eleanor shivered with guilt. Her fingers strained to tap their childhood tattoo of four beats to prevent her family dying because of her.

Eleanor loved her father: they all did. Eleanor loved Tim so much that they could leave each other alone. The love was taken for granted. Then they would find each other again and talk passionately about photography, he about technical developments, she about lighting; or he'd beg her to come walking by Wind Tor, and she would protest in laziness, then be persuaded, and they'd fall back into that old comradeship with its steady undertow. She was his first born, his funny little girl. He was dreamy and sweet-natured, abstracted – the root of the abnormality of their family, she thought. His social bearing was strange, as if he had never learnt the rules of conversation, as if he were still a child.

He wouldn't defend her against Paula. Eleanor thought he didn't even see it, wouldn't know what she was talking about if she said, 'Look, look what she does to me,' because his first love was Paula, inactive as it was. He was passive. 'You have no expectations of him, only of me,' snapped Paula to Eleanor.

There had been her special teachers. Miss Telemach thought Eleanor was pretty and nice, a pretty girl. Eleanor left the house plain, with Rolf chubby blue beside her, and in the chalk heat of school she uncoiled and talked about kittens and French with Miss Telemach, who found her interesting. Then the bell rang and Miss Telemach's babies poured in and Eleanor, age eight, ran to her lesson with Mr Beale.

Then there was Mrs Gledhill, who was just her class teacher and never noticed Eleanor, and Eleanor loved her for her unconcern, for never picking on her, and for her immense sensibleness. She dried Eleanor's hair vigorously, and Eleanor, chlorine cold, pressed her forehead into the towel, and felt the broad stomach.

Tim collected her and they held hands along the lanes, and Eleanor knew the world was safe, the lanes solid, the trees in their place, and Tim with his brown coat and his beard her post in the ground. His smell, the pace of his stride, were all brown, brown, like names and words were colours, Rolf was green and Mandy red-pink, Poppy darker green, Telemach grey or perhaps mustard on some days.

They passed Mrs Gormer, the glamorous lady who lived in Stink Farm but was never dirty, wore an unusual quantity of make-up, and waved at Eleanor as she walked by with Tim. Eleanor wished Tim could marry Mrs Gormer, Tim with a wife who wore nail varnish and flashed white and red smiles at you as you passed in the kitchen, but Paula was standing stolid in the doorway, and Eleanor touched the wall four times so that her parents would never die or divorce.

Eleanor dreamed, the locus of her dreams no longer London W1, but the Totnes Centre: a transfigured Centre, a different building in its place. Eleanor became thinner in her mind. Her hair was lighter. Her face pale schoolgirl, threshold of plainness, of prettiness. The pagoda on the roof was her haven, passing the slit of light on the way to it. Lingering, lingering, but what if Selma Healy had binoculars trained on her admirers and caught her straining at the windowsill? Eleanor volunteered often to fetch stationery: if Paula Strachan, the lifeblood matron of the Totnes Centre, would elect her the paper monitor, she could know of Madame Healy's moves without making the unfeasibly danger-ous journey up the back stairs. But up by the pagoda, she could breathe with ease again on the wet heights before descending armed with stationery.

Eleanor was an insignificant body in a mass thrown together in a four-storey building by the river, but she and Mrs Selma Healy had focused on one another; she was silently favoured. She was fraught with the knowledge of it, but could do nothing.

In reality, Eleanor was far removed from the schoolgirl of her imagination, a pale fevered flower who wore a collar buttoned to the throat and learnt submission in a seminary. On her off-days she gave an impression of mouse brownness; when she was more richly coloured she had bursts of affectation, of hair-tossing exuberance. After school she would appear buffeted by cigarette smoke and the rigours of academic and social competition, carrying an inky weariness. She had taken to missing the Widecombe bus and catching lifts home with Paula instead, so she was a regular visitor at the Centre, and the shoemakers and the reflexologist recognised her, but didn't seem impressed by her as she had once imagined they would be, by her refined style, her superior grammatical knowledge. Paula seemed nervous and edgy, as if waiting for her to go, though she denied it when Eleanor questioned her. Eleanor would wander off into the back of the building and revise propped against a radiator on the staircase, or arrange to meet Sean.

Sean was scrawling rhyming epithets in bed in his basement room at Joyce Cochrane's. He rolled over. 'Do you like my haiku?' he said. '"Eleanor Strachan, Her Hymen's Torn".'

'Very humorous,' said Eleanor. '"Sean Kenny . . . " I can't think of one. "He's One Of Many".'

'Probably true.'

'You know it's not. And they're hardly haikus.'

Sean was one of those thin men with whom she associated maleness. 'Skinny bodies, large pricks,' said Georgia. He was wiry and nervous, veering between the manic and the monosyllabic. His eyes seemed glittery in a thin face; his voice was deeper than his thinness. His legs were stretched out on the bed. She twiddled at individual hairs on his calves until they hurt, and then she licked his skin. He pressed his fingers into the bone below her ear until she jerked her head away. She relied upon the very irritation of such rituals. But beyond that, he irritated her more profoundly. His large shoes alone were enough to cause annoyance. They were so frankly male and inelegant. She didn't want to listen to his current opinions, and his sweaty cycling gear disgusted her. But she also loved him, admired him for his changeable blondness, and for his street-wise cynicism, and for all the things within his grasp that eluded her. He knew harmonies by instinct, and dealers by repute, and the implications of international conflict, and how to form squats, and rig meters, and double track on Portastudios. He was conversant with worlds that were a mystery to her, that she lazily knew to be the legacy of gender difference. She had thought men like Sean Patrick Kenny belonged to other people – normal people. Perhaps she had been right, and he was slipping away from her.

They went out to sit in the Bagel until Paula was ready to go home.

'I saw your friend,' said Sean. 'She was shouting at the road-workers on the Plains.'

'Who?'

'The madwoman.'

'Shhh!' Eleanor hissed and looked about the café where they sat. A smile pulled at the corners of her mouth. Sean noticed it.

'Who do you mean?' said Eleanor.

'Oh for . . . the feminist from hell. The darling of the Totnes Hippy Centre. This isn't her class of dive. Don't panic, she won't hear me.'

'Why didn't you tell me before?'

'What is there to tell? She just walked along the road, the roadworker said something to her, and she had a fit on the street. That's it.'

That same week, he had also seen Paula walking with an unfamiliar man on the outskirts of town. From his lofty vantage point in his van, he could see the world and remain invisible, which made him feel superior and excluded at once, far removed from the breezy network of despatch riders who met on intersections and shouted at one another between taxis when he drove into Exeter or Bristol. Paula flashed past him pink-faced against the wind, the man stocky and faintly proprietorial, and he drove on and neglected to tell Eleanor because there was nothing to tell, or out of instinctive wariness.

Eleanor was merry with ill-concealed smiles. She looked at him with an expression of love, but it was generalised goodwill only, bounteously bestowed, and beyond that her attention flickered.

'What was she doing?'

'Walking along the road.'

'No, I mean –' Eleanor laughed at herself. She gazed at Sean's features with a calm swell of affection. The pattern of the dots on the irises she never realised she knew now leapt out at her as familiar, the slant of hair on his forehead which became dull and fingered by the end of the day. She had always liked his voice. His intonations were like the weave of her bedspread or the smell of Poppy's hair, known to her.

Sean started to laugh, and Eleanor laughed, uncontrollably, both of them laughing at her in tacit acknowledgement of something unspoken.

'You know, Eleanor, this is your lovely time, but you don't re-alise that,' said Paula, turning to Eleanor abruptly in the evening.

'You mean, "Youth is wasted on the young"?' said Eleanor.

'Yes, if you like to put it like that,' said Paula. 'You'll remember this time always.'

'Why?' said Eleanor.

'Because,' said Paula, 'the world is very small, just home, school, you don't have to earn a living.'

'Yes, too small,' interrupted Eleanor.

'Yes, but that's what makes it lovely too, because then everything is very intense, and very big, and you can fall in love, have boyfriends, do well – as you do – at school, and so you can have these things . . . and, I don't know what I'm saying!' she finished off.

Eleanor focused on the table in case she blushed, but Paula was flushed and distracted herself. There seemed to be some common link, some joint allusion that bubbled unspoken beneath the surface of their talk, but outwardly Eleanor nudged Paula away from the subjects of Sean or love in her heated terror of emotional conversation with her mother.

If Paula was sullen in recent weeks, she was sullen in general; her frustrations were not focused on Eleanor, so Eleanor could blend with Poppy and Rolf and be treated as one of them. Paula didn't seem to notice anyone enough to single them out.

The Totnes Centre was shabby in the hard light of summer. The walls of Paula's shop were scuffed, revealing flecks of white paint beneath the orange-red of the surface. The smells from the communal kitchens in the annexe rose throughout the building.

'I'll lock up,' called Paula to Dilly the shoemaker.

'All right, darlin',' called Dilly cheerfully. 'Good weekend.'

David had arranged to meet Paula for a quick drink. Paula was relieved that Eleanor appeared to have taken the bus home. The ground floor section of the Centre emptied, the clangings and women's voices receding into the street. Paula locked the back entrance, and her hands played with stock order forms, but her mind wouldn't be stilled. The fingers of her left hand were dancing butterflies of nerves. She drew pictures in the corners of the paper, but her hand was shaking; she gave up and walked around the room.

'Closed,' she mouthed to a woman who was pressing her face against the window.

Another ten minutes went by.

People milled in the bus bay; the last buses for the afternoon left. The traffic quietened. A car reversed, a door slammed, but no one entered.

Paula tried to read. She looked up. David's stocky figure was silhouetted in the window. He came in, closed the door and locked it. Paula looked up, her heart thudding with relief.

He had brought Paula flowers, she who hadn't received flowers for years. She beamed at him, excessively delighted, fingering the petals. She couldn't look up from them to face his frankly male musculature, his fading strawberry blondness. His shoulders were tight packed beneath his shirt. She couldn't flirt; it was an impossibility. In her nervousness she became tight-lipped, and started clearing up, talking breezily of practicalities. David watched her, saying nothing. That full lipped, steady gaze that had frightened Eleanor and entranced Paula rested on her until finally she had to look up from the pamphlets on the counter.

'Please don't tidy up on my account,' he said.

'Oh,' she said in a high voice. 'No, I'm not.'

'What are you doing then?'

Paula said nothing.

'Denying a truth,' he said.

'Oh no . . .'

'Yes, you are. Come,' he said in the old authoritative tone. 'Come and sit on my knee.'

He leant against the table.

'Oh David, of course I can't!' said Paula. 'I'd – I'd crush you.'

'I could take two of you, three of you. You're beautiful, Paula, come here. Please come here.'

Paula leant against him. His thighs were thick with years of muscle, layers laid down on the slim young limbs she remembered staring at.

He rubbed the back of Paula's neck, and she quivered. His fingers moved down inside her collar, caressing between her shoulders, so she was shivering with desire or with the air that seeped inside her dress. He turned her round and looked at her with blue eyes, and they kissed, their mouths moving experiment-ally at first, and then faster, urgently, pulling trails of saliva between them, the wet surfaces of his mouth on her upper lip and round her nose, and she bit into his cheek, and he pushed his body taut against hers so they were rocking, his penis hard against her abdomen. David ran his hand up and down Paula's leg, his skin snagging on the tights, and cupped her buttock, kneading it till lust was mixed with pain. He lowered his hand and played gently, teasingly with the back of her thigh.

'David,' she swallowed into his mouth. 'Not here.'

He silenced her by laying a finger across her mouth, kissing her ear, and slipped away from her to the shop window where he leaned precariously over the displays and pulled down the blinds.

'Here?' she protested as he slid his hand beneath the corduroy of her dress and hooked the elastic of her tights on his thumb.

'Where else?' said David quietly. 'In your bed at home?'

'No,' murmured Paula.

'We can make our nest here. Just you and I. No one else.'

He crouched to the ground, pulled off Paula's shoe, kissing and

104

nuzzling her tighted toes one by one until she sank down beside him, and Eleanor rode the bus home and Poppy grouched without her tea.

In the evening, back at the house, semen dribbled inside her. Eleanor sat there looking very elegant and quite strange. Poppy had clearly been smoking. She wished they would all leave home so she could turn the whole house into a temple, or a brothel, whatever she chose.

Eleanor and Poppy galloped about neighing. Tim joined in as they approached the kitchen, his falsetto imitation causing Poppy to laugh excessively loudly. He walked over and hugged Eleanor. He made her feel sexy and childish at once. She was his grown-up daughter with a bearing acquired in the outside world: hugging, she was aware of their bodies, male-female, and how they couldn't press too hard. She was his little Ellie-Nora.

'Hi, Parentals,' sang Eleanor. The door slammed as they came into the room. Eleanor felt suddenly conspicuous: she had barely seen Paula all week, and Paula might comment on her more sophisticated appearance.

'So what's been going on round here? What's new?' said Eleanor after a moment.

Paula smiled. 'Oh what's new?' she said vaguely.

'Where's Rolf?'

'He went to the Scorwells'.'

'So . . . what else?'

'What else? Poppy's been doing quite well at school.'

'I have *not*!' protested Poppy. 'I'm proud to say I got the worst mark except Thick Brent in history, and Joseph chucked me out of pottery this week. *Pottery*!'

'OK, Poppy's not doing well at school after all,' said Eleanor. She babbled conversation while her mind grappled with other subjects. 'What's happened to Rolf's demo?'

'Jack – you know, Melly's friend –'

'Yes.'

'Jack's been listening to Rolf, and he says Rolf's really got something.' Paula's voice quickened.

'Yeah, I heard that before,' said Eleanor.

They were silent, animal-like, thought Eleanor. How could they possibly sustain such complacency? Paula looked positively dopy. Eleanor shot a look at her and wondered whether Poppy's verdict of senility bore some truth. And she loved them too. Her family.

She talked without thought. 'And are you, are you doing the Centre now? I haven't seen you all week.' Eleanor laughed suddenly, taking herself aback.

Paula looked hard at her. 'Yes, ' she said.

'But only part-time, or what? . . . are you thinking of giving it up . . . ?'

Eleanor threw out questions, comments. She seemed to sing: she was unable to control her voice, it flew high and not like herself. Paula did not anchor her flights, seeming similarly uncontrolled.

'So is Rolf – I mean, is Rolf looking for a job?'

Eleanor shouted above Tim and Poppy, who sang 'Norwegian Wood' in what they thought were Scandinavian accents. Paula sat pinned by the Aga warming her back, her response desultory.

'No, Rolf – I told you – Rolf's busy doing the demo,' said Paula.

David would take her to . . . to far away from this danger zone. His voice low like a hand on the neck. Another patch of wetness seeped through her.

'Oh.' Eleanor shut her mouth and said nothing.

'I find you a disruptive presence,' said Paula suddenly.

Seconds ticked and froze. Eleanor felt as though she had been slapped in the face. She slowly surfaced.

'I find you a disruptive presence, I said.' The jutting chin of new defiance.

'Why?' said Eleanor at last.

'Oh, I don't know.' Paula sighed.

'*Why? What?*' said Eleanor.

'I find you difficult, Eleanor. We were having a nice peaceful evening, nice and quiet, and you always bring in this – I don't know what. Disruptive questioning.'

'I wasn't even thinking –'

'No, you weren't. So what if I want to do the Centre on different days now? Does that affect your life? Does it make any difference to your life whether or not Rolf has a full-time job?'

'So you don't want me to be here?'

'Not particularly.'

'N-n-neigh,' whickered Poppy softly, and touched Eleanor's waist. Tim stood silently looking upset.

'But don't do your drama queen act and think that means I don't want you here generally,' said Paula, but Eleanor had gone.

When Eleanor lay in bed that night, she saw the lights of a car, or perhaps it was a shooting star, she didn't know, and she was in the dormitory at that dream place where they all worked and lived together in a building with a pagoda and interconnecting passages. The sleepers' breathing shifted. Eleanor heard doors shutting, snatches of talk; then the night sounds diminished and a breeze edged in through the window, keeping her awake. She strained to hear beyond the blood beating in her head. She made out windows shutting, suggestions of footfall. She spun a web of sound through the building, down the passages threading into the old section and heard creakings, sudden silences. She dozed, then jumped at a sound. Footsteps approached and faded. She woke again. At three o'clock she drifted into sleep. Fräulein Von Healy never came to her. Why would she? She had other concerns; she was oblivious to her in the old building. But Eleanor would wait. She shifted, and the light through the curtains was too harsh for starlight. She rocked herself.

'Of course this is, well, it's confidential,' said Paula.

'So tell me,' said Selma, although she knew already. 'How did you meet this man?'

'Oh, it was years and years ago,' said Paula. Her voice faraway. 'He landed in our lives and saved us from stagnation!'

'So why did you take so long?'

'Well, he was my *teacher*. Anyway, then he disappeared – we didn't see him for literally years – and then I heard of him again through a friend of a friend of a friend. He is . . .'

'Are you in love, perchance?'

Paula's chin set. She summoned courage. 'Yes, I think I am,' she said. Selma smiled.

'I never truly thought I'd have an affair outside my marriage,' said Paula. 'I mean, of course, I'm not – of course, I've often thought about it.'

'I think, really,' said Selma, 'we only live once. We should seize the right to what we want, regardless of all the . . . the supposed conventions of marriage.'

'Easier said than –'

'Yes.'

'I know I can trust you!' said Paula, reddening and turning to Selma.

'Oh yes. It's such a pleasure to see you looking like this,' said Selma, and she hugged her.

Poppy and Louisa had been upstairs discussing lemon vodka.

'Flapjack!' Paula called. Loud childish shouts floated down from Poppy's bedroom.

The stone walls and beams of the sitting room smelled perpetually of smoke, or of wet stone, damp granite encased in warm air. There were Poppy's drawings in bold felt tip on pieces of wood. A Jøtul wood burner, a tapestry warrior's mask, candles hanging in glass and pine boxes. Bob Marley, Fleetwood Mac, Joan Armatrading. Log piles rose above brown carpeting. Records played, voices from elsewhere; Poppy and Louisa came downstairs accompanied by Jason, a Dartington Hall child. The girls were fully made up, and blinked self-consciously under the sudden glare of parental observation. Paula talked with the children, and more voices, doors shutting, vibrated from elsewhere in the house. Selma lolled in a corner. Her work was currently so intense that when she allowed herself to relax, she wanted nothing but sleep. It was overwhelmingly warm: she fell into a momentary half-sleep, watching Paula move about picking up Poppy's belongings and throwing them into one pile, the image receding in dark grey lines.

Eleanor came in. Selma's sleepy voice floated in fragments to the hallway; Eleanor heard it as she closed the front door, then jolted with delayed recognition. She paused and darted upstairs.

She appeared in the sitting room wearing fresh clothes. Selma sat by the fire. She had bags under her eyes, and emanated an obvious and brittle weariness, but her appearance still suggested cities and vanity. Her hair was pulled back; she talked in the strange lulling monotone that made even Poppy stop her chattering; it made Eleanor shiver. Selma and Paula were discussing South African politics. Eleanor was amazed at how much Paula seemed to know. She sat in strained silence a few feet away from them.

'How are you doing, Eleanor?' said Selma eventually.

109

'Fine. How are you?' said Eleanor.

'Fine,' said Selma brightly.

There was silence.

Eleanor picked at her split ends. 'How's your book? I mean how's it going?'

'In fits and starts.'

'Did I tell you that Jude's sister's writing a book?' Paula interrupted.

'A magnum opus of the first degree, undoubtedly,' said Selma, and they entered into a hilarity-spiked discussion of Jude's sister's probable literary abilities. Eleanor focused on her split ends and hovered on the outskirts. Paula and Selma talked of motherhood, feminist novelists, of unknown people's lovers, and then in hints and codes they seemed to be referring to someone at the Centre. Eleanor hovered and then retired. When Selma left, she waved vaguely at Eleanor, throwing her a kiss.

'Bye, sweetheart,' she called through the hallway.

The end of the academic year came. Sean was leaving to go to Manchester, and with that knowledge he and Eleanor seemed to reach a truce. They relaxed in one another's company, and the strained attempts at conversation loosened to streams of dialogue. They would ride together in his van. The whole of the South Hams area, whose very name she despised, seemed to Eleanor to be touched with heightened drama as if she saw it consciously for the first time, and as they headed east, the roads unfolded in front of them as wide avenues and the light skies held premature excitement. Eleanor and Sean shouted over the music. She went for rides to fill in evenings with spurious substance; or perhaps it was the motion of the van that appealed to her, sitting up high in the front, vibrating along the roads in an open daze. She saw how all roads eventually led to Causton, that little gathering near the town where Selma lived, connected beyond their references on an ordnance survey map. Eleanor and Sean had spent a lot of their time bickering, or in virtual silence. They had both secretly looked forward to Sean leaving for Manchester. In those last few days they became closer again. His irreverence made Eleanor laugh. He drove fast and skilfully, and pretended to aim at old ladies crossing the road. He nudged cars along in parking spaces in town if he was impatient to park.

When Sean was leaving, he and Eleanor held each other tight with sudden new nostalgia, and talked tentatively of weekend visits.

Eleanor was resigned to living at home until her course had finished, but she was desperate to leave. Tim's phlegmy coughing; Paula's slurping, her loaded glances; Paula and Rolf. What she felt was a species of hatred. But without money, she was powerless. And although she didn't acknowledge it to herself, there was security at home.

There was this girl, and she lived on remote moorland, and her mother had a friend, thought Eleanor, and the friend was odd, beautiful, clever; the friend wore old brocades and had pale skin and took an interest in the girl, and then the girl began to think about this woman, who was a friend of her mother's, who didn't seem to like her own daughter very much.

In the summer, they were enclosed on the moor. The children had no means of transport, unless they caught lifts with Paula or Tim. The ferns leaked sap and then dried with acrid scents in the heat. Holidaymakers rented the cottage next door, the noise of their children floating up in bubbles through the still air from the river. The high blue skies on the upper reaches of the moor were cloud blown and restless, but down in the valleys, a haze of bracken fumes and sweating vegetation hung over the hamlets.

A new breed of lassitude prevailed. The apathy that nudged at Paula and Tim's schemes and projects swamped the general drift of life so they were all dispersed; even Eleanor was lethargic, her behaviour changed. The daily leaven of purpose had slackened in the heat. Rolf made no attempt to look for work; he used Webburn House as a convenient base for himself and his friends, while seeming to despise its inhabitants.

Paula's bookshop with its attendant clique had ceased to be her raison d'être. July in the Plains was frenzied with tourists. The women in the building were accustomed to the river breezes coming across the bus bay, but exhaust stained the heat. Engines whined at the windows.

It was, thought Selma, squalid on such days. Plastic tray stacks cluttered her desk, rising from a mountainous landscape of sliding paper. In winter, a cosy levity reigned in the afternoons, the work-place was animated under artificial lighting with the early blue of night pressing against the windows. Then they were industrious; their concentration grew to a point, banked up like an electric charge. Now there was only indolence. Figures lolled against tables, human effort futile. She wanted to shake the small town.

Selma was not the prodigy that she had once fully expected to be. The route that she had nurtured with such certainty at school had revealed meandering byways, just as her mental map of London had sprawled on arrival into a myriad of complications, so that her progress had not been precocious. And sometimes she feared her career had already seen its heyday.

Paula hired another helper two days a week, because Selma was writing, and went places, or stayed at home, where her mid-morning vacuum-cleaning whined and droned through the ceiling, filling Eleanor and Rolf with irritated guilt as they pulled their duvets over their ears. When Paula went to work in the garden, the outside world rolled away again and they dozed a sweaty rank sleep, and birds and life and trees shrieked at them if they emerged from the weight of their bedding.

Eleanor had sunk into lethargy as if exhausted. Rolf took inactivity for granted; Eleanor despaired over it, then was paralysed by it. Paula tired of this languor. She felt she should gather them up and demand they make money, help her, leave home. Eleanor cooked and did housework every day, dutiful and guilty, but Rolf viewed it as a doss house. 'Let's give them time,' said Tim.

In such clamorous heat, their parents' house was a fortress against reality. When Paula worked at the Centre, Eleanor gave in to the heated sleep that overtook her in the late morning after a night propped up reading. Poppy was out riding, Tim at work, the day stretched ahead barricaded against chinks of light and guilt, and Rolf was her accomplice in apathy, though they barely spoke to one another, merely grunted through their daze and watched lunch-time television with the curtains drawn and bowls of cereal on their laps.

Paula was out at weekend summer schools and other places she never talked about. She came back, and her children stayed in their rooms or with other people and there were days when no one saw anyone else.

Eleanor worked in the tearoom in Widecombe when they needed her, read *Madame Bovary* again under the counter between rounds with the cake trolley, and dreamt of more glamorous occupations, of her impending riches and success as soon as she could get to London. She had something, she knew she had something, that made people look at her, a delicacy or refinement that made people respond to her in a way that suggested a different vision of her from the one her mother had. She charmed, whereas she certainly did not charm Paula. Her place in the world was higher than her place at home, the position Paula had allocated her by implication, and as she grew older and closer to leaving home, she drew a new confidence from it, and tested out her power beyond Paula's earshot, revelling in its existence. She drew her two opposing certainties of miserable inadequacy and future fortune closer together, and in the gap she tasted power. She pushed the cake trolley round, shoved *Madame Bovary* under the counter, hooked back her snaking brown hair, and was smiled at and tipped by the tourists.

After a while, Rolf made gruff and desultory attempts to find work, but unlike his sister, he assumed his existence itself was justification for food and clothing, and beyond that for drums, mopeds, private schooling. Eleanor rarely asked for anything extra in case she was denied it, and because of an obstinate pride she maintained to protect herself. Self-abnegation as a weapon against Paula, a pre-emptive shield. And her pride kept her striving, revising, striving for the perfection of physical appeal so she could win in the world outside where she had failed at home, and it made her curl into herself at night when her defences dropped. She let her pride unfold and ache.

Paula remembered when Eleanor had been fourteen or fifteen. Suddenly almost beautiful. She wore a turquoise swimming costume, electric aqua like a swimming-pool, she ran about in it all summer, and she and Tim took photos, of each other, distortions of the magnolia tree, fish-eye vistas of the clouds. Whole afternoons they spent together, Eleanor always in that swimsuit, and it seemed to Paula that her rib cage was only there to support small shocking breasts, and her skin only to be marvelled at. Paula stayed in the kitchen washing up, and later she lashed out at Eleanor for playing with her food.

*

When she was old enough, Eleanor had attended the local comprehensive school. Rolf also went briefly to the state school but he had problems with work and discipline, so Paula and Tim decided to send him to what was termed a progressive school. Since Rolf was artistic and Dartington Hall would allow that to develop, it was a good decision all round. Tim worried about the fees, but Paula reassured him by reminding him of what both the Maharishi and David Harpur had said about money.

Paula thought that providing her children with the opportunities she had never enjoyed would make her happy. She saw them thrive, express themselves. At Dartington, Rolf confronted his fears, overcoming the shock he had suffered at state school discipline, and concentrated on his drumming and canoe-making. He was handsome and he stank: he wasn't bound by convention. Rolf was the artistic one; Eleanor was the academic one, and if that pleased Eleanor, Paula was pleased for her. Eleanor knew her mind; she was stubborn and clever. She would go far, that girl, thought Paula, watching her. She was lively, outspoken. Her brown-eyed Eleanor bloomed at the comprehensive. And little Poppy, her country nut of hair, her rounded cheeks, was prickly and naughty and untethered. Oh for such freedom, thought Paula, and made Poppy a nest at the top of the house, a haven of horses and drapes, but later Rolf needed it for his music because it could most easily be sound-proofed, so Poppy moved downstairs.

The summer after she met Selma Healy, Eleanor lay in bed in the mornings; on afternoons she walked, or hitched, along the high back lanes to Widecombe to work in the tearoom. The tourist traffic snarled up the road so she had to climb the banks to get past the honking queues, and middle aged men threw lewd comments out of car windows; the local traffic flashed by when the lanes were clear, and the telephone cables seemed to hum or ring monotonously overhead. She sweltered and coughed in the sun-hot exhaust, and now it was summer she was Tess again and wore her flower or reticulate print dresses, slightly dated, to be covered by the grubby frilly aprons of the tearoom. In the evenings she took strings of photographs with the films Tim received free from his suppliers, but the orange evening light, so laden to the eye, was harsh and red on film. She tried to write the novel that flickered so beautifully through her head month in month out, but when she read it back to herself, she could spot where she had been reading Nabokov, where Flaubert or Duras, the studied rhythms or the linguistic trickery now glaring back at her in flat imitation; her novel, concerning a schoolgirl who resembled a Hardy heroine and her English teacher lover, a patchwork of unconscious pastiche. She bit her arm, her fingers as she wrote to get the blood rushing to her head, to shock truth and clarity onto the page, but she threw it to one side and practised her French past historic. Her motivation had slackened.

Tim was at work; Paula left Eleanor alone; Selma never came to the house any more. She was working on her book and looking after Louisa; Paula said she was in London, seeing her husband.

Selma had been a part of the house, appearing bound in cosy conspiracy with Paula, yet different, so that Eleanor cleaved to her. The milky largesse that she emanated lapped over Eleanor; she loved the tea roses she wore with her paleness, the dark red lipsticks.

If Eleanor perceived her as glamorous, she was seen by others as simply older and richer. She was fractious beneath the tranquillity, tending towards self-absorption. Paula was beginning to find that Selma was not quite as she had thought, the woman she had first perceived trailing perfumed assurance into her bookshop as she emerged from the back staircase late mornings dazed from her computer, quipping in that sleepwalking voice. Paula found her convictions over-strident; she suspected their friendship was oiled by her own admiration, and wondered whether Selma viewed her with contempt. But still the friendship had lasted through conspiracy and affection and frequent contact.

At the end of August, Selma returned to Devon with Louisa. They travelled on the train from Paddington, weighted with suitcases, dirty from the journey, like immigrants Selma thought. She took Louisa's hand, and went to the little café like a beach hut at Totnes station to order a taxi to Causton. Then she felt lonely, aware that she had no one to collect her to take her home; she missed her husband. They waited half an hour for the taxi in the café that only sold tabloids and tea by the mug, and at home there was a dead mouse on the carpet and the hot water system had broken down. Selma kissed Louisa and told her to go and watch telly, then sat with her head in her hands surrounded by her cases.

The office at the Totnes Centre was Selma's comfort since work was the only constant in her life. If she could manage to be disciplined, then she achieved a near-guarantee of happiness. She watched the way light poured across a particular corridor in the early mornings when she arrived there after dropping Louisa off at school, and felt affection for the familiarity of its crisscross patterns before they blurred in the heat. She knew every indentation of plaster in that section of the building; she focused on each one, forming faces, angels, animals. She missed her husband, having been on better terms during the summer. There had been densely-textured conversations that didn't flare into aggression, sex again even. But they agreed that living together was an impossibility. And she would never tell anyone of those pangs of loneliness. So the women of the Centre thought her image-conscious and confident and a little intimidating.

It was early September. From her window, she caught sight of Eleanor Strachan with her familiar group of friends moving in a gaggle on the other side of the Plains.

She opened the window. 'Eleanor!' she called, but Eleanor didn't hear her.

They all looked too old for their uniforms, Eleanor and her friends, too much bosom and eyeliner though they stretched the notion of a uniform to its furthest limits. Eleanor's hair was heaped on one side as if she had just thrown it there with an actressy sweep of the hand.

'Eleanor!' Selma called again, and Eleanor looked up from across the coach park. She hesitated between a smile and an automatic gesture of defensiveness.

'I saw you like a waif across the Plains with your less attractive school friends,' said Selma when Eleanor arrived. 'All I could see was long swathes of droopiness – coats, hair, tights – walking along. And you the chestnut coloured starlet amongst them. Will you run down to the kitchen to get tea for us so I don't have to bump into the Tashas and Dillys and talk to them? It's cheeky of me, isn't it? You don't have to.'

'Yes,' said Eleanor, and ran downstairs in her army coat. When she returned with the Centre's bright chipped mugs, she sat in a pool of coat on the floor, because there was nowhere else to sit, Janine the assistant's chair a pile of files, Selma making no attempt to remove them. Selma's computer screen paled in a shaft of sunlight.

'Take that coat off,' said Selma. 'What is it with you girls? Why must you wear coats all the time, even in this heat?'

'Don't you think I look nice in army surplus, then?'

'A regular charmer.'

'Oh. Where have you been?'

'In London mostly.'

'With your husband?'

'Yes. Working. I've been working like a fiend, because I must finish this book soon or I'll have to sell my mink collection or put Louisa in an orphanage.'

'Have you *really* got mink coats?'

'No Eleanor, I have not.'

'I see,' said Eleanor, blushing. 'What can I tell you?' she said quickly. 'There was a break-in here but they only took some of the awful boots, can you believe. And . . . and the river's like a creek and has dried up. And Sean, you know Sean –'

'Yes.'

'Sean's gone to Manchester.'

'Heartbroken, Eleanor. Heartbroken, aren't you?'

Eleanor reddened again, so she talked on. 'There's a *Tree* Festival in Ashburton this weekend, can you believe it, with a "tree dressing ceremony". You have to celebrate nature by inventing a folksy bollocks woodland tale and dress your tree as the protagonist in your ecologically sound tale. Can you *believe* it! It's funded by the council, by the way, the most conservative council in Britain. They must have given in and just accepted that there are troops of raving hippies everywhere. Paula and Tim were hinting to Poppy – age eleven – that she might like to go, but Poppy said bullshit, so Paula and Tim are going with their sandal-worshipping friends Tiny and Pete, age about forty. Oh God.'

'Oh God yes. Let's go to supper.'

'Us?'

'Yes, you and I. I don't mean me and my least favourite roadworker out there, do I? I mean, you and I go to supper, and you can entertain me, you can tell me all your secrets, you can tell me all about what teen queens talk about.'

Eleanor frowned slightly, but Selma turned to her and smiled. 'Look, Eleanor, you'll have to go now,' she said. 'I only meant for us to say hello. I have to work.'

She turned to the screen. Eleanor watched her blankly and then left.

Eleanor waited in a restaurant for Selma. She wrote letters to appear occupied when Selma arrived, setting her jaw at the precise angle to prevent a double chin and denote concentration, but the letters degenerated into her own ramblings. 'Dear Grandma, How are you? I'm waiting in a restaurant as I write . . . I'm entirely, I'm . . .' The waiters hovered questioningly by her table.

A phone call for Miss Strachan. 'I'm caught up, I'm just leaving. Is it nice? Is it all right for you there?'

Eleanor would not look up. She would write and write until Selma arrived. Nerves beat through her pen and distorted her handwriting. She was close to indignation.

Selma's voice. The waiters were around her like a fur coat. Eleanor wrote. She was immersed in a sick calm.

'Do you have a tissue for my lipstick?' said Eleanor.

'If you blot it, you must give it back to me,' said Selma.

'Why?'

'Yes, you must so I can keep it. Here. OK, thanks.'

Selma looked tired, the muscles in her face pinched with the effects of work.

'That computer's not good for you, maybe,' said Eleanor.

'OK, so I'll get a cataract and have a miscarriage, but I'll produce a book at the end of it,' said Selma in the hard voice that Eleanor was beginning to dread, so Eleanor teased her and she softened.

'So – I'm honoured by your presence, elusive one,' said Selma eventually. She held Eleanor in her eyes, the restaurant's darkness diffusing the effect. 'What are you thinking, Eleanor?'

'That it's better to be here than at a Tree Dressing Ceremony. I want to be in restaurants, or somewhere, always.'

'With me, you mean,' said Selma calmly.

'You're the elusive one,' said Eleanor.

'Perhaps I'm not as elusive as you think. Just lazy. People call me, so I don't need to call them. It's bad, isn't it?'

'Give me something of yours,' said Eleanor. She cut her finger on the menu as she said it, and didn't know until she saw the blood. 'You've got my tissue. Give me something.'

'Alright. What? Here.' She pulled two rings off her little finger and handed Eleanor the lower one.

'Oh no! Of course, I meant something silly. Give me – your napkin.'

'That wouldn't be very original. This is yours. It's actually Victorian, from Camden Passage. And I send my love with it.'

When Eleanor returned, she couldn't sleep. She trembled and twisted as if she had been drinking black coffee. She could never sleep. It left her with a flushed and pathological tiredness during the day.

The flavour of this woman infected her, as if Eleanor could suck her dry. She was the essence of frustration: she was age itself, and belonged to a different world.

The romance of the pagoda at the Totnes Centre academy was eclipsed by the walled garden Eleanor thought of at night. Behind the whining exhaust of the bus bay down there, on the private north-facing side of the building, sprouted a dreaming garden. It was enclosed, all walled and espaliered, just as the Totnes Centre itself had become a closed order, and in the garden there were

SIX

AUTUMN HAD NOT YET TAKEN HOLD: IT WAS MORE A SEEP-age of summer, skies draining to whiteness, dogs slinking along the damp lanes, unsold gnomes and sheepskins put into storage until the following year.

Poppy and Eleanor had fits of hysteria about the rumours that circulated: there was a rogue badger on the loose near Bowlands Farm; the woman at the Post Office had taken to wearing a Harley Davidson belt with wing details; the garage owner's wife from Pondsgate with thousands of dogs was sleeping with one of the hunt saboteurs. To Poppy and Eleanor it was a soap opera that staved off the despair of mean-minded provinciality, of muddy fields sewn with the specks of birds and no other movement, hour in hour out, and of the daily rounds of drabber gossip that hemmed them in to that square mile on a water logged peninsula.

At the house, the disparate strands of summer converged and clumped, and they were cosier, enclosed; there was happiness, and they rotted. Eleanor thought she caught glimpses of decay. Their routines kept the voids and inadequacies under wraps: school, work, signing on, Totnes Centre, but Rolf kept forgetting his signing on day, and Paula worked variable shifts. Poppy claimed to be hoping for a suspension too so that she could take a little holiday.

But Paula was not always at the bookshop on those days. She who had once sat on the floor below the master physically trembling in anticipation of – what? Of his words, of his moves, was now in the inner sanctum. Fucking, fucking in a characterless male flat in Bridgetown. Fucking through long afternoons, while Dilly or Jude looked after the bookshop, and the women in the Centre used up her share of the tea. She got back in time for Poppy's return from school, and Tim who would sometimes arrive at the Centre must wonder about her, but then Paula, everyone knew, had taken to walking afternoons in the park, and was slimmer to show for it.

David would switch off the omnipresent phone, abandoning business just for her, the woman who had once been his disciple and crouched, attempting to sit cross legged, on a floor at his feet with a myriad others. They reclined in his matt speckled bedroom drinking tea, with suburbia outside the window, Bridgetown where the streets were blank and the windows empty in the day, and where they filled the vacuum with the rank juices and hot fumes of sex. He held her to him, so male, less blond, dulled, seasoned, and she found him surprisingly lacking in spiritual insights, or in the kind of perception that had once shaken her, but he thrilled her all over again with his calm masculinity and with it his assumption of power, and of her desirability, and of sex.

He kissed her, as he had so many times in her bedroom fantasy overlooking the saplings by the river, and her breasts sprang and budded. Her flab and stretch marks – those battle scars of nearly twenty years – dissolved to water, to nothing, as he touched her, and merged with the sheets, and the wet of it, the sore ridges of sheets she could embrace after they had finished for how they had been created. She licked the stiffness of his neck; his voice and its depth vibrated through to her lips in its maleness as he murmured to her, and they rocked as one, an antiphony; his penis was large, sometimes disarmingly large, inside her, and this was power, away from her children and the old geese and compost heaps and the Totnes Centre's grimy Area steps and Dartington Hall intellectuals. They fucked in juices until she felt his penis ramming at her cervix, their angles acute, their comings unrestrained.

At home, Poppy returned from school carrying blackberry tarts and a textile collage. She broke the stillness, Eleanor thought: Paula's gaze in the doorway was too loaded without deflection. Poppy smelled of school halls, smoke. She and Eleanor exchanged laboured innuendo. Tim walked into the room and hugged his daughters.

At the table, everything was the same, as if Eleanor had never worked or had sex or planned her departure, as if Rolf were not virtually adult. Poppy wanted to read. Tim munched, abstracted but more animated by having the Fambly all together. Paula served Rolf and Tim larger servings and rose above their verbal apathy with her energies.

'What have you been up to?' Paula asked Eleanor. She had barely seen her elder daughter during the latter part of the summer, only vaguely registering that there was some difference in her behaviour. She was too absorbed by the difference in her own behaviour. Paula looked at Eleanor directly, the pale brown irises steady.

Eleanor wanted to bolt, to gabble an answer and shut her up.

She wore a different perfume, Paula noticed. She was lit and closed-off. Eleanor could live only for snatched meetings, for new theories, the school of real life, of feminism, of social analysis. The school of pure silk clothes and feminine cabala. She was still driven by lofty ambitions, a tolerance only of the highest standards. But her aims had leapt in another direction. She would do nothing, prepare herself, rather than be droopy and idly contented like those girls in Sean's separate crowd who alternated cleaning with art courses, and ran market stalls in Totnes or sold their own jewellery at Hood Fayre and at the Health Centre. They seemed happy, happier than her. She could almost have joined their ranks, met her boyfriend for snatched breaks in adjoining cafés and shivered on stalls with the long haired girls in felt hats who were laid back and friendly – more normal than her, more casual. But she also resisted them and was driven by some other force: hours were not just for living but for collecting and distilling, moulding to her own machinations, and she could not bear even faint echoes of her parents' life, those grey flecked women who made flower pot bread to sell, those men in jerseys who enjoyed life for what it was. She despised them, and hated herself for not being famous, and aspired to some other life altogether.

'Perhaps you could use your A'levels in some way,' said Paula brightly as if imparting a novel idea.

'I intend to, don't I?' said Eleanor. 'How's your job, Rolfie brother?' she asked eventually.

Rolf looked blank.

'Which one?' Poppy guffawed.

'Rolf's been doing lots of guitar,' said Paula. 'Melly's neighbour – Jack, who's something quite big in the music business – says he'll listen to a tape.'

'Yeah, a proper demo,' said Rolf.

'Have you made one?' said Eleanor.

'Not yet. I'll be doing it in the next few weeks.'

Paula nodded. Where once she was enraged, Eleanor was merely contemptuous. Rolf's attempts at developing a half-hearted hobby were financed and embellished by Paula.

'Imagine them coughing up for studio time for a demo of me and my recorder?' A hot sudden whisper in Eleanor's ear.

Eleanor looked at Poppy, and for the first time it occurred to her that Selma was right. It was merely that Rolf was male, that was the answer to it all. She had a mother who preferred boys and respected them: it was as simple as that. Boys were dear little chaps, little fellows; girls were little madams. They put on airs. Amongst the children of friends, girls, even toddling girls, were subject to oblique judgement. Girls were manipulative or attention-seeking. Boys were uncomplicated bundles of energy.

Cake was served. Again, Eleanor noted, Rolf was cut the largest slice. The growing boy needed his food. Paula would love Rolf's son, but love his wife with reservations. But Eleanor also knew, quite prosaically, that she could never be loved like Rolf. He was simply preferred. It filled her with a sense of helplessness that rose inside her stomach and constricted her like a lump in the throat.

But there was some secret, some weapon. She could score in another world. She rose, insulated, above the Strachans and their munching. 'You,' Selma's voice came to her, flippantly, 'are like me.' Proofs and suggestions that were too terrifying, too joyful – she would hoard them now and examine them later alone.

Paula was picking over ideas. A sesame seed stuck to her lip. 'Perhaps,' she said, and again the eyes were frank and steady. 'Perhaps you – the thing is to enjoy yourself, Eleanor.'

'Yes, I do. Often.'

'I don't think you're really enjoying yourself, are you?'

'I thought you didn't care what we did as long as we didn't go into the Army. Oh, and I know you've got a thing about teachers as well.'

'That's not my *point*. And it's not that we don't *care*. We don't *mind* what you do as long as you're happy. I wasn't talking about that anyway.' She stared at Eleanor.

The silence. Eleanor clenched her teeth, made her expression blank. The thin disapproval. She held her breath against the next guarded judgement. She could not bear it. She could not tolerate the tiniest twitch of criticism if it came from Paula.

'Have a good time, if you're not –'

'What are you saying?' Eleanor almost screamed it, hushed herself. 'I thought you thought at Easter I should get more worthy work. I thought –'

'All I'm saying, darling, is that . . .' Paula prodded crumbs on the table so they stuck to her finger pads, 'perhaps you could let go? I mean, Eleanor, you don't really know what you're going to do when you finish school, so –'

'I *do*! I'm –'

'So, I was going to say anyway, you've worked very hard at school, and then again for your exams, and you never really just let go and have time for yourself. Now's the time to do it.' She looked at her brightly, decisively.

'Now is exactly *not* the time to do it!' Eleanor exclaimed. 'One minute you're . . .' Eleanor trailed off, looked down at the table. Rolf and Tim seemed calmly oblivious. Poppy had sneaked in her Dick Francis and was reading it on her lap.

'What?'

'Nothing,' she murmured.

Happiness shot through her despite Paula. It scaled her body and vibrated to her finger tips like lust. The knowledge of a world closed off to Paula lined her mind as a smug secret. For the first time, she was beyond Paula's judgement. There was another scale on which to measure herself. Thinking of Selma, she nearly murmured aloud, the sensation pouring to the base of her body; her warm skin, her cold features.

But Paula was needling at her.

Eleanor surfaced.

'Let's sort this out,' said Paula. 'I feel some grievance in you.'

'There's nothing to *sort* out,' said Eleanor, taut with embarrassment. Paula wore her expression, the one she adopted when she was about to tell Eleanor, in feigned casual tones, about some teenage child of a friend of hers who was thought to be pregnant, or the face she had worn when she had checked that Eleanor was using contraception, or when she attempted to talk love and emotions and resentments. The look that was preferable only to the pursed lips of unspoken criticism.

'I don't mean to get at you, darling,' she said. 'I only worry that you're not fulfilling yourself.'

'Well you don't have to worry.'

'I do worry about you, though, Eleanor.'

Eleanor pressed her nail into the table until she dug into its soft pine. 'Well, why not worry about Rolf or Poppy?' she said at last. 'They're not exactly doing anything.'

'Come on, Poppy's at school. And why do you have to drag Rolf into everything?'

'Why is it always *me*? Why do you just have these expectations of me? I mean, Rolf just oafs – no, sorry, Rolf – I mean, Rolf doesn't do that much.'

'He's not driven in the same way. Look, it's always hard to get this across to you, Eleanor, but I know what makes Rolf happy, and I know what makes you happy, and Rolf's somehow free of the – would you say this is true, Rolf? – the things, demons, that drive you. You're always looking. He's got something, some peace. He's a bit less hard on himself, if you like.'

'So in other words, Rolf knows himself and I don't?' said

Eleanor with irony.

'In a way, yes,' said Paula, missing it. She looked at Eleanor as if daring her to challenge her, the thin mouth set.

Rolf sat there, like a calf, thought Eleanor, the lips slightly parted as he looked up at his mother. Big eyes lashed, blank, complacent. He said nothing. He didn't have to. Just as he didn't have to help in the house to be loved. He was so utterly sure of himself, he was inert. He didn't have to do, thought Eleanor, he merely had to be. But his arrogance was combined with an innocence that set him beyond reproach. Big baby calflet suckling Mummy. Eleanor couldn't win. She didn't have blue eyes and strong forearms and a bullying certainty of her place in the world.

'Do you see what I'm saying? Really?'

'Yes, Paula.'

A pause.

'Don't look at me like that, Eleanor.'

'Like what?'

'Like a drama queen.'

Eleanor bit her tongue to stop tears rising in her throat. She wanted to shriek, kick the table, shout at that fat, freckled cow sitting in judgement opposite, but she was too scared of the pale hazel eyes, and banked it down, and knew, finally, she couldn't win. The years of it. She scrabbled against tearfulness.

She heard the echoes of a past regime: You are not spiritually in tune with David. It's your own choice, but you're missing out on good things. Oh Eleanor, try to open up your mind.

She looked away, so Paula's gaze was only a glint on the edges of her vision. She concentrated on the teapot with her own image distant and owl-like in it, so her thoughts were clear, and again excitement plummeted through her despite the pain, as if her body were primed for it, hit her abdomen with heat, so she was almost blinded. Her homely family munched behind lines of blindness. She was congested, thick-headed; Paula filled in the silences with questions and doubts, and Eleanor was dreamy, and Paula couldn't get through to her no matter how much she worried at the wound. Eleanor knew she was a pariah: she left her chair abruptly and went up to her bedroom.

'We're all invited to Selma's on Sunday week,' said Paula brightly. There was a note of pride in her voice.

Eleanor lifted her head from her book.

'Me too?' said Poppy.

'Of course. You can play with Louisa,' said Paula. 'Richard's down,' she said, as if she knew him.

Rolf declined the invitation. Eleanor had wrapped the blanket of defence tighter around her since her conversation with Paula; she threw herself into her work, but she was visibly distracted. It was as though she gritted her teeth against Paula: looking at her, there was a clash of irises, awareness and resentments like static electricity in the air; she said nothing and took on more than her share of household work, so Paula would be unable to fault her.

'Try to . . .'

'What?' said Eleanor, freezing. '*What*?'

'Well try to be sociable there, won't you?' said Paula. 'You've been like a wet weekend recently.'

Eleanor's mouth slackened. She said nothing, reached for a pen to fiddle with.

'Please don't ignore me, Eleanor,' said Paula.

'I'm *not*! Well what do you want me to say? What can I possibly say?'

'Nothing,' said Paula, her mouth clamping shut, the defiant mouth. 'I've made my point.'

'You mean you think I never talk?' said Eleanor in a strained voice.

'Now I didn't say that, did I?' said Paula patiently. 'All I said was if you're going to go to Selma's – my friend's – please do us all the courtesy of wiping that pained expression off and opening your mouth.'

'I do talk – I do talk to Selma,' said Eleanor, reddening slightly. She looked down and studied her pen.

'Yes, I suppose you do,' said Paula, and looked at Eleanor with her double gaze, the stare of frankness that masked some unspoken accusation.

'It's funny,' said Paula after a moment, 'but when we were young, we rebelled. We didn't want to hang out with our parents' friends. If we did, it was only to shock them.'

'You mean you smoked a bit of dope and sat on a few beanbags and said "fuck" a lot?'

'Well, we tried out all sorts of things,' replied Paula calmly. 'We wanted to up and travel, wear different clothes, dance, hang out – I didn't care so much about school marks, didn't take things quite so seriously, I suppose.'

'I'm sorry I'm a disappointment,' said Eleanor.

When they arrived at Causton, Selma seemed older, her figure just starting to become middle-aged. Two men and a woman sat at the table. Selma talked hectically, her hair tied back so that the focus of her face was her nose, a prominent nose on a white face with an ageing tiredness to it. Her eyelids were lumpy with mascara; it was as though she was flaking. She looked mad, Eleanor thought momentarily, then lost the reason behind the thought, and wanted to go over to her. Eleanor's body seemed to clamour physically for comfort. Paula stood beside her, slightly twitchy, beaming sociably, wanting to impress.

Selma's house was elegant in a way that made Eleanor yearn for such a home, though there were touches of make-shift, evidence of transience. It was as though she had imported London to the country, and it sat uneasily in its new surroundings, but it impressed Eleanor nevertheless. Number three, Causton, was a tall cottage in a terrace, like a town house. It was workmanlike, a worker's house, externally drab. There was a long garden; beyond which a field and then the road to Totnes. To Selma, it was her punishment and her salvation; the defeat of her marriage and the resurgence of her work.

The Strachans stood in a row, Tim's arm round Poppy, and Eleanor was acutely conscious of their scruffiness, of how they looked as though they were dressed for a CND march, Paula in jeans and trainers, Poppy in dungarees; and though Eleanor wore the cherry-coloured silk Selma had bought her, the scruffiness enveloped her by association, just as the lack of social bearing extended to her for being Strachan and therefore socially inept. Paula and Tim had never given dinner parties: instead, co-workers, devotees would roll up on a Saturday afternoon with their children, and Tim would fall asleep in a chair while Paula tried to join in the conversations centred around spiritual matters at the same time as serving up wholemeal pizzas.

Selma and Jilly, Selma's much lauded 'best friend' from London, talked at once. There was a bloom of camaraderie built on common references. Eleanor stood to one side as Selma talked, and Selma caught her out of the side of her eye as she gesticulated or laughed, greeting her only with the slightest eye movement of acknowledgement.

'This is Richard,' said Selma. 'My friends Paula and Tim Strachan.'

'Pleased to meet you,' said Richard.

'Richard's got to catch the train, unfortunately,' said Selma. 'Oh, and two of their children, Eleanor and Poppy.'

Richard Mecklen was clearly younger than Selma. He was tall

and energetic. There was an intensity or an anger to his movements in long strides about the room, the way his hair flopped over his forehead in animation. He seemed very certain of himself. Eleanor ticked with self-doubt. No longer cushioned by the pink buffer of extreme youth, she had no excuse. But if she was too old, she was also too young: squirming, dull with self-censorship. They all talked, and there were references to people Eleanor had never met, a natural cynicism whose provenance was largely unknown to her; beyond that an entire system of life that was outside her true comprehension. Selma was no longer her saviour from Paula, just another of that band of people from which she was excluded.

They walked into the garden. Richard held out his hand to Eleanor on the steps that led from the back door to the lawn, and she took it and jumped down. He was large and corduroy trousered, he smelt of alcohol and wallets on the steps. His air of bonhomie had an abrasive edge: after drinking, he was courteous to the point of belligerence. He was a large, male presence. Eleanor couldn't categorise him, or imagine what bound Selma to him. The image of Selma, somewhere in the garden, seemed frail and breakable in comparison. Picturing Richard, with the masculine planes of his face and his large gentle hands, tangled with Selma in the inevitable bed upstairs made Selma appear so ultimately womanly that Eleanor was filled with a poignant awareness of the quality, and when she descended through the double doors into the garden, she seemed bound by some secret of sex, and Selma noticed her and straightened a corner of the blanket for her. She patted it with her pale fingered hands. She made a questioning sound. She rested her arm on Eleanor's shoulder, proprietorially, as if gathering her flock about her, the Strachans and Richard, and Louisa skulking by the tree, Jilly, and Louisa's regular babysitter, Ben. Her scent moved over Eleanor.

Lights appeared in windows, pale in the fluid blue of evening. Selma walked around the garden with Jilly. The garden was hazardous with vegetation – neglected pots, a dusty tree, the grass uneven with clumps of flower and weed. Summer plants were fading, untended by Selma or Louisa. A siren wailed beyond the hill and disappeared towards the moor.

Selma and Jilly paced about the garden engaged in a horticultural argument. They prodded plants and disputed their names. Selma kicked a browning bush in an earthenware pot so that it rolled over and its roots were slimy with approaching autumn. Their argument became loud and childish: they giggled and held each other and kicked more plants. They paraded the garden skittishly, both of similar height and size, though Jilly was more worn with age, the layered tawny hair and sun-dulled skin of her generation's brittler survivors. They both adhered without knowing it to remnants of early seventies style. Jilly's kohl on the lower rim of her eyes, the eyebrows that never fully recovered from plucking.

Selma caught Louisa round the waist. Louisa twitched away, then lowered her head against Selma and they paced in long sloppy strides about the garden. Selma could not let go of her, Louisa dragging at her waist, her feet kicking out in more deliberate strides, and they sank together on one of the blankets, Louisa lying on Selma's calf, staring at the sky and then unwaveringly at Eleanor.

Selma spoke. 'Louisa has just got a beautiful new –'

'Shut up, Mum! Shut up,' said Louisa urgently.

'OK,' whispered Selma, and stroked her, drumming her finger pads lightly on her temple. Eleanor wanted to belong to it all, an integral part of the scene, as if the Mecklen family could adopt her. The mere three of them, Richard, Selma and Louisa, with their customs and their objects, were like a large enclosed order, and you had to be Mecklen or Healy to share it. If she could not be Louisa's sister, or one of the nieces, she could carve a niche of her own. She veered between roles: Selma's babysitter, Selma's servant, Selma's best friend. She wanted to know where all the kitchen utensils were, and direct guests to the lavatory, and stay the night in a room at the top of the house that was seen as Eleanor's room. She dreamed of moving to Causton to be a neighbour, so that she could wander casually in and out, contained by the stained railings with Selma's own blanket on the ground.

'I wonder what the poor people are doing,' said Selma.

Ben the babysitter began to protest.

'Ignore her,' said Richard. 'It's a favourite of hers.'

Hurt, Selma murmured to the world at large, making statements blankly without pause for response. She conducted monologues while gazing at Louisa, plucking at her skin and squashing her nose, tracing the folds of her ears, enfolding her.

'I have to go,' said Richard.

'Oh God, you do. It's quarter past already, for God's sake! Hurry darling.'

'Dad, *don't*,' said Louisa.

Selma looked pained.

Louisa burst into tears. Richard lifted her up from Selma's lap, her legs dangling too long as he held her, burying his head into her and kissing her. They walked to the house together. Selma looked exasperated, as though she might cry.

'It upsets her so much when he leaves,' she said. 'It upsets me so much when he comes.'

Jilly left with Richard to catch the last Sunday train to London. They said goodbye, Richard and Selma snapping at each other and hugging each other in a sudden valedictory outburst of recriminations, while Louisa sobbed and Poppy neighed in her ear and stroked her, making horse faces for her.

The day had been dull and warm. A gnatty rain fell. Selma pottered about making tea. She turned on the porch light and illuminated the drizzle. It wet her face as though she were crying, drawing real tears from her that the rain disguised.

'He, he gives me no confidence,' said Selma, sitting down. The drizzle thinned. She poured tea and blankly handed it round.

'I thought he was nice,' said Paula simply.

'He is nice. But that's not all there is to it.'

'He's quite a good-looking man,' said Paula.

'*Paula!*' snapped Selma. She shook her head, looking down at her lap. Paula's hazel gaze was rooted upon her.

'It goes well beyond that, can't you see?' said Selma. 'It's not just him.' She lit a cigarette and puffed, and the smoke edged gently over to Eleanor. Tim was deep in a conversation with Ben the babysitter. Poppy and Louisa appeared at windows in the house, sauntering round the path. It became darker. They wore Selma's shoes and giggled hysterically, conscious of Ben, who was oblivious of them and talked about glass-making and photography with Tim.

'I think it's marriage in general, the institution of it,' said Selma. 'I mean, any institution that legalises rape within it can't be exactly democratic, can it? I think marriage is fucked,' she said in a louder voice.

Paula looked nervous. 'Oh come on Selma,' she said with a little laugh. 'It isn't so bad.'

'Oh really?' said Selma, looking directly at her. 'Really?'

Paula laughed more nervously, fixing her gaze rigidly on Selma with a slight frown.

'Think about it,' said Selma.

'Yes, yes I will,' said Paula.

Eleanor watched them from her corner, alert for a subtext she couldn't quite fathom.

'It's not the women,' said Selma, 'though we collude. Really, we shouldn't support the system, we really shouldn't support their abuse of us, and that chip-chip-chip terrible undermining. God, Richard, he comes here and I'm pleased to see him because of course I love him, I do of course –' she sighed, 'but then he takes so much out of me because he storms about the place thinking he owns me, interrupting my work, just blustering, biting away at my confidence.'

Paula nodded, looking serious.

'I think women are just nicer beings,' said Selma. She rose above the liquid monotone, her voice becoming louder. 'Men, the way the world is at the moment, are fucked. Really, it's not worth being with them. Really . . . They eat up your energy and then sit there belching, and then they want to fuck you. I'm just going to be friends with women and get on with my work.'

'Selma,' Paula tentatively stretched out her arm and touched her. Selma's shoulder dropped and relaxed at her touch. 'Can I do anything?'

Selma ignored her.

Paula cleared her throat. 'Men aren't all so terrible, you'll see that when you're calmer, Selma. They can be quite nice really!' She laughed self-consciously.

Selma openly raised her eyes to the sky.

'Do you want to talk about this any more?' said Paula eventually.

'No,' said Selma. She clamped her mouth shut. Its top lip formed a passive curve against the straight line of the lower lip.

Louisa wandered over. She curled up to Selma and crawled onto her lap as if much younger.

'I'm sorry about Dad,' Selma murmured.

Louisa replied with a hiccoughing sound. She locked herself to Selma as if they were one. Selma put her forehead to Louisa's hair, and her movements were accustomed, unselfconscious. She teased and talked to her in a low voice, babying her while speaking in sentences that might have been directed at an adult. Eleanor watched them from her shaded position. It was silky, sexy. She wanted to be held by her like that, the calm efficiency of years in even the most affectionate gesture. Eleanor watched Selma talk and talk, smoothing Louisa as if moulding clay, pliant under her touch, and she was light-headed, mesmerised. Sometimes Selma was silent, and Eleanor caught her breath, waiting, as her silence was unexpected, she seemed to be waiting passively for others to take their turn, and she was all profile and nose, all white cut features in the dark looking down at Louisa. Her hand movements were frequent and light over Louisa, her long nails and the twisting of her wrist. She wove a different texture of smells from those to which Eleanor was accustomed, perfumes, face creams, Louisa, her skin.

Eleanor shivered but remained sleeveless: she was light and cold and the hollows of her arms seemed white on the grass, like the stunted white weeds that now glowed by the house. She was aware of her breasts and her heart beating with a hurting rhythm. Selma seemed to swing above her as if distorted by a lens.

She could say nothing. The double clamp of Selma and Paula silenced her. She strained, physically, to talk, but only the phlegm of a cough emerged and she tried silently to growl it away, all the muscles in her throat constricting in silent effort. Her heart began to thump as soon as a sentence rolled around in her mind, practised and perfected, but speech seemed to require a physical ability that she had lost. She remained silent. Selma's breasts hung low, her back arched to stroke Louisa. They were large, crumpled with fabric, the essence of all her femininity and maturity. The remains of lipstick stained her mouth, meeting in a darker line of wine on the bottom lip. The depths of whiteness of her skin, that tired translucency against flat brown hair, took on new paler shades, bluenesses, in the light. The clean angle of her jaw softened as she leant over Louisa, talking close to her ear. Eleanor ached.

'We were talking earlier,' said Paula brightly into the silence. 'About how kids don't rebel now. In the same way as we used to. Funny, isn't it?'

'They do rebel,' said Selma, playing with Louisa's ear. 'Only in a more subtle way.'

Eleanor let her hair flop; it hid the side of her face.

'I suppose Rolf's a bit of a rebel,' said Paula.

'I'd say he's a completely predictable product of his up-bringing,' said Selma.

Eleanor snorted faintly with laughter and twitched the curtain of hair further over her features, forming a shield between herself and Paula.

'I wouldn't call a modified punk look an act of rebellion,' said Selma. She slid a glance at Eleanor, who smiled unseen back at her.

'Well no, I suppose –' said Paula, at a loss. She looked over to where Eleanor sat, silently focused on the ends of her hair. 'Our Ellie here says –'

'Oh Paula,' said Eleanor.

'Well, you say what you said,' said Paula.

'I didn't say anything.'

'Exactly.'

Eleanor looked over at where Selma sat, Louisa in a semi-doze on her lap. The scents, or the idea of the scents Selma emanated, or simply her context, her house and belongings, were so various and adult that they contained only frustration. Eleanor clamped and slid her teeth and played with her hair. Being beside Selma in all her self-possession was unbearable, and yet there was pleasure in simply looking at her. Eleanor could lower her head and then look up and catch her in glimpses, and there she was, there she was herself, in all her curves and her exquisite rightness, every gesture and every intonation. There.

Paula needled at Eleanor to end the silence.

'Eleanor's an old soul . . .' she mused. 'You're set on your course, aren't you, no flex – no wavering.'

'Just because I don't go to slimming clubs one minute and T'ai Chi classes the next,' snapped Eleanor. 'No, I don't want to follow ten different bearded gurus and then give them all up and decide to go to University and then never go and then work in a shop. No.'

'Oh Eleanor,' said Paula.

'As I said before, I'm sorry I'm a disappointment to you,' said Eleanor, 'I'm sorry I'm – me. I –'

'Of course you're not,' said Paula gently. 'It's just I wish sometimes you'd experiment, loosen up a bit.'

'Oh Paula,' pleaded Eleanor. 'Please, I'm sorry.'

Eleanor got up suddenly. Her bladder burned in the cold. She needed to be alone to escape from Paula, to assimilate Selma. She got up and walked to the house, which contained its daytime warmth and smelt of other people's houses, proper houses, clean baking, sophistication, unlike her parents' home, which smelt only of the Strachans and their own familiar inadequacies.

Eleanor crept up the stairs, though she was alone in the house, and prodded doors to find the bathroom. Her legs jumped on a nerve as she sat on the lavatory, shivering with an overdrive of nerves though she was no longer cold. She was small and discreet and curious in the strange house. She pulled herself in. Her urine was a bright intrusion. She flushed it away and padded along the upstairs corridors, between patches of darkness and muted light, let in, finally, to Selma's workings. The home of Selma Healy.

Though Selma was in the garden, Eleanor had the space and incapsulated time to examine Selma alone, as if in a museum, her house with its photos and choice of colours, to feel her as if in the flesh, like touching the living warmth of recently discarded clothes.

The house was cool and bold, dark wood floors, pale walls, small folding chairs with woven seats, rugs of maroons and reds. A stone sculpture stark on a corner windowsill, mirror frames stained ebony. She nudged a door open: there were unexpected touches of prissiness in a bedroom, clearly Selma's, restrained white frothings, lace edging to shelves. Again, a different world. Eleanor ached with it. It excited her; she wanted to possess it; it was hers for the moments she stood there. She looked out of a back window and made out the glass planes of a greenhouse in the dark. Down the corridor were photos of Louisa as a young child, large granular monochrome prints. Their professionalism irked her. Suddenly jealous, in her instant absorption of detail, she felt as much an intruder as if she had rifled through Selma's underwear drawers. Family mementoes repelled her as an outsider, but she loved, loved, the silent house all to herself, her breath loud and slow, the Selma smells, she loved Selma; she put her cheek against the wall and its porous cool pressed her like a friend. She moved down the stairs, past a modern naked religious triptych, onto the first floor where she sat on a little window seat, again the stained dark wood, and lifted her knees up to frame herself in it, light-headed against the pane. The curtains were wine velvet, lined with cream. How pleasing, she thought, and eyed the books on the landing shelves, each title a facet of Selma, every mundane paperback a momentary choice she had once made. Each object belonged to someone else, its codes indecipherable to her. Perhaps in Selma's wardrobe there still hung the raincoat she had worn that afternoon on Totnes High Street when she had sat in a café with Jilly: Eleanor remembered exactly its cut, its exact impression, though perhaps not its colour, and thought of it hanging, a recognisable detail of her past, clung to it in her mind, it belonged to her, proof of something essential.

'You're up there, I'll come up,' called Selma. Eleanor jumped. Selma clattered up the stairs and appeared on the landing.

'Where's everyone?' said Eleanor.

'Down there. In the garden.'

Selma was beside her in the passage, vibrant with sudden details of breath and flesh and individual hairs that strayed wirily and caught the light, the living person quite different from her mental representation. She was casual, her hair falling down around her ears. They stood and smiled at one another.

'Was I rude to you today?' said Selma suddenly. 'I've been very preoccupied.'

'Well, you're difficult to talk to sometimes,' said Eleanor.

Selma turned round and half looked at her. 'Am I? Conversation isn't by invitation.' Her voice was light, without warmth.

'That's true,' said Eleanor. 'But people are frightened to talk to you because you don't acknowledge them, you barely even bother to look at them half the time.'

'Perhaps they're not worth looking at. It's more tempting if they're easy on the eye at least,' said Selma.

Eleanor remained silent.

'I'm self-sufficient perhaps, but I'm never rude. I won't tolerate bad manners,' said Selma.

'You are rude,' said Eleanor.

'How?' said Selma coolly.

'You're not responsive, you –'

'No, I innovate, I don't respond. There are quite enough responders around.'

'Yes, but people are scared of you, and then they bore you

because they're not themselves, they're afraid of your judgement or your lack of interest, and then you get bored yourself – I can see it.'

'Well thanks, sweetheart, for analysing my predicament.'

There was a lull. Eleanor shivered. They stood in the passage. Selma turned to her. 'Tell me – when I've ever been rude to you,' she said to Eleanor.

'I think you were today,' said Eleanor. 'You say to come over, and then you don't even say hello. So I don't know where I am, whether I should stay or go.'

'Of course I wanted you to stay. You don't need my assurance of that.'

Eleanor shrugged.

'It's up to you how you treat people,' said Eleanor. 'But I think you can't cope unless you've won them to you, and then you can afford not to bother with them.'

'That's not true.'

'You need to be *adored*. You don't care if you're liked.'

There was silence. Selma smiled over at her, her gaze disappearing in patches of dark.

'I hope people like me too,' said Selma calmly.

'Look, we're talking about *you* again, Selma,' said Eleanor, half laughing despite herself.

'I can cope,' said Selma, tilting her head back. She looked down at Eleanor. 'You're naughty to speak to me like that,' she said. She rearranged Eleanor's hair on her shoulder. 'And you, of course, are just a shrinking violet, no need for adoration, Eleanor Strachan.'

'Very funny.'

'You aspire to be like me –'

'What a lie!'

'And that's why I rile you.' She smiled at her. 'I'll show you my house,' said Selma, turning. 'You haven't commented on my house.'

'Oh, it's lovely,' said Eleanor, preoccupied.

'I'll show you my screen and my Listed fireplace. That's an old study or something up here – there's nothing to see in there – this is Louisa's room. I have instructions not to show it to guests. Look at the star wallpaper.'

They stood and contemplated it, gold stars on brushed blue paper lining Louisa's walls. Selma leaned against the door and they talked, lowly, blankly, all tension diffusing. Eleanor looked up at her and smelled her smell, again sharply different from in memory, or from its simplification in perfume testers in chemists. The voice lulled her.

'And this is Richard's old boot of a sister in some Austrian pig farm.'

'She has Louisa's mouth. Or chin.'

'Quite. I can't be blamed for it.'

She stood in profile. She looked down, calm and sculpted white. She held the doorpost with her arm above her head, so her body curved and lengthened, arching her foot on the carpet. The cold regularity of her features made her appear harder, more remote, than perhaps she was. She swum between distance and proximity, the face an impossibility, the emissions of breath merely human and close. She had a sister-in-law, a pubescent daughter, responsibilities. She had a life that had made her strained and nearly forty.

'Look – some strange and beautiful nutcrackers a friend brought me back from Morocco. I'll show you how they work – see that?'

She is glorious, glorious. The edge of her mouth shaped to a perfect closing, a crease of symmetry. Eleanor breathed through her nose and felt she was swaying.

146

'Let me see,' said Eleanor. She took it, and her fingers looked small as they held it curiously, carefully.

Cupboards in apple pie order, linens; Eleanor realised she had misunderstood, forgotten the controlled, domestic element in her admiration for all that was more flamboyant. She looked at Selma's back leaning over a slatted door, the arch of it, the womanliness that was her own possession and couldn't be touched.

'So, do you like my house, Eleanor?'

'Of course.'

'It's my anchor. Like my clothes.'

They wandered around, felt textures with a shared concentration, their hands meeting on wood and fabric. Eleanor saw her whole world sharpen into a knowledge, an awareness of that moment, the strange leisurely exploration of objects in a house, as if time were non-existent and there were no guests in the garden. They talked inconsequentially as in a dream, milky, unhindered. Everything was reduced to an object, and the tensions it carried, and Selma's nose and Eleanor's fingers.

'I'd only expect such a lovely screen as that in films.'

'Yes, it seems to bloom.'

The breath through Selma's nose a small hiss over the female hairs on her upper lip. Her voice, to Eleanor, was reduced to its components, its meaning lost in its tones and vibrations. It was tangible.

Touch me, touch me. Speak in the voice. The thick white calm beaded with tension. There was an electric heaviness outside. The weather was mobile and uneasy. Selma was moving through the sweet dense smell of the office, showing things. Eleanor caught an edge of awareness in her, an unusual loss of composure. Their gazes clashed; they looked away. Eleanor's nerves swelled and flared until she was sensory only. They looked at each other: they

147

laughed simultaneously, a hiss through the nose, and held each other, and Selma's mouth, fine and pale cut, buzzing by her ear, Eleanor's cheek below her collar bone, the cloth pressed hard and ridged. The rustle of hair in the ear thunderous, cartilage, perfume hot. Beats and breathings amplified. Each imagined gesture sprung into reality, hardness, the cloth on Selma's shoulder.

'You know —' murmured Eleanor.

'My "daughter",' said Selma, and laughed.

SEVEN

PAULA HAD LOOKED AT THE CHILD ELEANOR AND SEEN little glimpses of herself. She saw Tim's mouth, Tim's nose twitch, but she saw the essence of herself. Eleanor, like she, had many faults. She bristled with insecurities. And beyond that, she was rather a little madam, demanding attention. That stick-like child would grow big hips: Paula could see it already, laying down the fat in her mind's eye five years prematurely, remembering herself as a portly teenager who had stared in the mirror in distress, in screaming angry hatred, and thought of sloughing the fat off her own thighs with a butcher's knife. She worked at correcting Eleanor's faults, her guile, her untidiness, and was exasperated with her. She'd bend over Eleanor to brush her hair, so fine it was like plant-life, like sea-life, and her stomach protruded and her chin slackened as she leant. Sometimes Paula didn't know who she hated, herself or Eleanor or the world, and she tightened the clamp, glimpsing an excitement almost sexual, a frenzy of self-hate and guilt punctuated by pure love, pure love for Eleanor.

Then Rolf appeared uncluttered from inside her, a clean slate. He had blue eyes, strong boy thighs, muscle not fat. He was the dearest boy. She wondered where such beauty came from. His glossy head of hair, his long lashes, his little needs: she wanted to protect him from something. His screaming kept her up at night and exhausted her; he was slow to talk; he wet the bed; but her exhaustion was simple, simple physical exhaustion without twitches or complexities.

She loved them both, her children. She was lucky to have one of each: a boy and a girl, and both healthy, and growing up without rules or regulations, the freedom of the fields and spiritual richness.

Eleanor wanted a kind mother. She was the luckiest girl in the world with her house and her parents who let her call them by their first names, but she had problems, so Paula got cross with her. She wanted a mother who smiled down on her as she tucked her up in bed, serene, and stroking her. She wanted a dove, a glowing mother out of a Bible or an advert. Sometimes she glimpsed it in Paula. She thought then that her mother was an angel.

'I can't believe it's nearly November,' said Paula.

'I have to write a dissertation by next week,' said Eleanor.

'Are you going to manage it?' said Paula.

Eleanor shrugged. 'Yeah,' she said.

'OK, well I'm off then,' called Paula. She had lost weight. She had done it without trying. She put on her coat and went out to the car.

Eleanor curled up on the sofa until her ankles went to sleep under her. She shook them like a cat, and wandered off to the kitchen where the bright orange foam of the previous night's pasta settled in the sink as a legacy of Rolf's washing up. Bags of unwashed clothes emitted a stale smell by the washing machine. The phone rang; Eleanor jumped, but it was only her friend Georgia.

The house was at its most mellow in the autumn, its warm tones deflecting the cold outside. There was every comfort: food in the fridge, fires, music, people. Eleanor sat on the sofa, feeling her black-tighted legs, and the year drew on. Tim asked her if she was depressed, then left her alone, but Paula suddenly said she would pay for a new coat for her, and invited her to the Centre for lunch if she felt like coming.

The moor was losing its colour, like wasteland, its puddles rough with sky. The upper ridges were bleached, earth shaved to stone. Buzzards scaled the blankness, the sky wind-torn or wet and still, dissolving outlines with fog, dripping with a meanness, an absence of colour.

Some people with dogs on strings were camping outside Widecombe. They had sprayed 'Sin City' over the sign announcing 'Widecome-in-the-Moor – Please Drive Slowly Through This Village'. Rolf went to visit one of them who had played with him in one of his half-hearted bands, then came back and said he was moving into the field with them. Paula and Tim calmly assented, and Paula visited the next day with a tin of flapjacks and some quick-cook rice, picking over the field in her newly polished shoes, flecking her red tights with mud, and two days later Rolf returned home. The reeds near the pond softened and browned, and Poppy's pony covered its flanks with a permanent caking of mud like a cracked river bed.

Paula confidently flashed along the lanes in her VW overtaking the late autumn tourist traffic. She listened to Simon and Garfunkel's Greatest Hits, knocked over a badger one night, and was warned by the Ashburton police station not to drive so fast at dusk.

'It's the Rogue Badger!' said Eleanor. 'Poppy, Paula's killed the Rogue Badger!'

'What is this Rogue Badger thing you two go on about?'

enquired Paula mildly.

'Oh *Paula*,' sighed Poppy, 'you *know*. The famous wild humungous badgie-badge that's meant to hang out at Bowlands Farm.'

'The monstrous creature of local legend,' said Eleanor. 'Like a King Kong of Widecombe.'

Poppy snorted.

'You mean you invented it. More of that mindless, arch snobby gossip you two invent. I wonder what the neighbours would think if they heard you,' mused Paula. Their chatter barely engaged her. The van stereo had been blaring 'The Boxer' as she accelerated, the suspension floating along the long clear section by the Dart, David's face in her mind, on her body, and as the van juddered with a sudden metallic thud, her heart crashing into thumps, it was David's chest beating after the low yowl of his orgasm, his sweat and her sweat, the feel of the dead animal solid under the wheels.

Paula began driving faster. Everything in the country took longer in the winter: keeping warm, starting vehicles, cleaning the house. Simple actions required calculation: stumbling from a porch to a car in the dark, every bone in the back in a seizure of cold; taking out the Aga's ashes into a bang of frozen air by the yard, the dustbins only emptied weekly, weather permitting. Ashes left on the flagstones in the kitchen, the dog's water in unlicked puddles, and mushrooms, toadstools, slender fungi growing inside the pantry windows facing quarried earth at the back. Coal dust in circles round the freezer's legs, and always Gandalf smellier, wetter, even his breath a damp meaty slab of odour.

Paula caught the edge of her coat on the muddy rim of the car and cursed.

'See, I told you, it's like a ridiculous *punishment* having to live in this place,' said Eleanor quietly. 'It's a penitentiary. Remember what's here? The *prison*? Right? Ever wondered why? Why don't you buy a nice house in London? Tim could go to Hampstead Heath if he needed some trees.'

Paula's silence spoke assent. She drove with Eleanor to the Totnes Centre.

The girls of the conservatory composed fine prose and parsed sentences. Eleanor hid her paper in a section of her desk so she would have to travel to the stock cupboard and fetch more supplies. Paula Strachan remarked upon her extravagance: she would have to be more cautious. But the window on the landing revealed only grey across the roofs, and blank panes on the opposite side, and the sky behind the pagoda seemed thundery.

They had finished their work for the day, yet late afternoon tea was subdued, as if they were waiting, but no one ever acknowledged the reason for their unease.

Then Mrs Healy slipped into the room, her hair pearled with wet from the world outside, and with her arrival and the onset of evening, those fine strands of expectation that infected the hours before bed. The rigours of the day dissolved: they chattered and laughed for her to see, their darting eyes and tossing hair having a manic quality, but she calmed them too, drawing them together with the quality of her voice. And during the evenings, her favourites would emerge, but the patterns shifted, she heaped upon her chosen ones all her loving attentions and then became distracted, and it was all surmise. Then she would leave them to join her peers. 'I owe you your keepsake,' she said in a sudden intimate address to Eleanor before she left.

Paula bloomed. She bloomed behind her freckles. She bloomed behind her ample frontage. She had shaken off the cows and water meadows; her children were half grown up; her husband did not seem to notice her, but now his negligence was a gift. She walked about the edges of the moor, and the stomping country cousin that she had been had taken flight.

'I think, you know, love – lust, whatever, it can change your whole being,' she said to Selma.

She missed Eleanor by a matter of fields and walls. Eleanor, too, took to the moors for odd hours, and while Paula stuck to the footpaths, Eleanor forged inland through the gorse paths, and they never bumped into one another, though Eleanor once spotted a figure in the distance she suspected was her mother, and was about to run down to her when she remembered she was wearing pale colours, which Paula said did not suit her, so she turned away. The years of bottle green tights and bumble bee stripes had taken their toll. She sped on, and trippy flowers appeared to grow under foot, and the trees contained echoes of something unattainable.

Eleanor had filled out, her face fleshier. She frequently wore a large jersey over what was clearly a summer dress: old dark red silk that flapped and clung to her legs.

'Why do you wear that thing in the winter?' asked Paula. Rain darkened it in streaks. The texture of Eleanor's tights pressed against the damp patches.

Eleanor shrugged. Her breasts looked larger, lumpy beneath the jersey. Paula cast an eye over her and wondered whether her figure would become like her own after all. An aureole of fine frizz created by rain and central heating, rose above her hair. Eleanor hunched herself against Paula's scrutiny.

But yet she was delectable, thought Paula. Even the slight lumpiness of the breasts beneath the jersey, the winter frizz of her hair, were surface flaws on what must simply be perceived as sex, readiness, a plumpness of skin, an awareness of attraction, and

Paula thought then that men must look at her daughter with desire. They must look at her and find her appealing simply on account of her youth and her breasts and her liveliness and imagine fucking her.

Eleanor was mottled and edgy. She snapped, then tamed herself. She seemed to live in a frenzy of intolerance that lapsed to absent happiness. The lumpiness increased: there were days when she was dark and drooping in large jerseys, her hair hooked in ropy clumps behind her ears, her skin both drained and inflamed.

Paula noticed it, but her inner thigh muscles were tender from sex and obliterated much thought. If she worried, it was over Rolf. Poppy was a child and bolshy; Eleanor was an adult and bolshy. They had a toughness. But Paula sensed a hurt young man behind Rolf's bluff and sneer, a boy who still needed encouragement. Paula could see it in the way he held his thin chest defensively, in his loose-lipped silences, and it pulled at her heart.

Winter encased everything. It enclosed desire within the house. Lamps were little suns against the cold outside. They were jewels. The cold encased the scents of things, like cold pressed perfumes. The walls, the fires, moved and spurted smoke, but everything else was preserved. Eleanor was sick with excitement, and winter boxed it and magnified it. It was not like summer when blowsy emotions drifted and spread. She thought of Selma, and her breath became thin and faster. Her chest felt constricted as she breathed the warm smoky air from the fire. She imagined then that she could go outside and hike and hitch her way to Causton, but the shock of cold air, and the extreme dark, no lighting along the lane but the moon and rare specks of cars passing on the far horizon, made it an impossibility. Selma Healy, smelling of roses, smelling of her child, was tucked valleys away, the other side of the Dart, beyond the moors, past the A38 leading to Plymouth. She would be working by a lamp in her study while Louisa watched videos. To Eleanor, the world had contracted to symbols of her, the smell of her clothes by a heater or a theory casually expounded.

She hadn't seen Selma Healy herself since the Sunday at Causton. Her name flickered through Paula's conversation. She was the older woman of a fantasy. Eleanor could hardly tell where reality ended and where a fictional troop of women embodying the essential qualities of Selma Healy meandered through her mind.

Eleanor wanted to be a maid – a maid washing Selma's linens. A protégée under her tutelage. Or a boy, a young boy with his lover, Madame de Healy like Madame Léa, always French, a woman who scented her age with roses and enhanced it with powders, and stretched out on beds of pillows and tea gowns. She used dabs of cream from pots, unctions and preservatives. The demure wing of her hair fell over something more knowing. That blasé assurance, the very key to her desirability, was what Eleanor craved and feared she'd never attain. She thought that Paula half suspected the content of her fantasies, and moaned out loud alone in her bedroom in embarrassment. But then Paula seemed preoccupied.

The school Eleanor attended in reality was a breezeblock tribute to early seventies architecture, drafty and low-hung and vaguely Scandinavian. While Dartington Hall was set on grassy slopes, the Comprehensive was banked by a carpark and clusters of pre-fab language labs and maths huts. Its main quadrangle featured a squiggle of sculpture like a concrete turd or a snail. Its pine rafters, shiny with grime, lifted the Scandinavian-style roofs. The breezeblocks along the corridors were painted brown to scuffing height, graffiti'd white above, and rain spread into them and cigarette smoke seeped down from the toilets, and the classrooms were strip lit and vinyl tabled, and Eleanor Strachan could not imagine what she was doing at such a place, where eighteen-year-olds mingled with eleven-year-olds, the autonomy of the Sixth Form 'college' merely an administrative distinction, when her heart and mind had long since left the place, usually for London, sometimes Causton. And at other times she had regressed into fifteen-year-old submission to discipline and tradition.

Sean barely entered her consciousness. His function as a symbol of normality and popularity had been fulfilled; he had long since slipped from his place in her daily thoughts, except on odd afternoons when she thought of him and missed him. She completed her work automatically, and suffered odd panics in the night about forthcoming exams.

And it was in that other place that she lived, a different land, an academy where she wore her muslin night slip, her day chemise hanging ready for morning by her bed.

The clamour of girls preparing themselves around her. She sidled out of the door and made her way through the main building into the back corridors, which seemed to have thrown up labyrinthine passages; she found the stairs that led to the roof, and now the light flickered as she passed. Mrs Healy was here, in the building. Eleanor went back to bed.

Why did Mrs Healy take so long to come and see her? But why did Eleanor hope and go on hoping like this every night? Because the memory of her face would not leave her. Signs appeared every day, in half-heard comments, in the arrangement of certain wild things in the garden, and in hints less concrete but momentous in their symmetry.

Steps sounded down the passage, closer, and closer, passing. An hour, two hours, of creaks and silences. Eleanor dreaded it as she longed for it. It was too much. But her gut was in pain with waiting. Noise faded; distant shutters; silence. Again, wakefulness like a disease. Her senses so strained, a whole new life of sounds in her ear drums, gurgling like footsteps. There. A noise! Nothing. She couldn't tolerate this. Her heart beat in recovery from the false alarm, overlapping with what were now real sounds, sudden footsteps taking her by surprise. The loudness of the real thing behind her confusion. The steps stopped. A pause.

In the darkness, barely perceptible, Mrs Healy came in and checked on some harsh breathing, twitched a sheet back in place. She folded a dress. 'Eleanor,' she murmured as she passed by her end of the room. She placed her hand on Eleanor's forehead. Burning. The hand was snow calming a fever. 'Here is your present,' she said, and lifted Eleanor's head, fingers cold on the downy space of hair on her neck as she fixed a chain. Eleanor's skin leapt to goose pimple. 'It was my Christening locket,' she said. 'It's Victorian.' Her hand drifted over Eleanor's shoulder; Eleanor shivered and arched her back towards her, and they held each other in absolute communion.

Eleanor entered the Centre with Paula in the evening, for the first time since the Sunday at Selma's house.

'Hello, Eleanor sweetie,' said Selma. She smiled at Paula, betraying a slight awkwardness. 'Hello, Paula. Takings were comparatively good today.'

Eleanor looked dark and small like a child. Selma was shocked at how childlike she suddenly looked. The skin around her nose and mouth was inflamed.

'You need some E45 cream,' said Selma absently to Eleanor.

Eleanor's hand shot to her mouth.

'It'll soothe it,' said Selma.

'Paula's always rabbiting on about calendula and comfrey

cream,' said Eleanor.

'Paula rabbits on because Paula knows about these things,' said Paula.

'Yes, yes, death to hydrocortisone, ban the bomb, and feverfew on everything. I know,' said Eleanor.

Paula's eyes darted round the Centre. Selma shook her head slightly.

Paula and Eleanor were a study in contrast. They were of a similar height, but Paula's flesh was solidly laid down where Eleanor's was susceptible to change, lumpiness and slightness within the same month. Eleanor's jersey was stretched over her bottom, her skirt bagged out beneath. Her darkness was an impression rather than a skin hue or perhaps it was merely in the shade of her eyes and brows. Her mouth closed to a full feminine arch. Paula's eyes and neck had turtled with age, though her hair was still thick and her breasts full. Where Paula radiated plump good will, Eleanor emanated a more volatile self-awareness. Selma could barely see the mother in the daughter.

'So how are you?' murmured Selma to Eleanor when Paula had gone into the back to put on the kettle.

'Well, thank you,' said Eleanor.

'Where shall we go out?' said Selma.

'What?' said Eleanor.

'Well let's go to supper, shall we? There's not much choice round here, is there? But there's the Carved Angel in Dartmouth.'

'Which costs millions of pounds.'

'Only thousands, and I have it.'

Eleanor's flush spread from the inflammation around her nose.

'You're a blushing maiden,' said Selma. 'Not such a maiden. Oh you're lovely, Eleanor. You just need to . . .'

Eleanor opened her mouth. Paula returned with three mugs.

'Go away,' murmured Eleanor, a low moan, almost audible.

Selma glanced at her. The veins on Selma's neck were like the tracery of veins on roses, on inner arms, white and faint blue.

They drank their tea in near silence. The windows of the shop were dark. Last customers milled in. Selma sat against the heater. She wore eye make-up that day so her eyelids were large and in shadow, and fake Chanel earrings. She seemed to be amused: Eleanor could see laughter twitching over her lips.

'Well,' said Paula eventually. 'So no visitors for me today?'

'No,' said Selma. 'People know it's not your day, don't they?'

'I suppose so,' said Paula. 'Can you deal with things while I see Dilly a minute?'

'Yes,' said Selma. She smiled up at Eleanor, closing her eyes and half winking as if in conspiracy.

'Do you think she thinks we've got anything to say to each other if we're left on our own?' said Selma teasingly in her level low voice. A customer turned and looked at her.

'Well,' said Eleanor. 'She asked the other day – she asked about you, said did I think you were –'

'A suitable companion for you.'

'No! Did I – Well, she was asking about her, really, about whether I thought you were bored by people you knew here.'

'All except one or two,' said Selma.

'Oh,' said Eleanor. She pulled down her sleeves and held their ends scrunched in her fists.

'Cut out these awkward adolescent gestures,' said Selma. 'You'll be wrapping one leg round the other and pouting next.'

'That's so rude,' murmured Eleanor. She turned around and frowned.

'Sorry,' said Selma.

A nervous film separated them from the shop's two customers, ignored by Selma as she took the money for a book.

'I don't mean to be rude,' said Selma calmly. She glanced at

Eleanor, her hair falling over one cheek. 'I'm just telling you. Women should be strong, I can't stand kooky-goofy acts –'

'It's a wing,' said Eleanor, glancing at the hair.

'What Richard says,' said Selma.

'As for *acts*, I don't know what you mean,' said Eleanor.

'And by the way,' said Selma, without responding. 'I hope you're working bloody hard. Do you agree with me on that subject? Because the rest of this place doesn't seem to know what it means. What *hard* work really means. I can't stand mediocrity, just can't stand it, I'd almost rather fail than any 2:2, B-plus, blurred photo kind of stuff. It's not in our scheme of things, is it?'

'God, no. I'd rather fail spectacularly. Better than B-plus-ishness.'

'It's like big love. Perhaps it's the only kind worth having, though I don't know. It all goes wrong. Predestined to go tragically wrong, I think.'

'It *isn't*,' said Eleanor. 'It can't be.'

'I'd hardly call that young Shane, whatever he's called – Kevin – your big love.'

'God, that's so –'

'"Rude". But it's true, isn't it? Look, we haven't really got time to talk, you can see that – Paula, hello, I've locked the front door.'

In the car, Eleanor could not speak to Paula. She considered asking her to stop at the Meadowbrook carpark, where she could spew up her excitement in the toilets, claiming that the motion of the car made her sick. Paula shot through the dark lanes in comfortable silence, and Eleanor leaned against the window, light-headed, watching the looming walls speed past.

'What do you want out of your life, Eleanor?' said Paula suddenly.

Eleanor came out of her reverie. She tensed. 'I don't know, really. Well, I do . . .'

'There's no need to be embarrassed when I ask you about these things, darling,' said Paula gently. 'I just meant, are you happy?'

'Yes, thanks. Mostly.'

'Are you happy at college?'

'Oh yes. We were using different types of light reflectors in the studio this week, you know, as part of our weekly doss session. You can create a diffuse reflection on the face, or a harder one using foil and things.'

'Sounds interesting,' said Paula. The tension between them had eased. Eleanor kept to herself and was secretive. Paula longed now for closeness with her daughter. She wanted to make her peace, yet she wasn't certain of her crime. Eleanor flinched from eye contact with her; Paula was uncomfortably aware of subdued anger, layers of sadness. But perhaps she imagined it: Eleanor was cheeky to her too, outrageously rude at times, would sometimes talk for hours; there was even a gentleness between them as though those invisible battle lines were softening as Eleanor grew older.

'Did you know,' said Poppy to Eleanor when they got home, 'Rolf's getting a Gibson?'

'With what?' said Eleanor. 'His dole? You don't mean . . .'

'Yep. They all went to that shop in Exeter yesterday.'

Eleanor looked at Poppy and they laughed. Poppy's laughter was loud and hysterical.

'Yes. And I'd love a sopranino, please-thank-you-very-much, and I could really do with my own show jumper too,' said Poppy.

'Yeah, I'll have a Nikkor zoom, 80 to 200,' said Eleanor. 'And do you think I could have the kitchen turned into a darkroom? I mean, it's very *important*, my *hobby*.'

'I know it's Rolf's hobby, not his work, but he is talented,' said Poppy seriously.

'How do you know?' said Eleanor. 'He doesn't even practise,

162

does he? He just strums in his room when he feels like it. How do you know if he's good or not?'

'Well he *is*. Come on, Eleanor, everyone knows he is.'

'Yes, quite. Who?'

'Well . . .'

'Paula. Paula and Rolf. There's this idea that Rolf's *artistic*. Well why aren't I "artistic?" The idea is just that if I'm successful it's because I work hard.'

'Paula thinks you're clever too.'

'It's easy to be "clever". All you've got to do is get more than two CSEs or whatever it was Rolf got.'

But Paula had always been sure that Rolf was not quite able to cope. He was noisy, rough-and-tumble, but the world was hard for him, and Paula felt he needed extra encouragement to compensate. While Eleanor had gone through school making fairy cakes that rose, acquiring stars, Rolf was put on the Tadpoles desk, which everyone knew meant the slow group, and got into fights. Eleanor longed to ask him with feigned innocence, 'But Rolf, why do the Tadpoles get more play-time and reading when the other groups have maths and poetry? Why do you think? Why?' But Paula might smack her, and even she, the spiteful sister, was not sufficiently malevolent.

Paula was always terrified of Rolf being bullied, but she told herself her fears were unnecessary. Eleanor, she knew, would be fine. She didn't worry about Eleanor, though Eleanor was sometimes stiff with fear before school, fear of bullies, dinners, people teasing. Eleanor was like her, so she knew she would cope. But Rolf and Tim had no common sense; they were hopeless; instinctively she protected them since she was needed by them, their amazing helplessness exasperating and touching. It was the way they blustered and blundered through life. She chose Tim's clothes; she wrote Rolf's geography project herself; she took

Rolf's side in arguments, because he stumbled over his reasoning and used words incorrectly.

When it rained, Eleanor set off for school with her hood up, but Rolf stormed and clung, and Paula bundled him into the car, since she didn't want his hair wet in the classroom all day. Eleanor walked very fast, unthinking, because in the bright bright arena of Room 4 would be Miss Telemach, and at the entrance of Room 4 Eleanor's stiff wet back relaxed, because Miss Telemach would ask her what Whispers, the neighbours' cat, was up to, or remark upon her stars on the star chart, and then she would run to Registration. And then Mrs Gormer, the lady from Stink Farm, who seemed to like Eleanor, waved when she saw her, or even stopped to talk to her in her thrilling syrupy voice, and Eleanor had dreams that there had been a mix-up at the hospital when she was born, and Miss Telemach or Mrs Gormer was in fact her mother, and there was a giving-over ceremony on the village green, the authorities watching over to supervise, and Paula now tearful at having to hand Eleanor over.

But Miss Telemach and Mrs Gormer were elusive. They bestowed their bewitching attentions in passing, but they were grown-ups who owned proper houses; they disappeared into some twilight zone in the evenings. And later, Selma Healy was there to wave at her, flash scarlet smiles upon her, and there was the smell of her, the feel of her.

Eleanor and her friends' lives were circumscribed by Totnes itself, that pretty townlet (river and castle ruin) that snaked up a single cross of streets before it scattered into mini-suburbs. The narrow shops – brightly-painted wooden toys; fine art papers; supermarket; butcher's – the houses banked up on slopes and steps, spawned beaming visitors and an underbelly of hippies. A toytown: market, dairy, postcards. Beyond that, housing estates and a darker apathy.

The Comprehensive's final year was composed of those who formed the fabric of the place and had never considered leaving: 'Gloria Totnesia,' they mouthed to the school song on Founder's Day, and there their vision rested – and those, like Eleanor, her friends Georgia and Kate, who had come to despise it with a vengeance unmerited by its charms. To them it was claustrophobia itself, hemmed in by Dartington and its long skirted drama students on one side and the villages of ever decreasing size that lined the mouth of the river on the other. Their names – 'Harbertonford', 'Tuckenhay', 'Dittisham', filled Eleanor with a sensation close to anger. Didn't these people know London existed? she wondered. What made someone actively decide to live out their days in Ipplepen?

That High Street of clock bridge and narrow pavements was backed by housing estates, invisible to the tourists. Totnes's resident unemployed, a sizeable clique, sat on the market walls and in the Bagel Café, and held sway. They wore faded black, bristly wool and paratrooper boots and walked in long loping gaits between café and market, ignoring people like Eleanor, nodding acknowledgement to Sean when he was there, and setting the standard for mannerisms of speech, of philosophy, being indisputably the town's coolest faction.

Paula's friends would drift up from the lower reaches of Totnes, hailing greetings and buying sesame seed loaves. In this context, Selma was something of an oddity. To Eleanor, perusing the market for jewellery in the lunch hour with her friends, it was scarcely believable that she was there at the lower end of town at all.

The week was blustery and cold. Chip paper swooped in the market and the air down by the terminus was gritty.

'Isn't that your friend?' said Karen to Eleanor.

'Who?' Eleanor jumped. The wind blew her coat.

'Your mum's friend. Selma something.'

The back of a head disappeared into Cranks. Eleanor stood still.

'We'll go in,' said Kate.

'No!' said Eleanor.

'Why not?'

'Come on,' said Kate. 'I want to see what she's wearing. It's always something . . .'

Eleanor had subtly spun myths around Selma, so that now, to the girls, she was a local point of interest, like the embarrassingly handsome English teacher, the garage attendant reputed to filch underwear from washing lines, the girl at school's mother who had been painted by Picasso; a joking reference point that rumpled the routine of their existence.

They entered the shop. Eleanor lagged behind. The pale head turned and barely registered them. Selma stood in a queue by the till and seemed hurried and impenetrable. She was close to the completion of her book, and worried that it contained no cohesive message. She had come to fetch Louisa's peanut butter as a break from her computer. Her rings glinted as she handed money to the shop assistant.

'Oh hello,' she said absently to Georgia. 'How are you?'

'Fine, thanks,' said Georgia.

'Good. I've got to hurry back to the computer. See you.'

'Hello,' said Eleanor, as Selma reached the door.

Selma swivelled round with the same impersonal gaze she had directed at Georgia.

'Hello, Eleanor,' she said. She pulled the door open and left the shop.

'How can she do that?' said Eleanor.

'Do what?'

'Well, she was so *rude*.'

'She wasn't. She said she was hurrying to do her work,' said Georgia in matter of fact tones, and began a consultation about the purchase of herbal cigarettes as a joke for her boyfriend.

'Is she married?' said Karen absently.

'Yes,' said Eleanor, and walked out of the shop.

They straggled back to the school. Eleanor wanted to be out of it, these last delaying months in which she felt like an impostor in a uniform, in a parental home. Yet a part of her pined to be fifteen, and at that school, and with Mrs Healy.

'She *was* rude,' murmured Eleanor obsessively to Karen.

'Who?' said Karen, and Eleanor was silent, and all day, mechanically modernising Chaucerian English, sitting on the Widecombe bus, it ached and nagged at her.

Sean rang her that evening. He had been drinking. He flared up at a mention of Selma.

'She's a mad woman!' he burst out. A student-filled background clamour came down the line.

'You always say that,' said Eleanor.

'She's barking.'

'No she's not.' Eleanor giggled suddenly.

'If you weren't such a little *provincial*,' he muttered, 'you wouldn't find it all so exciting . . .' His deep voice, at odds with his thinness.

'Oh shut up *please*, Sean,' said Eleanor.

'Yeah, well it's true,' stated Sean belligerently, unsteadily, down the line.

'How much have you drunk?' said Eleanor.

'If you hadn't grown up in a *field*, you'd have met your fill of rich old bags who wear too much make-up and are always kicking up a fuss about something or other. You'd have met hundreds of them and you'd have seen through them all and saved yourself the bother.'

Eleanor wondered again whether Sean had another girlfriend. She assumed he did, but she put off thinking about it. She saw her whole world collapse into one vision of Selma, and gave in, and allowed herself months of mental grace as if she were sick. Paula enquired after Sean. She sent him some bright red ski socks in case he was cold in Manchester.

That week, the wind swirled on the open reaches of the Plains by the river before cutting up the High Street. 'The Mistral,' murmured Selma to her researcher. She felt as though she were sailing high up above the square with the wind cracking against the windows like sails. It was intense and pressured, the computer glowing in the low winter light, enclosed in her room with Janine trying to finish her book. The room became thick with concentration and breath. They worked hours at a time, the days darkening, Janine twitching with impatience to get home, casting dark unseen glances at Selma. Then there were whole days in a row when Selma could barely work, and wanted to cry because of the pressure of it all: she leaned her head against the computer, closed her eyes, and felt only vulnerability, as if her world had collapsed, her husband gone, her book unfinished and uncertain of success.

Then there was boredom, when moving a pen was like grinding stubborn machinery, and she felt literally sick, violently weary, clenched her teeth, wanted to kick in the computer, and all she pined for was company, for someone to distract her, though she had fiercely discouraged distraction.

The girls went to the Centre sometimes: visiting Paula, going to the café on the Plains, they looked up at the window and saw the light, or sometimes Selma's hair passing the pane. The days went by, blowy, inconsequential.

Eleanor walked alone in her lunch hour through the warren of lanes that led off the High Street to the methodist church. The wind tugged her coat and spurted raindrops at her hair. She wondered whether now, all these years after her longing, she should go into the church. She walked blankly along.

'Eleanor,' Selma's voice came from behind her.

Eleanor turned. Selma stood there like a ghost, colourless. The rain intensified her colourlessness.

'Selma . . .' said Eleanor.

They were alone in the lane. Eleanor hesitated momentarily, then they stepped towards each other and hugged. Selma's skin was mushroom cold, mushroom white, shining with rain. Her nail scratched Eleanor's hand.

'I'm happy to bump into you,' murmured Selma. 'I rarely do.'

'The other day . . .'

'Oh, I was in a hurry then,' said Selma. Her hair blew.

They walked about the warren of lanes aimlessly. They passed the old house called The Shambles.

'Shambles means slaughterhouse,' said Eleanor. 'I wonder if it was.'

'I've been thinking recently . . .' said Selma. She stared down the lane in her cold blue-eyed way. 'I wish these houses were called The Manse, The Old Manse, and that was Narragansett Bay, or some Indian-sounding Sound. Nantucket. I want to travel. Not back to London, but away. I think it's just my work. I really can't bear my work at the moment, I just can't stand even turning on the computer. It makes me feel sick. If I could look out of my window, and there was a Sound or a Cape it would all be all right. It's just hopeless.'

'Is there anything you want me to do?' said Eleanor. She ran her hand through the spray on her hair and looked at Selma. She shivered.

The wind threw a shower of small raindrops against Selma's neck and cheek. 'You could come and visit me occasionally,' said Selma. 'Make sure the shoemakers don't come with you, and bring me, bring me tea. No, bring yourself and all the fragrances of the outside world, and all the sweet things you've done at school.'

'You really think I'm about twelve, don't you?'

'No, you're nearly a free woman. Then we can travel to Morocco and buy silks. Or we'll take a little house in Cape Cod and write novels.'

Eleanor darted a smile at her, and a flush spread through the sallowness of recent months. She looked around the lanes, the wet brick walls that gave off a smell of damp soot, or something more rancid, cat urine and old moss. They passed the cobbled section that led directly to a council estate, and the gas works beyond that, then turned off, back to the passage that ended in the Plains. Eleanor walked in fast little steps, suddenly lively. Selma was slower and more contemplative.

'You know,' she said. 'Eleanor –' She pressed her hand momentarily.

'What?'

'Nothing. I don't know what I was going to say.'

Eleanor looked at her.

'Oh, let's go away,' said Selma desperately. The river glinted below behind the trees, beyond the river pubs.

'Where to?' said Eleanor. She breathed quickly.

'Oh, nowhere,' said Selma irritably.

There was silence. 'Did you know,' Selma said, the blue eyes mascara-lashed sliding a glance at Eleanor, 'did you know that Paula's invited me to supper on Friday, and I've accepted, but I know that while I'm talking to her I'll be wanting to talk to you. You'll be sitting there all brown-chestnut and receptive and I'll wonder what you're thinking, and you looking so sweet and pretty.'

Eleanor blushed a deep red. 'I'm meant to be going out on Friday,' she said.

'Oh,' said Selma. A small silence. 'Well,' she said, sounding hurt.

'But I –'

'Surely you prefer my company to Georgina's or Kevin's? Am I not a more exciting proposition?' she said in a low voice. 'What on earth am I doing out here, anyway? I've got to get back to my appendices.' She turned towards the Plains. 'Bye, sweetheart,' she said without looking back at Eleanor, and she half ran towards the Centre. Eleanor looked up across the Plains, and there was Paula, watching her. She caught Eleanor's eye with a knowing glint visible even from across the square; Eleanor waved, then turned away and pounded back to the college building.

On Friday, Eleanor caught the bus home, the four o'clock Widecombe bus that daily climbed the back of the moor, sitting by Georgia in a daze as the Dartington arts students were replaced by the garage workers and farmers and B&B owners who lived in the villages scattered about that section of the moor.

The bus accelerated by the river, the driver always double declutching in the same spot for the slow ascent past the escarpment of Pondsgate. The bracken lay in brown frozen heaps. 'I don't know what to do,' said Eleanor, leaning her head against Georgia's shoulder momentarily. She looked out of the window. The road was saturated with the grey of the sky. 'I don't care that it's a woman,' she said. She laughed. 'I just don't care. Isn't that funny?'

'What would Sean say?' said Georgia, her casual acceptance of the situation making her Eleanor's sole confidante.

'Who cares?'

'Can't you just confront her?' said Georgia.

'No. No. What would I say?' said Eleanor. A lurch of sickness hit her as the bus mounted the last hill before their drop-off point at the end of the lane. Three hours later, Selma would follow the same route.

'Selma Healy, take me down to a place by the river,' said Georgia.

'No. Really,' said Eleanor.

'Well.'

They pounded down the lane, their hair trailing behind them, their tights picking up a spray of dried mud and dead fern and grit. They ran faster. They felt sick from gulping so much fresh air, their cheeks red beacons. Eleanor leaned over by the gate, a scum of thick saliva lining her mouth, and tried to heave, but she was only nauseated and trembling, her lungs stretched with cold.

There was no one in the house except Rolf, who stayed in his room. They put on a record and went upstairs, for Eleanor to change her clothes. The fields were frozen and darkening about them. The headlights of Tim's car shone down the lane.

'Do you think, do you think she likes *me*?' said Eleanor. She stared at her reflection.

They sat with their knees pulled up against her bed, the sisal carpet making indentations in their flesh.

'How would I know?' said Georgia.

There was a knock on the door. Tim opened it, letting in the sounds of Rolf's guitar.

'Hello,' he said, smiling at Georgia. He stood there in his baggy worn cords. 'Ellie-Nora,' he said, 'I'm making supper, and I wonder if you know, how long do you have to boil kidney beans for before you get rid of the poison?'

'The poison?' said Eleanor.

'They're toxic,' said Georgia. 'It's meant to be ten minutes minimum at a high heat, but I'd do it a bit more to be safe.'

Eleanor drifted into thought, her heart beginning to thump.

'Thank you,' said Tim. 'It looks cosy in here,' he said, lamplight on the Laura Ashley paper, the brown walls.

'Oh God,' said Eleanor, when he had gone. She began to laugh. Georgia began to laugh too, and they became slightly hysterical, making jokes about Selma, about Eleanor.

'Eleanor!' cried Tim again, from below the stairs. 'Can you help?'

'God, you're such a culinary burk!' shouted Eleanor. 'OK,' she groaned. 'Coming.'

'You're *so* rude to your parents,' said Georgia. 'If I said half the things you lot say . . .'

'Oh, Tim likes it,' said Eleanor casually.

They went down to the kitchen, where Eleanor cut up garlic and Georgia tried to curl Poppy's short hair with a curling tong. They happily sang along to a record as they worked.

'Tim, I can see the shape of your willy through those trousers!' called out Poppy. 'That wally old corduroy's wearing thin.'

'Really?' said Tim, looking down. 'Thank you for telling me. Should I get them mended?'

'On the willy bit?' cawed Poppy. 'You can't have a patchwork patch there; you'll look like a clown.'

Eleanor's heart jumped with the music. She cut herself, the blood staining the grain of the garlic. The garlic's juices pricked her flesh.

The door slammed. Eleanor jumped.

'Smells good,' said Paula, arriving, all coat and keys and shopping from her van. 'I bought some pudding. I'll help in a minute, just make myself a cuppa first. Ooh,' she sighed, sitting down, 'that drive's a real bugger when you're following a tractor. How are you, Georgia?'

'Good, thanks.'

'Is Kate – or is it Karen? – coming?' said Paula.

'Yes,' said Eleanor. 'Kate. A bit later.'

'Good,' said Paula cheerily. 'So we'll be – five of us, seven, nine. Go and get the hall dishes out, can you Pop?'

'Yes, Ma,' said Poppy.

Eleanor could hardly believe that she would soon see Selma. The clock said six twenty-five. Paula and Rolf had lit the wood burner. Soon Selma would walk through the door with her confusion of scents and her sleepwalker's voice, her slight strangeness amidst the solid wood and log smoke homeliness of Webburn House, and Eleanor savoured the moment now, the anticipation, because she had come to realise that anticipation was the happiest state. She froze the moment, whole drifts of seconds and minutes in which she thought about the gift she was going to receive, Selma's presence itself a gift, and she tweaked at the wrapping, looking at the clock, seeing the minutes go by. She remembered the first day she had met her, in the hallway, and thought she was somebody else. The memory had been so rubbed and loved that now it was unclear in her mind.

'I do declare you've put on weight,' said Paula looking at Eleanor when Georgia had left the room. 'You're not really looking your best, darling.'

Sometimes when Paula spoke, it was as though a part of Eleanor died. Her flesh stiffened. Hit me, hit me then, and it won't hurt me.

'Only a little bit,' said Paula, looking at her again.

Paula had been at the Farrier Inn, not far from Two Bridges, that afternoon. Selma had encouraged her: they had conspired together, Selma offering to take over the shop for the afternoon as an excuse to avoid the book that now loomed and spread cancerously in her mind. Even the mundanities of Janine were a relief.

Paula had driven cautiously to the Farrier, looking out for Tim's Citroën although he returned from work along another route. The Honda was already there, on the gravel carpark by the swings like the symbol of so many family outings, now a sign of something dear, and all she had to do was find the room he had booked, self-conscious by the reception, a housewife buttoned up plump in her coat with her children at school.

David was lying in bed reading, wearing only his pants when Paula arrived, laid the car keys on the dressing table and went over to kiss him. They kissed gently, rocking one another, his arms closed behind her shoulders while she leant over him as though he were her child.

'Darling, darling,' he said, and she was already wet as he placed his mouth on her breast, nibbling through the cloth of her blouse and her bra. She leaned over, then she toppled heavily onto the bed beside him, their shin bones knocking as she fell next to him. She was embarrassed, and lay staring at the ceiling to calm herself.

Then they stayed there, just talking, as the two o'clock afternoon drowsed to grey, and again she wondered where his electrifying wisdom had gone, that philosophical light he had poured into the sealed-off darknesses of her life a decade before. Now when he talked she was excited by the tone, not the content, because of the sexual codes it held, a key to the times when the voice had vibrated by her neck and ear muttering animal lust as he slid into her, or pumped almost violently, or lay across her and fondled her breast with total concentration. She focused closely on the golden hairs of his chest, like a boy's, though he was stocky now, his solidity amazing her anew every time, with his heavy calves, his taut fleshed buttocks. She imagined him as a horse, or a centaur, a golden animal of Greek legend.

His penis pressed against her tights, repelled by the elastic of the crotch, so she gripped it, and rubbed its girth between her legs. She liked such words: 'girth', 'thickness', 'penis' – they were faintly rude and perversely stimulating. She put both her hands around his penis and kneaded it firmly and insistently, and they were kissing without stopping, their tongues moving in rhythm with Paula's hands, while he pulled her tights down, her knickers now cold wet, and she lifted her legs to struggle out of them, tilted her hips forward and inserted him inside her, gripping him hard with her legs tucked behind his buttocks. They were both slippery, wet, they moved frantically, and he came within minutes, grunting a deep echo, his throat thick, his hair wet, and he collapsed on top of her, his lips splayed against her, and dozed through mere seconds, seconds of deep sleep, Paula still in her coat, David lying on her chest.

Then he woke up, blinking his eyes without knowing whether he had slept or when, and turned her over, undoing her bra.

'Stay like that. You mustn't move,' he said. He straddled her, perching on her buttocks, and slowly inserted his fingers inside her bra. He edged towards her nipples, cupping the weight of her breasts, inadvertently squeezing the flesh as her weight against the mattress impeded his movement.

'Don't move,' he said again in a quiet voice. His fingers travelled around the areolae of her nipples, slowly and patiently for several minutes. Occasional cars crunched the gravel outside. The school bus would be on its way back to Widecombe. David licked his fingers and kneaded the nubs of her nipples with saliva until Paula moaned into the sheets and pressed her pelvis against the mattress.

'Don't move,' he commanded.

He felt inside her skirt, and his hands space travelled in imperceptible movements, a minute glide across her buttocks towards her crotch, and finally nestled there, not moving. Then he fluttered his finger tips on the pink flesh around her clitoris as if padding the surface of water, flickering and fluttering until sensation began to bead and swell. He stopped. He dribbled his fingers again. His own semen ran between them onto the sheets. He pressed her flesh with insect touches until she groaned. 'Shut up,' he said. She was silent. His flutterings took on a steadier vibration; he moved his finger round and round, travelling the whole area, then focusing on a point, on and on, and as she panted involuntarily, he slid his finger into her vagina from behind, and she shuddered and cried out in a staggered crescendo.

Half an hour only until Selma was due. The time had the thick and suspended quality of a dream. Eleanor's calm was the biley lining of hysteria. She changed her clothes again, choosing black that lay close to her skin despite her supposed weight gain. Paula glanced at her. Her hair had been washed and hung without snaring behind her ears. The look of intensity or slight sadness she carried, that appealed to others and irritated Paula, was heightened.

'A good day?' said Tim, putting his arm on Paula's shoulder.

A flicker of guilt. She blanked it. 'Yes,' she said. She shrugged. 'Yes.' There was a slight ring of soreness on her buttock where David Harpur had grasped her.

The fire was burning. Poppy's hair stuck out in glossy tufts. Eleanor hugged her. 'You been smoking?' she murmured.

'Can you smell it?' said Poppy in a whispered grunt.

'Faint,' muttered Eleanor. She fetched Poppy her perfume.

Woodlice ran over the log pile, drawn out by the heat of the fire. The plaster on that wall shone with damp when the fire was lit. Music played, garlic drifted, the cold settled in for the night, and Gandalf came back from the sheep fields with a bleeding pad and arched against the Aga, his leg vibrating with dreams.

A car engine thrummed outside the window. Minutes went by. There was a knock at the door. Eleanor paced, plucking books and twitching with involuntary movements, but it was Kate's chatter that filtered through from the hall, and again there was silence outside to her strained ears, only the river in the distance, the wind.

'Is your friend Selma coming over?' Kate asked Paula.

'Yes,' said Paula.

'Yes, I think I saw her behind me on the A38. Does she drive a dark grey —'

'Yes.'

Eleanor's heart thumped so hard, the beats hurt her chest, and her head pumped with dizziness. The fire licked logs. The kitchen clock ticked.

There was a ring at the door, and again time went into slow motion, everything dreamlike as if events took place behind a milk skin of unreality: the doorbell bleeding into the dream, a silence, sounds from the hall, minutes passing, then Selma finally entering the room, the contrasts of her dark lipstick, her pale skin, her pale brown hair.

'Eleanor,' she said behind the mute film. 'You stayed.'

Her smile was a symmetrical formation of curves, the fleeting white of her teeth, the upper bow settling firmly on the pad of the lower lip when she stopped smiling.

'I've never seen you wearing anything like that before,' she said. 'You usually hide your body. You've got this lovely figure — you should show it off.'

'Yes, doesn't she look good in that dress?' said Paula, as if in reparation for her earlier comment.

'Didn't you bring Louisa?' said Poppy.

'No, sweetheart,' said Selma. 'She's at a friend's tonight. She sends you a – a neigh.'

'Neigh,' said Poppy. 'Send her snorts and hoof stamps.'

'Come and sit down,' said Paula.

They sat by the fire.

Selma half-smiled at Paula. She pulled off her gloves and smoothed out the fingers. 'So did you have a good afternoon?' she said quietly. She twisted the glove and looked up at her.

Paula shot her a look.

'Were the takings good?' said Selma.

Paula nodded. 'Mmmm, well yes, lots,' she said. 'Would you like a drink?'

The girls were moved to self-consciousness in Selma's presence. Their usual display of giggles and gossip and intense sudden seriousness tailed off into near silence: they were polite, or showed off, making efforts to impress. Poppy was similarly moved, but rebelled against it by turning peevish and demanding Paula and Tim's attention. Kate, Georgia and Eleanor sat on the floor, as if at Selma's feet, their age alone lending them a certain uniformity, a surface impression of confidence.

Selma sat in the corner and talked to Paula, sometimes to Tim, her voice seemingly dislocated from her speech, lulling and distracting. She glanced at the girls as she spoke. Eleanor's black dress revealed the shape of her breasts before it fell and clung to her stomach. She had tired shadows under her eyes, bruisings of purple and nerves. Her slightly wide or fleshy nose still flared with the remnants of a rabbit cold.

'Where's Rolf?' enquired Paula.

'In his room. Can't you hear the guitar?' said Tim.

'No,' said Paula, looking up. A log fell in the fire spurting lines of flame. 'That fire makes noises.'

'Paula, you're bloody deaf,' said Poppy. 'I keep telling you. She should get a granny hearing aid, shouldn't she?' she said, turning to Eleanor.

Eleanor shook her head and smiled.

'I'm *not* deaf,' said Paula. 'Poppy, go and get Rolf, will you, tell him we're having supper.'

They wandered into the kitchen. Paula had laid out a cloth over the pine table and arranged candles in a cluster in the middle.

'That's pretty,' said Eleanor. 'The candles. Tim, your kidney bean ethno-bake had better be good and refined. No half potatoes and whole carrots floating about, thanks.'

'Tim's quite a good cook,' observed Paula.

'Yes, strangely good at times,' said Eleanor. ''Tis amazing.'

Rolf arrived, dark block of hair, and strode through the kitchen. He flinched at the largely female company. 'Actually,' he said, 'I'm not hungry.'

'You've got to eat,' protested Paula.

'I'm not hungry,' said Rolf. He picked up a banana and walked away.

'Have something, darling,' said Paula. 'Ready Brek? Go and get – I'll whip some up and bring it up.'

Poppy sniggered. Eleanor suppressed a smile.

'Oh, for God's sakes, Paula, he's a six foot man,' said Selma. 'He knows when he wants to eat.' She cast a glance at Eleanor, but Eleanor looked studiedly blank.

Paula shook her head. 'Yes, yes, you're right. Of course. But I said – Oh, I'll just do it quickly.'

Selma leaned under the table and nudged Eleanor, reaching the side of her thigh, but Paula's eyes were moving about the room, and Eleanor looked rigidly to one side.

'I'd smack him round the arse if he was my son,' said Selma when Paula had taken Rolf his Ready Brek. 'Not boil him up a bowl of baby food!'

'Poor babelet Rolfie might die of starvation or hypothermia in his room, you see,' said Eleanor.

Tim looked at them thoughtfully, but said nothing. 'Don't be hard on him,' he said eventually.

'Really, I must say something to Paula,' said Selma.

Eleanor looked delighted, but cast nervous glances at the doorway. 'Does anyone want any soup?' she said. 'It's my watercress. My friends know how famous and excellent it is.'

Paula returned, smiling. Eleanor left her friends to their own devices and ministered quietly to Selma, helping her to bread, to butter, passing her requirements with unobtrusive movements.

'Well,' said Selma quietly. 'So here we are en famille. Famille Strachan.' The lines on her neck tensed and relaxed as she spoke, moving infinitesimally with each word.

'Yes, it's not the Carved Angel, is it?' said Eleanor.

'No, but it's quite lovely, I think. You take a lot for granted, Eleanor. Look, you can even see the edge of the thatch hanging down over the window, so idyllic, see that darker shape in the dark. And all this, flagstones, pictures, warmth. I never did take you to the Carved Angel, did I?' she added vaguely.

'It doesn't matter,' said Eleanor.

Selma said nothing. Eleanor's fork froze while they remained silent.

Selma looked around.

'Here's to my beautiful friends,' she said. She swung her glass in Eleanor's direction, then in Paula's. 'You look so beautiful. All of you,' she said.

Paula flushed with pleasure, resistance flickering across her features.

'Selma!' said Paula. 'Would you like kidney bean bake à le Tim?'

'*Au* or *à la*,' said Eleanor.

'So very clever, madam, aren't you?' said Paula, pointing the serving spoon at Eleanor. She served the food, while Tim offered salad, and Georgia and Kate, who liked Tim and frequently teased him, made salad jokes with him, and Poppy sat eating with her round cheeks rotating, her round top of hair like the cup of an acorn.

'Did you like my fake pearls I bought at the old clothes shop?' said Selma to Paula.

'Oh yes. Well yes. They were lovely. A little bit much – over the top, would you say? – for me, though,' said Paula.

'You should be braver, Paula. You'd look good in more body hugging things, more –'

'Oh, pwah!' said Paula. 'With my figure?'

'Yes,' said Selma. 'The female body is a beautiful object. And that means curves, stomachs, breasts.'

Poppy sniggered and looked at Tim.

'I mean it,' said Selma. 'You should wear more colours and non-draping fabrics. Others would agree with me.'

'Who?' said Poppy.

'Well,' said Selma. 'Most men, I'm sure. Tim? Not that I'm suggesting Paula dresses for men rather than for herself. So what did you think of the peacock feather earrings, Paula? I want your opinion on all my latest acquisitions.'

'Did you get them at that shop we went to?' asked Eleanor.

'Which?'

'The one where you got me that dress?'

'Which dress?'

'You know, the dark red silk dress.'

'Did I buy you a dress?' said Selma. 'That was nice of me, wasn't it?'

Eleanor felt her talisman, the cherry silk dress she wore even in winter, disintegrate. She tried to secure Selma's attention, but Selma rarely caught her eye, addressing comments to Paula and the room in general. She flirted and flattered, but her talk had an idle, inconsequential flavour that implied her listeners didn't interest her, their attention all that was required of them. It was nine-forty. Georgia caught Eleanor's eye. Eleanor shot her a look of panic. Georgia shook her head slightly. Eleanor absorbed Selma's profile in brief surreptitious glances, the nose that rose so pleasingly from a curving mouth, the pattern of veins and hair and flesh that was known by heart.

Another half an hour, and Selma largely ignored Eleanor's presence beside her. Her scent reached Eleanor in strands. She was silent, seeming bored, interspersing her silences with topics that indirectly drew attention to herself. She rode rough shod, or elegantly shod, thought Eleanor, over the Strachans, and over Georgia and Kate for being young, and over Eleanor for being compliant. Eleanor looked at Paula's round frank face, and felt a spasm of love, an instinct to defend her against Selma.

'How is your book going?' said Eleanor at last. The smell of garlic eased from the Aga.

'Fine,' said Selma with a flicker of distress.

'When are you going to have it finished?'

'Do you always have to ask questions?' Selma turned to her and looked down on her. 'Tell me something instead.'

There was loud talk at the other end of the table, though Paula, always concerned with her guests' wellbeing, darted glances in Selma's direction. Georgia and Kate were involved in an argument about twentieth century literature, fuelled by references to people at school. Poppy threw in comments about Dick Francis and *The Catcher In The Rye*.

'I wonder –' began Eleanor.

'Initiate. Don't always react.'

'*Selma*,' said Eleanor. She looked up. Paula was talking to Tim. 'I just don't – understand,' she said in a quiet voice.

Selma was silent.

'I don't understand you,' Eleanor hissed, her boldness growing in panic. 'After all, that Sunday – do you remember that Sunday, at your house, afterwards,' she murmured, glancing at Paula and Tim. 'Well, *do* you remember?'

'Of course,' said Selma lightly.

'Well –' said Eleanor, blushing. 'Well then.'

'Well, yes, I suppose – of course – but – you go through different stages in your life, and I'm very preoccupied at the moment, very preoccupied with my work.'

'So what?' said Eleanor.

'So what a lot. It means a lot. It's my livelihood – everything.' Selma frowned. The look of distress that accompanied all mention of her work passed over her face again.

'Yes, but let me help you then,' said Eleanor.

'You can't. No one can. Not even Janine. Just help me by being supportive and knowing when I want to see people and when I want to be left alone.'

'It's very hard,' said Eleanor.

'Well,' said Selma. 'Yes. That's the way it is.' She looked across the room with her habitual focus on the middle distance. Eleanor shivered.

Selma said nothing. Eleanor wanted to claw at her in panic. She wanted to cling to her physically, to grip her.

'When can I see you then?' said Eleanor desperately. 'I mean . . .'

'You're seeing me right now.'

'Yes, but . . .'

Selma sliced her fork through tomato and kidney beans. Her

physical presence wore Eleanor out, she was worn out with her body, her smell. She almost wanted to kill it if she couldn't have it – it was too much – to put to death the thing that quivered and lived minute spaces away from her. It was like looking down on the pure bland flesh of a baby, perfect, so white and oblivious and mewling, you thought momentarily of stifling it, of pillowing that round wet mouth, gagging that saliva wet life because you couldn't have it.

They were silent. '*Please*,' said Eleanor desperately. 'Talk to me. Tell me something.'

'Look,' hissed Selma. 'You're much younger than me. You must have loads of things to do – boys you're interested in, other friends. I'm literally twice your age. More. And very busy, and a friend of –' she nodded at Paula. 'I can't deal with answering all these questions, I really can't.'

Eleanor sat there, and despair trickled through her in stages. She looked at Paula, then back at Selma.

'OK,' said Eleanor.

'Really?'

'Yes, fine. You're right, I've got plenty to do.'

Selma turned to her for the first time, and saw the bruise-coloured shadows, the melancholy strained prettiness like a Victorian painting. She softened. She held out her hand under the table, continuing to eat with her fork. She took Eleanor's hand, limp on her own lap, and held it in hers, moving over it and pressing the flesh.

Eleanor looked back at her in tired amazement. Selma's artificial air had softened a little. A string of baroque pearls, and one of evenly cut amber, tumbled and snared on her breast, and fell against the table cloth. There were several grey hairs by her ear.

Eleanor could say nothing. She breathed deeply. Selma pressed her thumb into her palm.

'I can't carry on with you saying things like that,' said Eleanor at last. There was a sob in her voice. 'I just can't, so fuck off if you're going to be like that.'

Paula caught sight of Eleanor while stretching across the table for the pepper, suddenly glanced at her, and fine tuned as she was to her, she saw desperation.

It was as though she were feverish. An anger or tension so concentrated it became a kind of serenity.

Paula smiled to herself as she realised that Eleanor would love to be thought feverish. There was a delicacy about the shape of her skull. She looked beautiful, thought Paula, quite beautiful, that plant soft skin, those shadings of brown, dark eyebrows, full lips. It lasted perhaps three or four years. In a year, two years, it would begin to tarnish, but now it was quite ripe, its glory only partly conscious – in the twitching of the hair, the movements of the mouth – but carelessly worn, little knowledge of either its existence or its transience. It was as though she offered up those breasts, that flesh, without any true knowledge of their power. Sitting beside her, Selma looked like a repository of all experience.

Selma made no comment, but finally she looked at Eleanor, as if in compliance.

'You're so sensitive,' said Selma. She slid her hand from Eleanor's palm onto her leg and moved it over her thigh, still cutting food with her fork. She left her hand outstretched on Eleanor's leg, moving her thumb in a circular motion, squeezing the flesh minutely as though soothing her. Eleanor barely breathed. She inched her vision to where Paula and Tim sat, unsure whether they had observed her. Selma and Eleanor formed one pocket of conversation while the others dipped into a ragged general dialogue that rose and then fragmented.

Paula watched them, but they had spun a web around themselves. A blue vein on Selma's neck throbbed with her blood.

'Anyway, I'd rather be here with you than with the shoemakers,' murmured Selma. 'I mean, shoemakers has become almost a collective term for them all, Jude, Dilly, Tasha. When I got there I thought they were friendly, not intrusive, but,' she rubbed her cheek, 'I don't seem to get on with them. They seem mistrustful of me. It's not that I don't like them, it's just that there's no meeting point, anywhere. And I know it'll never change.'

'Exactly,' said Eleanor calmly. 'It's like that with them all. All the people we've had to grow up with. I never did get on with them, never. You know, there were these years of street parties – or farm parties, whatever – with these people who'd paint kids' faces into bright clowns and unicorns and tigers, and we were supposed to love it. But I didn't. The women had plaits and whacky make-up even though they were probably in their thirties, and everyone, all the children, seemed to want to join in except me. Then there was an older version of this whole lazy, laid-back life that eludes me, at Dartington – you know, where Rolf went to school – where I'd see these rooms with spider plants, big cushions, and records playing, and people dancing around or lying round having conversations in cool grunts, and I wouldn't be able to do that, I just wouldn't. And then, a couple of years ago, I realised that if I could just achieve certain things, there is after all the whole world out there. And then . . . then I –'

'Met me,' said Selma. Her hand had slackened.

Eleanor opened her mouth.

'You focus on this place,' said Selma, again becoming dismissive. 'That's just a minute part of it, it's missing the point.'

'You'd put it down to adolescent melancholy. Or some incipient socialist feminist outrage,' said Eleanor.

The corners of Selma's mouth curved. '"The mind is its own place, and in itself can make a heav'n of hell, a hell of heav'n",' she said.

'*You* make it that,' said Eleanor in a mutter, clinging to Selma's now limp hand.

'Do I?' said Selma, her gaze on the middle distance. She dropped her voice.

'Sort of, yes.'

'Well, madam. What are you going to do about it?'

'You see, I . . .' murmured Eleanor. 'I want to be with you,' she tailed off. Her face was a deep red. She trembled steadily.

'Oh yes?'

'Yes.'

'That's very flattering.'

Eleanor said nothing. Selma glanced briefly at Paula and turned and looked at Eleanor. 'You're so gorgeous. You're very naughty,' she murmured. 'And your hand is very hot.'

Their hands moved over each other, shifting and uncurling. Selma moved further along Eleanor's thigh. Kate turned and watched her.

'So you didn't answer my question,' said Selma.

Eleanor glanced at Paula. She shook her head, her eyes fixed on stray kidney beans, on the glaze of the plate.

'What are we going to do with you, Eleanor Strachan?' said Selma teasingly. Her hand moved near Eleanor's hip bone; Eleanor could feel her long finger nails through the cloth of her dress as her fingers shifted.

Paula now turned and watched them, the conversation in the rest of the room thinning to spurts and silences.

'I don't know,' muttered Eleanor, aware of Paula's gaze.

'Maybe you have to take risks,' Selma murmured to her.

She looked breezily up at Paula and smiled. 'I'm having a wonderful evening, Paula,' she said.

EIGHT

ELEANOR SAT UP AGAINST THE WALL WRITING AS SHE HAD when she was younger and her bedroom was her sanctuary; she stayed in bed so she could lift the sheets and smell her own desire in fleshy wafts.

She wanted her. It was simple. She wanted Selma Healy. She plotted and devised. She never saw her. A sighting had the quality of celluloid, like an actress glimpsed in the flesh; she lingered over the image until it was distorted again, and always the reality was a revelation.

Eleanor wore the necklace hidden beneath her dress like a secret wedding ring on a string, because its giver had been absorbed back into a world that was barred to her. She endowed it with talismanic significance, certain in her lucid moments that her image was lodged somewhere in this woman's mind: her own flower face, like the plants from the garden or the cool movement of the locket against her chest. And things were trying to tell her. Events held serendipitous echoes: in music, in the chance significance of someone's words, and in Selma's initials, which were formed by live things in the garden.

Madame moved amongst the elevated pastures of upper floors and colleagues. The girls were cloistered beneath. They were passionate and jealous. They were uniform in age, station, aspiration, united in competition. Eleanor gloried in their anonymity, her little fantasy growing wild hot limbs in its grey culture, like her secret secret – she had grown beautiful underneath, for no one to see, her scraped back hair was a curtain of scents at night – but now such anonymity angered her. She felt her feet were bound. And they had begun to stink hot with pain. The grey girls perambulated their cloisters, and she who had once found hard delight in submission kicked against it. How dare that woman be preoccupied with her own life only when she, Eleanor, moved and breathed mere feet below?

'Tell me, tell me,' she said to the woman who cleaned the staircases at night. 'Where does she go in the late afternoons when we are working?'

'She is in her office, but those are her private hours, and no one must disturb her.'

'Tell me how to get there,' said Eleanor urgently.

The woman looked puzzled. 'Why, up the stairs and along the passage way,' she said.

But the passages had twisted back on themselves into dizzying warrens, and where Eleanor thought the third floor had once led into the fourth, she was plunged downwards along sloping linoleum, catching bewildering glimpses of the garden, which today flashed fierce and speckled. Onwards she went, until she was quite tired, but now her bound feet were unfurling, the stench of anger drifted about her, and she stumbled upon the office on the fifth floor without knowing which turn she had taken. This girl was beautiful. Her hair was pulled onto the nape of her neck. She had a milk flush to her skin, and blood on her feet. The collar of her uniform buttoned precisely at her throat; her eyes were trained to inscrutability, yet she exuded something animal and womanly, which inspired rage in the assistant who opened the door.

'She is not here,' she hissed.

'Where *is* she? Is she there?' said Eleanor.

'No, no, of course she is not,' snapped the woman. 'She is in the Sick Bay nursing the sick girls.'

As an eight-year-old, Eleanor had chased after her mother in her dreams, or in the half-textured passage between evening and sleep. She had travelled through the village, past Rolf, past David and the devotees, through glimpses of green and tile: she was searching for Paula, who would stroke her head and say she wasn't difficult after all, it had all been a mistake. Paula who would lift her up and hold her firmly against her shoulder, patting her back with long lingering movements while Eleanor clasped her mother's shoulder with ten fingers in a row. Sometimes Paula was a mother who made sponge cakes, and bought her nylon hairbands and took her to Sunday school, and loved her; at other times she wore her own corduroy shifts and cooked millet pilaf and meditated, but still she loved Eleanor, thought her as pretty as Rolf himself, as good and beautiful and lovely.

In the day, Eleanor kept a space between herself and Paula. Rolf ran to Paula and butted her, or ignored her.

When he was a baby, Rolf lay with his limbs flung out like a starfish warm with sleep, his woolly jersey, his lips wet where his thumb had flopped out.

'My starfish,' murmured Paula.

She wanted to sew kisses like roses on his mouth.

He lay in his cot with his arms splayed, his hands curled. She found it inexpressibly exciting that he had come out of her new minted and independent, a boy who would one day grow a deep voice, no womb or periods or mess or hips.

The children watched telly together, Eleanor taller, spikier, Rolf rounded. Little boy bunch plumped on a sofa with his nappy and peaspod lips.

'Let me be with you. I've got to see you,' said Eleanor to Selma.

'No, I can't. Get on with your work. That's what I'm going to do,' said Selma.

Eleanor would die that day. The day would be dead, a death in her memory afterwards.

Obsession is madness, refined madness. It washes the brain with a different chemical, like lust, that distorts perceptions. You are trapped in a cage. There is nothing else. There is no vision outside it, nerves shaved for the sound of the phone. A little room. The mind a little room. Jumping at the movement of dust. You pour your whole self into another person until there is nothing left of you, and they are coloured and alive and you are a phantom in their shape.

At the weekend, the house was filled with people in bulbous Totnes lace-up boots. Eleanor surveyed them in horror. Even one of the younger women from the Centre, who could have been elegant, wore them under a skirt. Paula and Tim were happy and relaxed. Even Rolf was sociable. Eleanor wanted to bolt from the contagious mediocrity of the young bearded men with thin white midriffs en route to Findhorn, older horsey women with greying curls who were still, cheerfully, despondently, talking of getting together the funds to set up as travelling storytellers-stroke-performers.

When all the friends had gone, Tim kept yawning and saying what a good day it had been, but Paula was quiet. She cleared away Rolf and Tim's plates. Eleanor pushed rice around, building it into piles and patterns with her fork.

'I really liked that guy – Jake,' said Rolf.

'Did you, darling?' said Paula.

'He's a good bloke,' said Rolf.

'I'm so glad you enjoyed yourself,' said Paula, smiling at Rolf. His spots were clearing up and he was looking handsome in a large new jersey she had bought him, hand framed by someone at the Centre. Rolf was tall. His teenage thinness was filling out. The indigo in his jersey caught the blue of his eyes shaded by his thick lashes as he looked down at Paula.

He smiled at her. 'Ta for the moussaka, Ma,' he said.

She smiled back. 'Welcome.' She chided herself for not having made more effort recently. She'd look through the *Western Morning News* later that evening for suitable jobs for Rolf, because she knew he would put off doing it himself, and he'd been depressed lately about having to go up to the dole office. She made a note to update his CV on the Centre's computer. Rolf could be a little brute at times, selfish and uncommunicative, but when he was himself, when he was happy, he made her laugh and awed her with his strength of will; he touched her soul.

Eleanor washed the plates and wiped all the kitchen surfaces. Karen and some friends had asked her out, but she was suddenly violently bored by all company. There was no point to it. She wanted to stay at home by the phone. She curled up on the sofa and read about the life of Mary Shelley.

Paula and Tim came into the sitting room and started playing rummy. Poppy returned from her friend Alice's house smelling of roll-ups, dropped her coat on the floor and made a pot of tea. Paula had been unusually silent since her friends had gone. Eleanor sifted through all that had been said that day for blame.

She constantly worried that Paula felt left out. Even silently reading, she wondered whether her presence irked Paula.

'Would you like more tea?' Eleanor asked Paula, stretching over to the pot.

'Oh yes. Thanks,' said Paula.

She placed a card on the table. 'So did you enjoy today, Eleanor?' she said.

'Yes, it was OK,' said Eleanor. She shrugged. 'I mean, it was nice.' The phone rang. She jolted. Poppy answered it and started chattering. A lurch of disappointment.

'Do you remember a woman called Lorna from when you were very little?' said Paula.

'Who babysat us sometimes?' said Eleanor.

'Yes, that's right! Your memory's so good. She was a follower – a follower of David Harpur – and it's amazing, but she's a good friend of Kady's. I mean, Kady's a Londoner born and bred, but she knew Lorna. I only found that out today. Isn't that strange?'

'Oh. Yes, it is, isn't it?' said Eleanor.

'What did you think of Kady?'

'Who?'

'The one I've just been talking about!'

'Yes but *I* don't know which one she is, do I?'

'Well were you taking any notice of who anyone was?'

'Yes, but they all look – they've all got the same names, so I mix them up.'

'No they haven't,' said Paula. 'You're going to beat me,' she said to Tim. 'There wasn't *one person* with the same name as anyone else.'

'You know what I mean, I mean the same kind of names. Joshy-Jakey kind of names, and Tasha . . .'

Paula was silent. 'Well anyway, Kady had a good idea. She's thinking of selling window boxes, but wild seed window boxes, woodland flowers and garlic plants so people can have a bit of the countryside in the town . . .'

'*Kady* – see. What's she really called?'

'She's called Kady. That's her name.'

'But is she actually called Katy, or what? They've all got these names . . .'

'It's completely irrelevant!' said Paula. 'Why's it bothering you?'

'It doesn't. I'm just saying I don't know which one "Kady" is.'

'She says disdainfully.' Paula raised her eyebrows tolerantly. Eleanor laughed.

'She had kind of plaits,' said Paula. 'And she was wearing . . .'

'Nearly dreadlocks you mean,' said Eleanor. 'Yes, I saw.'

'She was wearing –'

'An enormous jersey made out of a yak and some big lace-up clown's boots.'

'Oh Eleanor, honestly!' Paula said, still mildly amused. 'You're so intolerant.'

'Is it intolerant not to want to smell of patchouli and speak like I've been knocked on the head?' said Eleanor.

'No, but I do have to take it a bit personally that you don't like any of my friends.'

'Watch out, you're getting beaten,' said Tim.

'I do,' said Eleanor.

The hushed squeals of Poppy in the hallway became open guffaws.

'I feel it's a criticism of me,' said Paula. 'You've never liked my friends, have you?'

Eleanor smiled slightly.

'Not one,' said Paula.

'Yes I have,' muttered Eleanor. She smiled and studied her lap.

'Well name one,' said Paula. 'You don't even like Melly.'

Eleanor fought a childish giggle. Her mouth twitched.

'Oh – Selma,' said Paula. 'Of course I know you like *Selma*.' Her voice hardened.

'Well, she's OK,' said Eleanor, shrugging.

Paula was silent. Eleanor stared at her knee. Paula looked directly at her from the card table. Tim waited for her to place a card. Eleanor remained silent, but Paula stared at her.

'Well at least she doesn't moon around like a hippy,' said Eleanor at last.

'No, that's true, she's a fraught workaholic instead.'

'At least she does something.'

'So do my other friends,' said Paula.

'Yes, but Selma's got a career, she works –'

'Is that a value judgement? Mothers work too, you know. People who work at the Centre work.'

'OK, Paula, OK,' said Eleanor. 'I agree.' The thought of Selma still made her smile.

Paula caught the suppressed smile. 'Honestly, the reasons you like Selma . . . distress me,' she said.

'Why?' said Eleanor.

'Because you respect her for all the showy bits, her career. You're snobby about my friends, you're snobby about their clothes. What about all her affectations? I mean, the woman's pretty self-centred!'

'*You're* her friend!' said Eleanor.

'Yes, or used to be,' said Paula. 'You just don't see it. She's so selfish, self-centred – you see only the glamour, the clever talk, the fact she writes books – unlike those people who only work in the Centre, of course. Did you know that Richard's already walked out on her twice before?'

'No,' said Eleanor.

'No, I shouldn't think so. So Selma's quite successful, or used to be, I should say, and wears some designer clothes and gets quite a lot of attention from people. Is that what you value? Is that why you don't value me?'

'Paula!' said Eleanor, shocked. 'What are you talking about? Why are you attacking her?'

'Because I don't like what she does to you.'

'What?' said Eleanor. 'What do you mean?'

'If she encourages your snobby attitudes and makes you think about nothing but clothes and the glorious bloody career you're going to have and her – let's face it, Eleanor – then no, I don't like the effect she has on you.'

'Paula! Why are you attacking me like this?'

'I'm not attacking you. Your idolisation of Selma just makes me feel a bit sick.'

'Well at least she doesn't burble on about stupid gurus and wear ugly *disgusting* boots and live through her son,' burst out Eleanor. She stopped herself and reddened.

'What do you mean by that?' Paula turned to Eleanor. Her lips thinned.

'Nothing, really.'

'What did you say?'

'Nothing.'

'What did you just say?'

'That she doesn't live through her son.'

'Nor do I. Get out.'

Paula slapped her card down on the table, dark shadowed, shaking. 'Idolise that silly woman all you want, air your chips in public, but don't do it in my house.'

Eleanor looked towards Tim. He appeared sad, older. He said nothing, as was customary. Eleanor wanted to shake him. Poppy chirped on in the hall. Eleanor fetched her bag and her coat and found a jersey, and left through the side door. She crossed the lane, walked through the growing cold of the evening up the hill that led towards Widecombe, blankly covered the mile to the village, and lay against the wall where the Saturday bus stopped. She pressed her face against it. She shivered violently and waited an hour and forty minutes. The bright lit windows of the bus appeared in the dark up the hill, thundering towards her. She raised her arm, but she was invisible, it swept past, drumming grit at her, and she sat on a hummock of grass by the lane and put her head on her knees. Her head was blank. Selma would look after her.

When Eleanor was eight, she read books about children who ran away to circuses. It sounded exciting. But she didn't know where to find a circus. All the glamorous homes for *orphelines* were in France, so she sat in the fruit shed instead. There she dreamt she was a circus girl who wore white socks. The rain came down and plattered on the window: it was the people cheering her. A moth was caught in a cobweb; she let it free to stumble away. She curled up small in a corner, because it was cold, and if she kept still, spiders came near her and weren't afraid. She curled up smaller, like the old flower heads that lay in corners in the shed, and some slimy mould like dark earth began to frighten her. It was so cold, but Paula had bought Rolf's school photo, not hers – 'It's not the best one of you, Eleanor' – the shame of returning it to school unbought, Mrs Gledhill saying she had a pretty smile, and then in the evening, Rolf on Paula's lap, kicking his feet, showing her his wobbly tooth, Tim at work, and there was nowhere to go, because Paula didn't want her to spend so much time in her room. She made herself smaller in the shed. The spiders were her friends. It was cold. She wanted to crawl into a plant pot, hibernate, die.

'Oh Paula, Paula, please,' she wanted to say at these times. She wanted to beg her, break through the rubber thick skin of resistance between them.

'I promise I'll be good if I can stay,' Eleanor had said as a child.

Paula sighed. 'You are good, mostly, it's just . . .'

Eleanor bit her nail.

'Stay where, anyway?' said Paula.

'I mean,' Eleanor blushed, 'here, in the – house.'

'What? You've been reading too many of those bloody orphan novels or something Eleanor. For God's sakes, darling, this is your *home*.'

Eleanor hung her head in shame. Then she went to her room, lay on her bed and invented a new episode in her current soap opera of florid daydream sequences: the saga of a mentally-retarded boy and a mother who patrolled his bedroom like a matron issuing appropriate punishment. The matron became a half-demented tyrant; the boy wet himself and was whipped; armed with the insurance of her tattoo of four beats on a wall so that people wouldn't die as a result of her misappropriations, Eleanor dreamt up increasingly improbable scenarios.

Paula was highly irritated by Eleanor, but she felt mystified pangs of sadness. She looked for her, but Eleanor was shut in her room.

Eleanor hitched a ride towards Causton with a farmer's son whose sister she vaguely knew. He made half-hearted passes at her until Ashburton, then gave up and wouldn't look at her.

She heard Selma coming down the stairs. The house was dark. An unexpected echo of Richard's voice reached her on the front steps. He sounded abrupt. Footsteps towards the door, lights. Selma's voice, whining sleep, came closer. Eleanor suddenly grabbed her bag and bolted, hid behind the dustbin corner, and again she made herself small, waiting until they were gone, Selma jowelled with sleep and bemusement.

Selma there to take her in her arms. Those delicate arms, but strong, over her body, cold white, but strong. She would hold her and there would be first the frisson of her gloriousness, then the strength of her holding her. The perfume, and underneath her skin's own warmth. Eleanor crouched by the dustbins. She could see the street lamps on the road across the fields.

Bitch, bitch Paula Strachan. The venom of those watered hazel eyes, freckles, fat solid mother cow. Eleanor would hate Paula, slap her, but the skin would bounce like rubber and repel her, send her away. She had no mother. Paula had gone to Amsterdam with Rolf and left her behind when she was a child. She walked down the lane and cried against a wall on Causton Road, and felt the grit indent her forehead. Smug bitch, bitch twitching with smug secrets. She ran half a mile along the road to a phone box and dialled Selma's number, but there was only the inhuman whirr and pause of the answerphone, and she pressed her head against the glass pane, and thought that if she pressed harder, the glass might give way, and the bones of her forehead splinter a mess of bloody head on Causton Road, and Paula would come by and gasp, but all the while she would be twitching still with her smug hard secrets.

This was outrageous. How dare Selma, who had murmured more than promises, not be with her? Where was she? Out with colleagues; pressed for time; exhausted; so many demands on her schedule. Eleanor rested against the wall of the phone box, and recalled now with absolute clarity that late Sunday afternoon at the end of summer at Selma's house, when they had held each other as if they couldn't stop, held on tight and stroked and whispered; their faces were together, and their skin and their hair, every sensation amplified. They had hugged on and on, pulling each other tighter, their embrace a relief and a need. Then Selma had kissed her – Eleanor had traced the progress of her kisses in her mind so many times, the reality was blurred, but now she recalled with a shock of renewed certainty the sensations of lips on her jaw line, and by her ear, and finally half meeting her mouth, Selma's lips moving over her lips and the skin on her face at once. Her legs weakened in the phone box, and she reeled with excited queasiness.

It was preposterous that Selma should carry on her life regardless. Eleanor's anger fuelled her resolve. The despair of rejection – Paula's eyes, Selma's indifference – hung all around her, and she could yowl like an animal, or cower in the corner of the box waiting to be hit. She saw the despair in glimpses that caught her off guard, like flashes of her own madness, but she still lived in hope.

Eleanor rented Sean's old room from Joyce Cochrane for a couple of weeks with all the money she had, the room now nominally under the tenancy of Sean's brother Nick, who rarely showed up. Joyce, large in a velour tracksuit, reluctantly let her take it on the condition she didn't spread her clothes around, and would vacate it on Nick's reappearance.

'Yes, yes, of course,' said Eleanor.

Eleanor returned from school. 'ES – Selma Healey called' said a note by the phone. She stopped. There were roadworks going on somewhere up the street and *La Bohème* filtered down on a bad reception from a neighbour's radio. The afternoon turned slow motion.

Eleanor punched Selma's Totnes Centre number into the phone. 'Selma, it's me,' she said.

'Eleanor,' said Selma. 'We should meet. Do you want to come

to my house?' The somnambulant voice casual.

Again, no sleep. Eleanor moved around in bed; her head buzzed, composing ideas, weaving patterns of conceits that twisted one theme in ingenious or trivial ways. She held mental dialogues with Selma in which she told her life story: she explained herself. And Selma was moved and fascinated, and questioned her intensely.

She dozed. At six in the morning she got up. The communal bathroom spawned pubic hairs and old shampoo bottles. The basement's mould and the patch of nettles outside the door retained the damp rank scent that characterised the flat.

Eleanor ran out into the dark. The cold cut her lungs. She could not sleep; if she ran, she might be slimmer, more beautiful, by the time she saw Selma. The smell of petrol was preserved in the frozen air. Solitary vehicles whined up the hill. The milk van passed. She walked along the Dartmouth road, the cold pumping into her lungs, and imagined she was strolling through the Tuileries Gardens with Selma.

She back-tracked, ran around the edges of the Methodist churchyard in a weak light, the grass in frozen clumps, and she suddenly knew she was happy. Some men rolled metal barrels outside the nearby pub. She jittered with tiredness and adrenaline. She loved the top she wore. She had bought it and invested it with totemic significance: this was the object that would make Selma notice her, just as everything new, a piece of clothing, a book, fitted in with some mental notion of what would please Selma Healy. She returned breathlessly to Joyce's, and light shone thinly from the bathroom.

When Eleanor arrived at the house in Causton, her eyelid was twitching with lack of sleep. Her tired skin contrasted with her hair and her brows. She rounded the corner, the scrubby garden where they had all sat one Sunday visible from the side entrance. Selma had left the lights blazing. When Eleanor knocked on the door she turned some of them off. She wore a long silk dress from the forties, plain and almost girlish. She looked more womanly today, less ethereal, the whiteness of her skin less marble and more flesh-like. Her disturbing mix of scents moved about the house with her.

Eleanor so pined for Selma's company that by the time she secured it, she was exhausted with anticipation, and spilled minutes with her silences. She was perpetually made up and ready to go, topics for discussion memorised in abbreviated form in case Selma should happen to ask her out. Her best clothes lost their freshness. Her mascara was hours old; her interesting points rarely met with the intrigued response she had dreamed up, and were therefore delivered abruptly; she was lively to the point of mania, or had nothing to say.

'You don't have to entertain me all the time in case I get bored,' said Selma. She leant back and the silk clung to her hip bones.

'I don't do that as much as some people,' said Eleanor.

'I know you're scornful of people who attach themselves to me,' said Selma. 'But perhaps I need them, if that's all right with you.'

She stretched. Eleanor followed her hand as it moved through the air. The hand looked older than the rest of her.

'Yes, but do they have to giggle stupidly at every minor witticism and bake you heart-shaped loaves of bread?' demanded Eleanor.

'That was one person once,' said Selma. 'Anyway – the more the better. Why don't you bake me heart-shaped loaves of bread, Eleanor?'

'Ha, ha,' said Eleanor sarcastically. She pulled her knee up to her chin. 'I just wish you'd see that they pick you because, because you make them feel good, you build them up. You're something they're not – they think they can imbibe some of it just by being with you. They're like – ivy, it's not symbiotic.'

'So you tell me.'

'Can't you see!' replied Eleanor raising her voice, so fraught she would inadvertently flare up and express virtually the opposite of what she felt. 'They're weak! They think they can *be* you. Because all things seem possible for you.'

'Well – you overstate terribly.'

The phone rang. Selma made no move. The answering machine clicked and shook. There was silence between them. The room's dark wood floors reflected splashes of watery light on the polish. The cold from outside edged through the window. Eleanor shivered. Newspapers lay in piles against the walls. Richard's raincoat was draped across a stack of bills and envelopes. 'Where's Richard?' said Eleanor at last.

'He's here,' said Selma, nodding.

'Yes,' said Eleanor.

'He took Louisa to Torquay to see some terrible teenage film about drama students.'

Selma smiled at Eleanor. 'How's your sex life?' she said.

Eleanor jolted her head.

'That did it!' said Selma.

'What?'

'Got your attention.'

'Oh.'

'So how is it?'

'Er – I don't know. Good usually. OK, anyway. But Sean's in Manchester. How's yours?' Eleanor dared herself.

'Oh mine . . .' said Selma. 'Mine is – many splendoured. But not always. What do you make of that?'

'I don't know. I don't know what you mean.'

'So do you like sex?' said Selma idly. 'Tell me everything,

Eleanor.' She swivelled her eyes around the room, as if looking for something. Her dress made a pool of grey-blue folds between her legs.

'Well what can I say? What can I tell you?' said Eleanor. Her eyelid flickered minutely. She blinked to still it.

Selma shrugged. Eleanor paused.

'OK, so you don't have anything novel to say,' said Selma, looking down and picking at the folds of her dress.

'*Selma*,' said Eleanor, her voice distressed. 'Stop being so rude. You're always rude to me.'

'Isn't it interesting that we choose to fuck men?' Selma said.

There was a short silence.

'Yes, I suppose it's interesting,' said Eleanor. Her voice issued thin and self-conscious.

'What an emotional sweetheart you are,' said Selma, with irony.

'You're mocking me.'

'No. You're a delicate little flower.'

'I'm not,' said Eleanor.

'And I'm logic, as I said, with a little bit of heart thrown into the mix. Anyway . . .' She looked at Eleanor directly, sitting back against her chair so that her dress now fell demurely over her waist, and Eleanor watched the progress of its folds as they moved about her body. 'Isn't it interesting that we choose men to relate to sexually?'

'Well yes – but – well, why?'

'I don't know. Is it our conditioning? Have we simply never questioned it? I wonder for what logical reasons we'd choose men other than for children. Maybe there aren't any.'

They were silent. The phone rang again. Selma instinctively leant towards it, then sat back.

'Well then,' said Eleanor. She trembled as she dropped her

hand on her knee. 'Why did you get married?'

'It seemed like an exciting thing to do at that time with someone I found wonderful,' said Selma. 'And because, I suppose, it's much easier to be married in this society than not to be married. I got married, and I'm sometimes with a man. Does that define me once and for all? I think, hypothetically, we should all expand our boundaries, for want of a better way . . .'

There was silence. A car stopped outside. Richard opened the side door.

'Don't you?' said Selma as Louisa's voice carried through from the kitchen.

'Yes,' said Eleanor. She could not look up.

Eleanor wanted to be with Selma always, to cling to her and feed from her, have her flesh all over her. She missed Poppy, she missed Tim, but she had frozen all thought, her mind a blurred point of craving.

How did you punish Paula? She who was unpunishable, who would bounce back like rubber, matter of fact and capable, with her darting glances and set mouth. And nothing would get through to her. Only hysteria, blood, self-laceration might kick her out of her fat, blank course of indifference.

Tim had turned up at Joyce Cochrane's two days after Eleanor had arrived there, standing waiting for her in the street in his faded blue work shirt with thirty pounds for her in his pocket, and a hug, and some reflection, and no message from Paula. No message, because she was a pariah. And Eleanor thought that it no longer hurt her, that she would view the inequality with the objectivity of an experiment, collecting proofs like sores or hand grenades.

A week went by. Selma didn't ring. Eleanor lay in bed for three days. Joyce tapped on the door.

'You'll be ready to hop it if Nick comes back, won't you?' she said.

'Yes,' said Eleanor.

Eleanor wanted to dribble, cry over Selma's dress and say sorry, sorry, love me, like me. As a girl, too, she worried she had let Paula and Tim down. She wasn't pretty, and unlike Rolf, she couldn't perform clever tricks such as running up banks and into hedges making jet noises.

Her party dress was from India, tea brown with tiny mirrors sewn onto the cotton in pink and yellow embroidery silks; for school she had a hessian smock made by Paula over ribbed tights. Her friends wore lovely flowered dresses from C&A, and white socks. She dreamed of white socks. Forbidden. One day it occurred to her that Paula must hate the colour, that was the answer – white socks, white sugar, white rice, white bread, all forbidden. But even above and beyond the socks, her dream was long hair. Long hair kept off her face with two clips, or hooked behind her ears so sections of it fell forward forming glossy pockets, but Paula said she had problem hair, keeping it short would thicken it, so she wore a kitchen scissors page-boy cut that stuck out on one side instead of curving under, and she could never be one of the popular girls with gleaming nutty plaits or blonde wisps down their backs. She dreamt she was Rapunzel from the Ladybird illustration, her plait so thick and long she could pretend at school it was a nuisance, and wind it round her feet in bed to keep it out of the way. Mrs Gledhill and Mrs Gormer looked after her at Malory Towers, the finest school in the kingdom, where she was a boarder every night before she fell asleep. Her hair grew to her ankles, and they were concerned that she might trip over it.

*

Her friends rang.

'I'll come back next week,' said Eleanor.

'Shall we say you're ill?'

'Yes. Flu.'

She was ill with flesh, rose flesh beneath cloth and seams. Lying in that narrow bed, her body was liquid beneath the sheets. She thought of a woman hard with authority, with older scents of skin and expensive perfume, lying upon her, in the fug and breath of four days. The woman was more coloured and complicated than the marble creature of her mind. Tinges to the hair, details of pigmentation: faint freckling beneath the powder. Fine lines radiating from her lids. Flesh came away from itself, peeling back like chicken flesh as Eleanor grasped at it, pulling, lumps coming off in her hands and disintegrating; Paula's flesh harder, the balloon rubber of resistance.

There were sounds outside: reversing cars, builders' drills in the distance, the swell of the market on Friday. Nick might return.

When they lived in Somerset, Paula had earned her diamond chip at Weight Watchers. But the following fortnight she gained two and a half pounds, and didn't dare return for her Maintenance Programme check-up. Penny from the farm gave it a miss too, and together they celebrated with a box of Almond Slices each. Several women in the village were cajoling Paula to join the committee that organised the parish hall Christmas party for local children. Meetings took place fortnightly from the first week in June, but they clashed with the Sangha's new Initiation Workshops, so she had to decline, and sensed a steely resentment amongst the local farmers' wives and the woman in the Post Office.

But David Harpur suffused Paula with harmony in the face of

adversity. She tried to persuade Penny to sign up for an Initiation Workshop, but Penny didn't fancy it. This was Paula's light, and her love, and her reason for being – no, not her reason, but the vision that enhanced her existence, and made her see for the first time the heaven that was inside herself. Tim agreed, but he expressed doubts: 'Difficulties in understanding,' Paula called them.

The Sangha was doing great things. Satsang now took place daily in eleven West Country towns. Paula was granted an admin assistant to help her co-ordinate the booking of venues and fundraising efforts. Ravina was only nineteen, but she took on the burden of the index file herself, adding rainbow coloured cards for each new area, and soon the ICF had spread to Wiltshire and the first London meeting was in its planning stages.

Eleanor found that Paula would suddenly say strange things with the conviction of someone else, in the voice of someone else, and Eleanor was no longer hers until she learnt the shibboleth. Paula now beyond reason, the staring blankness of somebody else's certainties. Panic that she would go away. The tenor of the house changing, a new religion in the air, strange new words appearing. Their resistance; her disapproval. Know the ways of dreamers. Create your own reality.

Eleanor loved Selma, loved her. She couldn't sleep at night, woke harsh with life, then became swamped with tiredness later in the day, a thick film of it she moved through, and felt moments of madness. Her very name a possession to her, loved and complete. She matched the letters with letters from her own, made anagrams of them, wrote them side by side.

A mother, a very mother. A spiky grande dame. She was horrible, Eleanor realised, quite horrible – the beauty, the scatterings of strangeness. And beyond that, so sweet and loving,

Eleanor was almost moved to tears by her generosity of spirit, the touches that charmed and endeared.

The Strachan house in Somerset had been David's main base when his work took him to the Quantocks and Mendips regions. So that David himself was present at their morning meditation session, though Paula knew increasingly that she must not expect to communicate with him as she would communicate with a friend.

David had a long row of straight teeth that showed when he smiled. He talked of fairies. There were fairies in plants, he told Eleanor, and she was enchanted, under his spell for whole hours. He took her to the end of the garden to show her the plants where spirits lived: they were in humble dock leaves and crab apples too, not just the pansies on the borders. But he seemed to Eleanor to focus beyond her, and the smiles of his followers echoed his in a uniform serving of friendliness which frightened her, and Family Satsang frightened her, and when her dreams were not in Malory Towers they were in what she imagined a Sunday School to be, earning points towards a book prize.

There were more changes in the house. The Playroom had become the Meditation Room, and Rolf and Eleanor's paints were moved to the potting shed. People came from outside most nights to use the room. Sometimes they came in the mornings too, and stayed on for breakfast, so the kitchen was full of the gentle morning voices of strangers. Eleanor ceased to notice each individual change, because change was all about her, and Paula was always out in the evenings.

Eleanor had classes to attend most mornings, but she didn't sleep, and then she stayed in bed at Joyce's. She heard a party winding down, a distant lavatory flushing, birds in the early hours. She dozed through the arrival of the dustbin vans and woke with a sore throat in the cold. She twisted the garnet ring round her little finger until it chafed a circle of skin, another ring.

Selma hadn't rung. She got up, and in a daze, she walked to the Totnes Centre. She crossed the road to ignore the stream of people walking up the hill on the school side.

Those people, that time. Eleanor loved the peculiarities of the Totnes Centre, the staircase, the shape of the window frames, the rows with the roadworkers. Selma's outrageous demands. Her reputation. It was like a place you once belonged to and loved very much, and years later you came back and all the details of its plasterwork were so strikingly familiar, yet changed by time, and it was part of you because it was part of your past, and therefore part of what made up your life, like your hair colour or your O'levels or your lovers.

The Sick Bay was in another wing of the school at the Totnes Centre, a wing that seemed to have evolved since Eleanor had first known the building. Its corridors were not familiar to her. It was strictly forbidden. She hesitated by the door and watched the girls who lay there, imagined the air raddled with scarlet fever, tuberculosis, fits of fainting. Mrs Healy seemed to glide from bed to bed, her slim waist clearly visible, but then she would disappear and Eleanor was not sure that she was there at all. She saw her in parts: a bending waist, a hand on a head. What did she have to do to get to her? Collapse? Become anorexic? Her heart beat with the danger of being in forbidden territory, where the Fräulein quietly moved. She was bleeding and wild. What more did she have to do? The blood seeping and stinking. She stood there. Mrs Healy moved about marble white and severe.

'Madame!' she called finally, urgently. 'Madame!'

Mrs Healy was pulled out of her calm. She was taken aback.

She turned to the girl Eleanor with her wounds and her womanly smell. Eleanor's hair had unravelled from its tight bun. It hung down wild and snagged. Selma observed her.

The other girls lay watching with their gauzy eyes through fevers. Mrs Healy's hand rested coolly on the layers of regulation cotton on her shoulder. The girls watched them, the older woman, and the younger in her uniform and piety, silently shrieking, bleeding, vomiting love.

Eleanor tied her hair back and arrived at the Centre as she was, in crumpled jersey and old tights. She hadn't had a bath for several days. She slipped in through the side entrance, ignoring the woman in the kitchen, and worked through the back staircases to Selma's office. She felt like throwing up, her mouth coated with no sleep or breakfast. She knocked on the door. Selma continued her phone call while Eleanor waited.

'Hello,' said Selma finally, looking up.

'Hello,' said Eleanor. She trembled. 'I – just felt like coming in to say hello. I haven't seen you for so long.' She tailed off.

'Listen,' Selma sighed. The phone rang, its electric warble streaming into the pause. Selma grabbed a pen and scrabbled for paper. 'Eleanor,' she pleaded, then snapped. 'What is it with – can't you try to empathise? I can't see anyone. Especially not uninvited in my office. I'm telling you that now, OK? Fuck that phone! If I don't tie up this work in a couple of weeks, I'm done for, and then I'll have a nervous breakdown. OK? Can I make that any clearer?' She snatched up the phone, there was a knock on the door, Eleanor hesitated momentarily then left. She leant over a sand bucket in the back staircase, but all that emerged was a slick of dribble.

*

213

It was December, and colder. Eleanor found places in Totnes she had never known existed: wasteland near the railway, fenced off and overgrown and scattered with oil drums; an area of squat water towers, a sewage plant, truncated rows of houses; then the long slopes of watermeadow where the Dart began to widen, overhung and gold-green in winter like a Pre-Raphaelite myth. She walked them methodically every day when she was out of bed, and attended some classes, but she could not get warm, a core of her frozen: she shivered more violently in the heated school than in the basement at Joyce's, where it was so cold she was numb. It was so cold, she couldn't think.

When Paula had first met David, he had been blonder but less seasoned, less glorious even; though then, too, Paula had looked on him as on a twenty-eight-year-old god. An alchemist who could turn Weston-super-Mare into Mecca. She began to wear hats then, but below them her trouser suits puckered over the ridges on her hips, and she felt fat and mean-faced. She bit the skin on her lips and darted her eyes at David.

'Paula,' he said. 'You have a beautiful mind.'

Her mind was beautiful, even if her body was repulsive, he said so.

She expounded her views to her family. Eleanor and Rolf chewed on forbidden Curly Wurlies and fidgeted. Tim nodded and asked questions and said he was still searching. But that summer, Paula had found it. She helped set up the offices of the International Chavan Foundation in Taunton and put herself forward for extra shifts on the admin rota, and though it meant David used the house less and less as his base, the spread of his teachings throughout the West Country gave Paula profound pleasure, as though she had personally engineered it, and when the ICF took over a house in Bristol, she drove herself in most days, because the hierarchy had since tightened and she was now ICF Administrator.

Paula knew she must not love David in the earthly sense. She loved him as her teacher. She knew now that what she saw was truth, and eloquence, and bright prismatic light. It was all around her. She had just been blind to it before, the blindfolding that starts with birth in Western society.

Eleanor couldn't understand. She mourned her own stupidity. Why was she second in reading and got blue stars on her stories when the teachings of the Sangha were as Sanskrit to her? Rolf accepted them. He asked no questions, but he lived the teachings: Rolf seemed to have a direct line, as Paula joked, to the source of it all. Other girls had Sunday school or piano practice, while Eleanor Strachan had only freedom, and gouache, and barefoot gardens – for Satsang was not compulsory. As Paula explained to them, they had the choice.

But then she was no longer asked. Paula stopped asking her, as if her eyes didn't see her. They flicked over her and focused on some further horizon. On Saturdays, Rolf sat in the front of the car with the safety belt on sucking his muesli bar, and they drove off to Bristol, and Eleanor was left in the house with Tim. Or sometimes Tim went too, and then Eleanor was left downstairs in the ICF with Simi the Children's Officer, who let the children squall and dribble while she made dhosas and coffee for the Sangha upstairs.

There were hints that Paula might leave. Where? Who with? Eleanor tried harder, but by now it was too late. She was gangly and stubborn. She scratched her sun browned legs sitting on Simi's cushions to see how white she could score them with her nails. If she pushed harder, perhaps she could make her mind open up after all.

Paula was always flushed and exultant when she emerged.

Eleanor sat in the back of the car on the way home and knew that just by being there, invisible except in the rear mirror, she was an intrusion. Paula looked her over suddenly in the hallway, and Eleanor contracted in defence; but Paula said nothing, and Eleanor sat with her tree in the garden.

At Joyce's, Eleanor's breath was white in the air of the basement. She blew breath under the sheets, hot for seconds, then damp, and lay for hours, and only Selma's body would be able to warm her. The cold stripped her body: she was blind and peeled as a new born child, and where she had once climbed into the goat pen in Somerset, or dreamed that she had, she was never sure – the fruit shed where she hid too cold and ticking with insects – and sat, smaller than the goats, Zippy and Goatèe, her head tentatively against their hard haired coats, an angel child, like a holy child in a stable, the goats with their big calm eyes looking down on her, hoofing the hay around her, nudging her closer to them, till she was so near she could nuzzle them, suck love from them: lying in that bed at Joyce's, the air outside a frozen stillness of tarmac and frost, the world became more brightly coloured and hallucinatory, and Selma was hers, hers, rubbing and loving until they were only flesh. Selma was always there, beside her in that bed, nipple brown, powder flesh, their nest of butted hay, never leaving her, never flirting then rejecting her. She was mother flesh, her lover, her love.

Paula had thought, earlier in the summer of David Harpur's miracles in Somerset, that this was life at its sweet, painful pinnacle, but then she reflected upon the young people in the Sangha who could devote the cream of their energies to the project because they had no domestic ties, and came to see, in a shock of realisation, that she was not truly dedicated at all, that she had compromised and bodged what David was teaching her, and that fulfilment grew out of discipline. With that she bloomed again, and lost her added pounds, though she had already sold the diamond chip badge from Weight Watchers for ten pence at a Sangha sale to raise funds.

She seemed to fly, her mind rising, crying, jubilating, above silos and sedge swamps, above hamster food, PTAs, *The Forsyte Saga*. In October, Paula went to Amsterdam to join the new International Sangha, where there was room for her and her son in one of the members' houses.

Eleanor had known that Toggle the hamster loved her, but slowly she came to realise it was because she was the person who fed him. She was aware that she didn't deserve equal love to Rolf, but she wondered why she couldn't change herself. When Paula left Somerset for Amsterdam, Eleanor thought of the dogs, Malachai and Rover, who had been put down, and tried to banish the vision of their legs erect in death on an operating table, but she still feared Paula's opinion from two hundred miles away, unable to rid herself of the idea that Paula might take her to the doctor for an injection that would make her body go stiff. She hit her head with one of Paula's old shoes from the shoe cupboard, but she was a coward. Tim cooked her frozen meals and Mrs Gormer's sister, Mrs Pollack, stayed with her after school until he returned from work, and then she went to stay for a holiday with Anne, Tim's sister, in Hastings where the sea air would be good for her.

NINE

'SHE HATES ME,' SAID ELEANOR TO SELMA.

'Oh she doesn't. Of course she doesn't,' said Selma.

They had met in the town, the sight of Selma's raincoat like a hallucination in the cold.

'But she doesn't contact me.'

'She just can't find fault with that rather gangly and unimpressive teenage son of hers,' said Selma. 'It doesn't mean she hates *you*. She's been so upset since you left –'

'But she does, she really does,' said Eleanor. 'Anyway, I don't care. What's the point of caring about it?'

Nick had not returned. It might be weeks, it might be days. Eleanor could not now get out of bed until the afternoon, when the school bell was announcing the end of the day: it was too cold, too brightly coloured in the frozen room.

'Anyway . . .' said Selma, looking about her.

'What?' snapped Eleanor.

'Well,' said Selma. 'I really . . .'

'You want to go, don't you?'

'It's not that I want to, it's just that I really should –'

'Do some work. Yes, I know, you've got to go and do some

work.'

'Yes, sweet, I should.'

'No! Come with me to Webburn.'

'But,' said Selma. She turned to Eleanor. 'But you're not staying there.'

'I know, I know. No one's there. I want to go there.'

'How do you know?'

'They're all out – work, school etcetera.'

'Well –' said Selma. She looked confused. 'I don't know what to say.'

'OK, don't,' snapped Eleanor.

'*Eleanor*! What is the matter?' said Selma.

'Oh come with me, come with me *please*,' said Eleanor. She put her arms around Selma, buried her face in her shoulder. 'You've got to. Please.'

'Well –' said Selma, exasperated. 'Why *now*? Why can't we just have tea here?'

'No, I want to go to Webburn,' said Eleanor. 'It'll be warm up there, it's so cold – I just want to be there. You don't want to come, do you? You don't want to be with me.'

'Yes I do, it's just I'm busy. If it's warmth you want, there are plenty of other places.'

'You always are.'

'Always are what?'

'Busy.'

'Oh come on then,' said Selma at last, cautiously. She looked at Eleanor intensely, staring at her with the minutely uneven focus of her blue-grey eyes. 'Come on, let's drive to Webburn House. Only for a couple of hours, and then I *must* get back to work.'

The house was peaceful. It was nearly four weeks since Eleanor had been there. Logs were piled up between the house wall and the garden wall, Tim's country habits, spawning lice and moss. The remains of wood smoke hung in the cold air of the sitting room. Gandalf thumped the floor with his tail when he saw Eleanor. The house seemed still, empty, as if preserved since the day Eleanor had last been there, few changes, Poppy's coat in a corner, a larger pile of letters to be dealt with. Eleanor built up the fire and turned on the heating. She and Selma were quiet. Eleanor moved silently around the kitchen and handed Selma a glass. She glanced at the clock.

'This house is beautiful,' said Selma.

'I know, it is, isn't it?' said Eleanor. 'Come here,' she said to Selma. 'Let's go to the telly room.'

'I don't want to watch telly now!' protested Selma.

'Not to watch telly. It's just more comfortable in there,' said Eleanor. She walked through the hallway. The hall clock ticked. Selma sat for a moment then followed.

'God, it's cold,' said Selma. She looked around the room.

'It won't be,' said Eleanor. She switched on a lamp on the floor and a heater. They sat on the sofa, Selma drinking from her glass. The heater gave off a smell of burnt dust; the lamp emitted a low orange light. Eleanor saw the family photo wedged behind the frame of a painting, and Paula seemed to laugh directly at her through the darkness, but with some reserved glint of judgement.

'You really didn't want to come here, did you?' said Eleanor suddenly. 'I don't know why you ever see me at all. You're just interested in your work, or in other things, I don't know.'

'Eleanor, for God's sake!' said Selma.

'Well? You really can't be bothered with me if you've got anything else to do. Well it's true, isn't it?' she persisted. 'Tell me it's true! Tell me you don't like me, then you can go.'

'Oh, for God's sakes!' said Selma, losing her patience. 'You're ridiculous.'

'I know,' said Eleanor. 'Sorry. But Selma, there are all those times when you don't see me. I mean – You know, so long when you don't see me, weeks at a time, or when you seem to get angry with me if I walk into the room; and then suddenly you take me out to supper and say nice things to me. I think basically you don't really want me around.'

'Yes I do, I'm just busy.'

'Always busy,' said Eleanor.

'Yes,' said Selma. 'Nearly always busy.'

'But you don't like me!' The oblique glint in Paula's smile from the wall. Eleanor shivered. Her voice was raised. 'I can't stand people not liking me! That bitch Paula.'

'You stupid little –' said Selma. She rested her hand on the back of Eleanor's neck and kneaded the bone at the top of her spine. Eleanor slackened momentarily under her touch. Drafts seeped through the window frame in plumes of cold air. The lamp gave off a weak orange glow on the floor as the afternoon closed in. Selma kneaded Eleanor's neck more and more firmly.

Eleanor shook her head away. 'You're hurting me,' she said.

'It must be because I don't like you,' teased Selma.

'Go on, hurt me then.'

'No, you stupid cow, I won't hurt you,' said Selma.

'Stupid cow yourself,' said Eleanor recklessly.

'No I'm not.' Selma pressed Eleanor's shoulders quite roughly. 'Come here.' She pulled her towards her.

'What are you doing?' said Eleanor.

'I'm holding you. Like this,' said Selma. She held Eleanor to her, squeezing her below the ribs, holding her firmly against her, and they sat there for moments, Eleanor's back against Selma's chest.

Eleanor's heart thumped against the pressure of Selma's arm, vibrating through her own body.

'I can feel your heart,' said Selma, her mouth close to Eleanor's ear.

The unreality of sitting against Selma, in the warmth, hearing her breathing, left Eleanor numb, unfeeling, only the hard beats of her heart filling her body. Time, silence, ticked slowly by. There was a slight wind, the background pounding of the river beyond the trees. A car started up somewhere along the lane where the holiday cottages were, but the house was silent. Cold dribbled through the window frame, but the heater glowed on the floor in front of them. Selma turned to Eleanor after some time and looked her more directly in the eye, then enclosed her fully in her arms, and Eleanor lay against her, but simply, like a friend or a child being comforted. They lay there for minutes, looking at the walls, listening to the river, Selma only shifting the pressure of her hand on Eleanor's arm.

'Well . . .' said Selma eventually. They were peaceful, sitting in stillness against one another. The clock struck in the hall.

'Mm?' said Eleanor.

Selma was silent. 'What are you thinking, Eleanor?' she said.

She extended one hand, paused in the air, skimming the outer strands of Eleanor's hair so lightly that Eleanor was uncertain whether she had touched her or only disturbed the air about her.

'Hold me,' said Eleanor.

'I am.'

'No, like this,' said Eleanor. She lifted herself strenuously on one elbow, leaned against Selma's chest and buried her face in her shoulder. She buried her face as though burying her head, sightless, cloth pressing against her eyelid. She opened her mouth. All the rustlings of Selma's hair moved in warm friction above her ear. The smells were familiar, sharper in such close proximity. Eleanor paused. Nothing happened. She was caught there, clinging, breathing into Selma and unable to let go gracefully. She felt dribble escape from her mouth onto Selma's shoulder.

Then Selma moved her hand along Eleanor's back and rested on the nape of her neck, and they lay there, their warmth and breathing magnified to each other. They held each other. Eleanor's hair slowly flopped, section by section onto the arm of the sofa, her neck exposed, and Selma seemed to touch the wisps of hair at the top of her neck with the tips of her nails, but every nerve in Eleanor's skin was alert to sensation, her brain struggling to distinguish the prickling of her imagination from reality. Selma continued slowly, until Eleanor knew that her fingers were there, moving on her neck. Her nerves rippled in response.

'Your hair is full of chestnuts,' said Selma whimsically.

She drew a finger nail up the base of Eleanor's hair line, grazing the surface of the hair, pressing the skin. Another strand of hair flopped onto the arm of the sofa.

'Now they're tumbling chestnuts,' said Selma.

Eleanor moved her mouth up to the arch of bone behind Selma's ear, and pressed against the warm skin there, smelling of hair. They moved together and lay against the arm of the sofa.

'What would your mother say?' murmured Selma.

'Mmm?' whispered Eleanor. 'What does it matter?'

'You're – she won't come back?'

'No, no, not till much later.'

Their cheeks were against one another, Selma's skin warm. Selma enclosed Eleanor's face in her hands, stroking it with the dry pale fingers, older, of a Causton garden in the late summer, that had patted the blanket beside her, drumming on Louisa's brow bone. Her finger tips moved over Eleanor's ear, playing, making thunder there; Eleanor breathed out hard through her nose and began to see spaces of luminosity, Selma's face blanking. Sensation suspended in disbelief.

Eleanor turned to Selma and watched her white face, incon-

223

gruous in her parents' house, the odd juxtaposition of Selma's features with the ethnic weave of her parents' sofa, where Tim had stretched out with hibiscus tea, and Paula had sat watching afternoon television.

She lifted and untangled herself, sat beside Selma's feet on the floor, still holding her, and Selma followed her. Eleanor kissed the base of Selma's neck, and pulled her fingers through her hair for minutes on end, stroking and combing it.

They pressed their faces together, and shifted their bodies. There was a noise from the house next door. They paused. Selma ran her hand lightly over Eleanor's hip, stroking the cloth of her skirt.

'You're beautiful,' she said simply.

'No, it's you who's beautiful,' said Eleanor. She opened her lips and pressed them against Selma's shoulder, mouthing at the cloth, and moving to the skin beneath it. She made it damp, circles like morning pebbles, round and wet. Selma lifted Eleanor's head, and kissed the back of her neck in small warm kisses.

Then Eleanor, looking at Selma, was momentarily distanced, as though watching the scene without emotion, suspended only in disbelief that this was happening, the surreal apposition of herself and Selma Healy after the fevered distortions of fantasy. Her mind felt numb, matter of fact almost, stunned with too much emotion. It was somehow laughable: the rest of her life was without plot, without ambition. Then Selma, as if sensing her blankness, flopped her arm and stayed motionless, and Eleanor surfaced to the present and drew her to her, and Selma ran her finger across her collar bone and under the neck of the top she wore, and she quivered, and involuntarily moaned. Selma trailed her other hand down Eleanor's upper arm, and lines of response rippled the length of her body.

Eleanor did not dare look at her in case their gazes caught; she buried her head again in her shoulder, and sensation sprung over her body, her limbs light headed. She sucked at her, at every fragment of a movement, greedily imbibing it.

'Did you notice me when you saw me here? When you first saw me?' murmured Eleanor. The familiar smell of the carpet, or of the house, next to her nose.

'Yes,' said Selma, and kissed her lower lip.

'Did you like me then?'

'Of course.'

'Why didn't you seduce me then?' She kissed Selma's ear and tasted her skin.

'You were a child.'

'Not really.'

'You're more beautiful now.'

They stroked tendrils of sensation over each other's skin, plant-like, pulling off clothes as a continuation of a movement. Selma's nails were long over Eleanor's body. Her breasts unclasped from her bra, shockingly large in their whiteness, and Selma's neck, the little lines and creases close up, and Eleanor's smoothness, together.

They moved their mouths towards each other, half together, edging and resisting, the cool of saliva as Selma's inner lip brushed against Eleanor, and they moved together, tongues and lips igniting fire, and Eleanor's leg shifted between Selma's, their bodies rocking. The base of Eleanor's body was liquid. A pool of sensation, molten and mercurial, rolled through her groin. They were embracing, their bodies moving in harmony, hard and fluid.

Selma in all her pale poise suddenly animal and alive, her white skin glowing, shedding layers of clothing, of resistance, and she cried out, and their limbs bumped into each other, they became fast, urgent. The dark afternoon tugged at the glass, the carpet was rough under their bodies. Selma pulled off Eleanor's tights, peeling them down the length of her body, kissing her toes, murmuring into her feet, and their clothes were crushed in a mess beneath them, their bodies heated.

Sudden saliva on Eleanor's tongue. Their mouths urgent together. Eleanor drank cucumber from Selma's skin, her translucent sweet flesh, vegetable to fire, the Strachans a distant memory, Selma's curves a shock of contrast with the hard chest and thighs of Sean.

'Love me,' said Eleanor.

'I do.'

'You were horrible to me.'

Selma bit the mapwork of veins in the crook of her elbow. Her leg drawn up, the stubble mature, exciting on the younger skin of Eleanor. She ran her hand over Eleanor's waist, over her thigh, following the curve, and back again, and stroked again, and again, stroking flakes of touch. Her fingers rippled across Eleanor's breast, teasing its swollen flesh.

'I thought of you,' said Selma.

'Did you?' mumbled Eleanor into her skin. A brief memory of despair.

'I was only busy.'

'"Busy. Busy",' said Eleanor.

'Always.'

'You barely saw me for months.'

'Didn't I? I gave you a garnet ring. I thought of you.'

Madame, severe, austere, beside her on the carpet with wet on her flesh. This was the flesh beneath the seams, beneath the cloth. The bandages that bound Eleanor shards at their feet, stained, smells lingering.

'It's only that I have phases of – preoccupation.'

'But you must live.'

'Yes, I want to live too.'

She clasped Eleanor, and they kissed hard, long hard kisses, and ground into each other's bodies, urgently, instinctively, their pubic bones circling, hard, the metallic scents of lust rising on currents of warmth. Outside, night would be falling, with frost and farm cats. The nettles in the yard. Circles of wet, like plant spittle, on their skin, a map of mouths. Selma quivered. Eleanor was circling, teasing, stroking. Selma's breast in her mouth, the nub of it, sucking, kissing, and Selma pulled her head harder to her and cried out. They breathed fast, their breaths mingling. Milky, harsh, their lips banging and bruising, and Selma quite different, the jewellery, the refinements, the mesmeric voice, lost in the planes of her flesh, in the urgent sexuality, animal, fast. It was all sex, sex; lust rising from some deeper place, her voice thicker when she moaned.

Eleanor clasped Selma's waist, circling it with her arm. Selma's nails on Eleanor's thigh. New boundaries evolved. Eleanor glimpsed black-out. The burn of the heater near her returning her to consciousness. Their bodies sticky, crushed. Their skin lit from inside, from a different place. Hands moving, meeting, passing. Heat of thighs, and their hands moving downwards, the whisper of Selma's finger drawn over the pink flesh of Eleanor's vulva, open as it was like a flower, and Eleanor moaned and pulled her harder against her, rubbing into her. Heat of thighs, moving downwards to strange tropics in the hollows, hot flowers, rolling, swelling.

They slipped into a different level. Visual detail was submerged in a physical drowning, an indistinct pool of sensation. Eleanor trailed her finger across Selma's vulva, rubbing the nub of flesh above it, the harder hair, pushing her legs open, and then disappearing inside her, molten, wet, the glory of it, the beauty of that wet moving space, ribbed like the roof of a cat's mouth, bending and caressing, and Selma moaning high and not like herself by Eleanor's ear. Dry lips opening to wetness. Their bodies moved trance-like and urgent and unhindered. I love you, love you, murmurings into skin, dipping to faintness, rising to a bead of pain or of pleasure. Drowning, Eleanor lost all sense of space, time, emerging suddenly, in spasms, to the clarity of physical detail, the sharp nail of Selma's finger against her tongue, sculpted structure of nose and mouth, this alien maturity.

This was home, here with Selma. She was returning. Her face against her skin an inevitability, returning to the teacher, her Madame who had taught her, her shoulder stiff with cottons, her flesh pearl beneath. The unattainable one with her mouth gliding, as in a reverie, over her body, and she felt a moment of heady power, sharp glory.

Slipping, not knowing it, into other levels, the body now sensory only, each gesture pooling into one. Space, pure blue and airy, or heavy white. Eleanor was hungry, desperate. She moved downward, she bit and suckled, the flesh over her face to eat, drink. Their breath hot and mixed, one breath. Frantic for relief. Climbing, planing. She glimpsed blue cliffs. Or violet. Hands on thighs. A mesh of mouths. Stroking, stroking; stroking flames, her toes belonging to some other creature distant on the floor, then budding to life, her body fire burning, igniting ganglia, veins, sleeping nerves. She saw creatures in sightless depths, her body touched by heat and alchemy, this woman stroking her, her clasping her, caressing her, saw higher cliffs and blue speeding night, climbing, climbing to a different plateau. A breed of trance, no sound or space.

Paula entered the house, and saw the lights. She walked into the sitting room and saw the wood stove burning. She shivered in the sudden heat, and looked in the kitchen. Gandalf thumped his tail in a half-sleep. She moved silently back to the hall, and opened the door of the telly room quietly. A low amber light fell. She blinked floaters in the semi-darkness until she was accustomed to the shadow.

She saw two figures on the far side of the room. A back gleamed dully in the light, a twist of limbs; with sudden clarity she made out the naked body of Eleanor entangled with someone on the floor. The figures swam in front of her, then with a surge of shock the details rearranged themselves, and she saw stomachs and breasts pale in the lamplight, and Eleanor stared up at her through Selma's hair.

TEN

PAULA AND TIM HAD ROLF'S BEDROOM SOUND-PROOFED
and equipped with a four-track recording deck, and consequently
Rolf was even less inclined to communicate with anyone about
anything beyond his domestic needs. Poppy sulked and made
dark comments about her recorder. There were four days until
Christmas, yet no one had mentioned the buying or cooking of
provisions in the assumption that Paula would take responsibility.

'We need something done to that garden,' said Paula, looking
out through the grey to the mass of sodden foliage and weeds.

'It might be an idea to hire a goat again,' said Tim.

'Tim! It's a front garden, not an overgrown field in Somerset,'
said Paula.

She went out with a rake and Strimmer that tangled in the wet
stems and short circuited. Tim continued to ponder over goats.
Paula decided to invite Sean over for Boxing Day, then remembered she must go out and buy him a present. She looked around
the kitchen. Poppy and her friend Jason had stolen some garden
gnomes on a school sports trip to Salcombe, and now their soil
covered bases sat in pools of muddy water by the washing-up

liquid. Packets of paper chains remained unopened on the dresser, the family presuming Paula would enjoy making them up now that Poppy was too old.

On December the twenty-third, Tim looked up from his cereal bowl and enquired whether the food was in yet for Crimble. Paula felt her breasts, alone in the kitchen when no one was looking, and admired her new shoes, bowed her head and closed her eyes.

Eleanor was informed by Tim on Christmas Eve that Paula had run off with David Harpur. She had expected to be the object of scandal herself, but her mother had pre-empted her.

Daily existence at Webburn House had collapsed into the void Eleanor had always suspected lay behind Paula's ministrations. Tim was moonish and haggard, Rolf incommunicative, Poppy veering between outrage and distress. Poppy cried in her bed-room. The kitchen, which Eleanor and Poppy had always called the 'mellow yellow room', now had grease splattered over its walls; the dog had escaped and chewed the Afghan rug in the hall. Paula, currently in Hannover, rang the house but made no attempt to contact Eleanor at Joyce Cochrane's.

'Oh sweet,' said Selma. 'My poor love. But she probably knows what she's doing.'

'She's a fat, stupid cow,' said Eleanor deliberately. 'How anyone could fall for that raving conman – stupid cow.'

'Has she spoken to you?'

'No. Has she spoken to everyone else? Yes! Rolfie needs reminding to take his homoeopathic pills for his eczema – he's only sixteen, you see. It'll be food parcels next, or she'll get Torbay Council to organise Meals On Wheels.' Eleanor snorted. 'Forget about Poppy, shall we, she's a big girl of eleven and can look after herself.'

Selma took Eleanor's face in her hands and stroked her, holding her. 'It doesn't make it any easier for you,' she said into her hair, 'but this particular story occurs the world over. Mothers undervalue their daughters and respect their sons. Because everyone is taught to undervalue women, including other women. That's all it is, sweet; it's not some personal conspiracy against you.'

'Oh,' said Eleanor. 'I love you. You make everything so clear in a way I can't see it. What's the use of knowing that when you're growing up with it, though?'

'None. That's what makes it sad.'

Selma was milk-skinned and placid. Christmas had leached the nervous energy and left her with a sense of strength. But within a week, she was again the centre of a series of deadlines and dramas. Richard, staying at the house over Christmas, had rebelled against these crises; he had tried to understand them; now he was frankly bored by it all.

'I wish we were away from here,' murmured Selma into Eleanor's ear. 'I wish we were in a clapped-out old wooden house by the sea . . .'

'So do I. I wish we were on the sand, at night, and we never had to come back, ever.'

'You're a daydreamer, Eleanor.'

'So?'

'So nothing. It's nice. I have to make some phone calls.'

'I'll wait for you.'

'I have to phone Janine at home and my accountants.'

'I can wait,' said Eleanor.

'No!' Selma said. 'What I'm saying is I want some bloody peace from everybody, including you. I've got to meet Julian at eight. God knows when I'm going to prepare this speech for the WA – why am I telling you all this? Why do I have to explain?'

'Yes, yes,' said Eleanor. 'I'm going.'

Selma suddenly stood outside herself and saw herself descending into a temper. 'I thought of you as I was in town today,' she said quietly. 'I think of little Poppy, too – would she like me to come and see her, do you think? I got you some earrings. A bit like mine but smaller. I knew the amber would be more glorious with your eyes than with mine – yes, look.'

'Oh!' said Eleanor. 'How beautiful.' Her heart thumped. Selma softened and held her against her breast, as one of the Totnes Centre women circulated outside.

And lying in bed, fragments of the old obsession peppered Eleanor's equilibrium and kept her awake. She was scared of Selma and her power. She was gripped with panic in case Selma should stop contacting her. The old panic. She breathed deeply. She was hate-worthy. Paula had run off with David Harpur. She had given her to her aunt when she was a girl. She had hated her. She wasn't bothering to speak to her: there were no Post-It notes on Joyce's mirror for her. She stroked herself, the proof of something in the shape of her body, whose curves had been outlined again by a woman.

She dreaded speaking to Paula. She feared her silence more. It was the stifling of emotion behind a tight mouth and a too-direct gaze, a look that sent her daughters mentally gagging. That flinty gaze; a barely perceptible twitch that suffused Eleanor with more dread than a full-scale rage would have done. A failure to comment. And then there was the other extreme of quivering emotion distasteful in one so large and mature: Paula turning round wet eyed with a barrage of sentences starting, 'I really resent . . .' and finishing in querulous tones, Paula weighted down with her feelings and resentments because she hadn't anything else in her life, no career or ambition. Eleanor dreaded Paula's judgement. This silence would drive her mad. She wanted

233

to barricade herself against any possibility of contact, and she wanted to root Paula out and shriek at her, shriek at her for all the injustices she had ever perpetrated upon herself and upon Poppy and Tim, for all her bitter judgements, for being fat, for not being vain enough to do something about it. And the guilt, the guilt prickling under her skin every day of her life: Paula might die of a heart attack; Paula might be feeling left out; Paula seemed slightly on edge: had she done something wrong?

Eleanor could not get used to the cold of the basement. It hurt her throat. Sleep evaded her: she was clenched with hatred for Paula, or Paula's judgement, Paula the liberal, the laissez-faire, with her shuttered resentments and oblique disgust. That she could fall, once again, for someone of such mediocre and specious charms, made Eleanor despair. Paula the impressionable: mouthing cant, swallowing the dreams of others.

Eleanor blessed the state of adulthood, in which there was no fear of being put into a children's home: you could earn your own living. If your mother judged you you could, physically, stand up and walk away. There were others in the world: Selma to turn to, Selma who was her adult peer and yet would protect her and stand by her. Or snap at her and reject her. In her mind, Eleanor scored her legs with her nails, as she once had at the International Chavan Foundation when the Children's Officer wasn't looking. But that wasn't enough. No one wanted her. Paula ignored her. Sean made no attempt to contact her. Selma gave her jewellery and shouted at her. She plunged into panic: Selma, body tangled with hers, buying her suppers, murmuring confidences to her, was now back at work surrounded by the hundreds of people she knew, was again absorbed in herself and her monomania. And her husband. And her Julian somebody dinner appointment. Selma had already snapped at her. Nails, no. She stared up at the ceiling, imprisoned by absolute wakefulness, and imagined knives. She considered stabbing herself in punishment. For what? She didn't know. Stabbing was too easy. She imagined scoring herself with a red line along the thin flesh between her breasts. If she went beyond that, she could punish them all, Selma and Paula, while she herself drifted into blankness – no pain, only punishment for what she was and what she was not.

The next morning she woke in the empty basement, and felt, as one does on waking after a nightmare, a flood of gratitude that that was all it was. It was all terrible exaggeration. She wondered if she possessed some deep flaw: perhaps she was mad after all.

Poppy's skin was shiny and blotched. Eleanor went to Webburn House and lay her head on the back of the sofa in the telly room. The memory of Selma there shot through her in a frisson. It was glorious. She was filled with such violent hatred towards David Harpur, she felt little for Paula other than a kind of diluted disgust. She spent an angry hour vacuum-cleaning the house, then realised what she was doing and stopped. And her saviour wore old forties dresses and narrow Fiorucci skirts and embraced her and evaded her.

And later as she roamed the house, her arm around Poppy's waist, she caught sight of Paddington Bear in a weak shaft of sunlight by the window, Poppy's childhood teddy dressed in stout denim dungarees with zigzag hemming, and she mourned for Paula, who had once sat alone at a sewing machine making her daughter bear-sized dungarees, running up a present now forgotten to give Poppy pleasure.

'Eleanor! Ca-a-all,' Joyce bayed drunkenly down the stairs to the basement in the afternoon, and Eleanor darted up the basement steps shot with automatic hope that it would be Selma, and it was Paula.

'Hello, darling,' said Paula.

'Hello,' said Eleanor.

'I'm coming to Devon.'

'Oh.'

'We're on our way to Edinburgh.' A slight tremor. Stubbornness.

Eleanor was silent.

'Can I come and see you?' said Paula at last.

'Not with that fucker.'

Paula paused. 'On my own.'

Eleanor was silent.

'Can I?'

'OK.'

Again Eleanor didn't sleep, dreading Paula arriving in her basement needing a cup of tea and a quick trip to the loo. Dreading her references to Selma. Selma was her talisman: they were like sisters, moulded of the same stuff. Eleanor kissed the crook of her elbow to emulate Selma's kisses of only days before, the unbelievable truth of it. She could not sleep. She feared Paula like no one else: she flinched from emotion, balked at confrontation, a minefield in every conversation. She could hear filtered talk from somewhere in the house, or from the flats next door. She could smell Sean's family's smell on the mattress. She could see Paula's eyes darting about the basement taking everything in.

'This is very nice, Eleanor,' said Paula when she arrived after lunch. 'Do you know – I've never been here.'

'Of course you have,' said Eleanor.

'I saw it when I helped move Sean's stuff, but never after that.'

'Oh,' said Eleanor. A twitch of guilt. She had known that Paula would calmly accept Sean's boyish mess, his ever-present socks, but her own rolled-up underwear and perfume bottles might subtly offend.

Paula wore a new coat. She was the same – frank and large and freckled – and yet not the same. She has been fucking another man, thought Eleanor in amazement. She glanced at her crotch area and tried to imagine it.

'Do you want some tea?' she said at last.

'Oh yes, I'm gasping,' said Paula.

Eleanor filled the kettle and moved in silence.

'I just arrived,' said Paula after a while. 'David – I had to take the bus, the trains weren't –'

'Don't mention that man!' Eleanor banged a mug on the draining board. 'I don't want to ever, *ever* hear about a stupid charlatan – fuckbrain who brainwashed you and who's now ruined our family.'

'I didn't come here for a shouting match, Eleanor,' said Paula. 'I came to see how you are – and to try to explain to you – to explain to you what I've done,' she finished uncertainly.

Eleanor's heart thumped. Paula was a solid presence on the side of the bed. Eleanor momentarily feared that Paula might hit her. The electric heater had its one functioning bar switched on, but cold seeped in through the double doors smelling damp and fungoid. Paula's new coat brushed against a stain of damp growth on the wall.

Eleanor placed some tea on the floor in front of her.

'Thank you, darling. Oh Eleanor, look at me!'

'I am.'

'You've avoided my eye since I got here.'

Eleanor sighed. 'Paula,' she said, 'I've got loads to do. I've got to see the bank and sort out some work. I don't want to talk about the slimy prick you've run off with –'

Paula flinched.

'And I don't really want to talk about anything. Do what the fuck you want. Just remember Poppy is only eleven, and Tim's *ill*, I'd say, and that man is the biggest stupid bastard you're ever likely to come across.'

Paula's lower lip was unsteady. 'I think about Poppy and Tim. And Rolf. I really do. I'm going to see Poppy this evening.'

'I don't think she wants to see you.'

'What can I do, Eleanor?' said Paula with the sudden determination Eleanor dreaded. 'What can I say that'll make it better as far as you're concerned?'

'"As far as I'm concerned"? It's not just a matter of my opinion.'

'Yes it is. It's all about that. You're attacking me for what I've done. I'm not expecting your approval – I'd like it if you'd just open your mind and listen to me. You're my harshest critic.'

'You ought to hear Poppy's opinion, then.'

'Yes. Well, you two are always in cahoots. Think of Selma. She's never judged me.'

Eleanor blushed at the name. 'Why should she? Anyway, she agrees with me about the bastard. And anyway, how do you know what she says about you?'

'She's always been honest with me. And very supportive. Well . . .'

'What are you talking about?'

'Selma's opinion of me – doing what I wanted. It's very different from yours, even though she appears to be your guide in most things.'

'Have you been talking to her?'

'Not recently.'

'Well when then?'

'Oh I don't know. A couple of times in the last months.'

'What? You mean she knew before –'

'We've discussed lots of things. I thought you two told each other everything – didn't that bit of gossip get to you?'

'She knew that you were . . .'

Eleanor reeled as though Selma had slapped her. Betraying, calculating bitch. She had known all along, and supported her and loved her and listened to her stories and offered insight and advice. Eleanor was dizzy. The adult world she had entered snapped shut again, people like Selma and Paula older and richer and beyond her league. She summoned up her constant talisman: Selma. Selma to protect her from Selma. And the image slipped and shifted and left her with nothing.

'Don't you love me?' Eleanor had said flippantly the day before. 'Very much,' Selma had said. 'And I love Richard, and Louisa –' 'Enough, that's enough,' Eleanor had stopped her. And then later Selma had snapped again that she needed space for herself, and lost her temper, and later still, passing by with Janine, she had gabbled into her ear a string of erotic tendernesses. But a hint of rebuke, and the old terrors, the old obsession, ticking through slow afternoons at Joyce's, and Eleanor pleading with Georgia for advice she couldn't give. She would go mad. Perhaps there was a symmetry in it too: she could collect the indignities like sores, a hobby, secret sores sticking to her underwear like hair cloth.

She saw Paula looking at her with the old appraising glint and kicked the end of the bed, jerking her as she sat. Fury wiped out her fear.

'How dare you,' she said in tight anger. 'How dare you talk to Selma about him? Run off with that monster – again – and leave everybody behind, just run off as if you had no responsibilities at home. No one needing you? I mean, that's just outrageous! It really is –'

'Oh darling,' said Paula.

She began shouting, her voice barely controlled. 'How dare

you leave me like you did before? I've never complained about that, never *once*. You just left me, age nine. So there's no one to look after me and I have to go off to an aunt's.' She began to sob.

Paula reached out a hand.

'You gave me away,' said Eleanor.

'I –'

'It's terrible, Paula!' shouted Eleanor, high-voiced. 'Don't you see how you're prey for any loony who comes along? You've always done this – all that stuff about meditation and self-transformation blah, and you do them for eighteen months and they're *It*, you've found *It*. And we all have to listen and join in, otherwise we're outcasts. And then something new comes along and off you go, and the last *It* is never heard of again. I mean, it's absurd!' She laughed incredulously. 'Why haven't the Moonies got you yet? I often wonder that. It's just like that. Can't you see? You're a bit tired of the Totnes Centre now, and Rolf's always in his bedroom, so you fall for the smooth talk of this failed mystic who says he fancies you. It really frightens me. Did you enjoy fucking him, then? Being unfaithful?'

'Well. Did you enjoy it?'

'What do you mean?'

'Do you enjoy what you do with Selma? And the nice little surprise you gave me?'

Eleanor cringed with embarrassment, then there was a momentary kick of pleasure. But Selma could go to hell.

'I'm sorry, I'm sorry for what maybe it did to you, me going to Holland,' said Paula.

Eleanor was silent.

'You've got your so-called guru too, though,' said Paula gently.

'What?'

'You've got one too, Eleanor.'

'No I haven't. I have opinions of my own.'

240

'Developed by Selma Healy. There's nothing wrong with that. You learn from her, you copy her, may I say, and –' she laughed, 'you follow her, just as much as I do David.'

'It's not the same at all,' snapped Eleanor.

'Why not?'

'Because she's not some phoney mouthing rubbish and setting herself up as a deity.'

'I'd say that's pretty much what she does do when she can get away with it.'

'Anyway,' said Eleanor, 'it's not the same at all. You know damn well it isn't – I'm not leaving a husband and children at home.'

'Hark at you!' said Paula richly. Eleanor winced. 'Such feminism.'

'Yes, well,' said Eleanor.

They were silent.

'Well, it was your choice to get married and have children, so you should fulfil your obligations.'

'You're so moralistic, Eleanor,' objected Paula. 'You take this tone with me, and yet you – you feel *entitled* to have an affair with whoever you want and do what you choose. Absolutely entitled, no question about it. Whereas I'm supposed to stay at home at a dirty sink all my life, am I, because nineteen odd years ago I chose to get married to someone? And so things can't change? You're judging me just as a mother . . .'

'*Me* judge *you?*'

'Yes,' said Paula patiently. 'Just your mother, just your father's wife, stuck at home. Well you can take your avowed feminism and stick it somewhere.'

Eleanor stood in silence. She looked at Paula with her coat and her new slightly cosmopolitan air. 'Yes . . .' she said at last. 'But I still think you should consider the consequences before you just do something; you never do.'

'Did you? Before you slept with Selma Healy?'

'That's different.'

'Yes, everything's different as far as you go. Your theories don't extend to mothers, though. I had to get away, Eleanor!' Her face trembled. She looked as though she might cry. She raised her voice instead. 'You don't know what it's like, you have no idea. You may think I've spent my time dabbling, but to me it feels like I've been a slave to some grinding routine, some house or another, for twenty years. Why is my running away so much worse than yours? It just is – because I'm a different generation and I've got children. You've always berated me and scorned me for following – ch-charismatic leaders, for exactly what you've done. I make no judgement about what you did. And plenty would, I assure you.'

'You make judgements about everything else,' Eleanor muttered.

'You've had your freedom, your special person,' Paula appealed. 'So can I.' A tear began to form on the edge of her eyelid. 'I had to get away, Eleanor,' she said. 'I really did.'

'Yes,' said Eleanor. She saw an image of despair, and of raging excitement, of herself on a floor in Webburn House, and white arms and a peculiarly monotonous voice. 'Yes,' she said.

'You understand?' said Paula.

'Yes. Partly,' said Eleanor.

'Oh Eleanor,' said Paula, 'I'm so glad. And I'm sorry – how can I say this? – sorry that you thought I'd left you when I went to Amsterdam.'

'You did,' said Eleanor.

Paula hesitated. Heat rose alongside damp drafts. The afternoon closed in on them, blank January light turning dun. 'I didn't really leave you.'

'What did you do then?'

'I went to follow a spiritual guide,' she said.

'You left me behind, and you took Rolf.' Eleanor shrugged. 'It was your choice.'

'He was younger.'

'He was seven and I was nine.'

'He seemed much younger.'

'Look, Paula, after all these years I've given up. You prefer Rolf as a person, and you're entitled to that. I'm beyond it. I don't give a toss now, because it doesn't matter any more. But I wish you'd bloody stop pretending. You made your choice: you preferred Rolf, you took Rolf with you. Just as you're making your choice now.'

Eleanor folded her arms and spoke to the ceiling. Her voice was hard. 'All I hate is that you deny it. It's so obvious, it drives me mad!' She turned to Paula.

'I never *preferred* Rolf,' said Paula.

Eleanor stood, arms folded, waiting. She fought a sob that constricted her throat.

'I found him an easier child,' said Paula at last.

'*Easier!*' screamed Eleanor. 'He whined and hit and was spoilt all day long. All I ever bloody did was do the washing-up and try not to grow out of my clothes, and *still* you didn't like me. What more could I do? What more could I possibly do?' She shouted at Paula, straining her voice. 'I never took a *thing*, not one present, or living in that house, for granted, whereas Rolf just assumed everything. Tell me – what more could I have done?'

'Nothing. You didn't need to do all that. I –'

'And then you criticised me all the time, and praised Rolf to the skies every time he opened his mouth, and what was I to do? Tell me, Paula!' she shouted. 'What was I to do? I didn't *know* what else to do, because nothing was ever right. I thought all the time you were going to put me into care, I thought –' She broke off and leaned against the wall, sobbing, ashamed. 'I *know* I wasn't beautiful, I know I couldn't ride Choppers with no hands, and I didn't understand David's teachings, and I wasn't charming or anything. But I tried. I promise, I really did,' she said pleadingly, then slumped. 'I tried and tried and tried. You'll never know how hard. And you still gave me – that look.'

'I always loved you,' said Paula simply.

'What? You don't have to lie now, Paula. You never even praised me about school, because you thought formal education was a farce, or whatever your theory was, I don't know, and yet that – that educationally subnormal bully gave you orgasms if he managed to write his name. The great genius – Rolf Strachan. Don't you see you've emasculated him, your little princeling? He can't leave home, he doesn't do anything, he thinks the world – or his family – owes him a living. You still feel you have to stand up for him now – I'm accused of making trouble *still*. You know, you even give him bigger meals – it's laughable! The Boy Rolf's comforts are first and foremost. Why do you *respect* him so much? You know, I even think you're afraid of him. You defer to him. Don't look at me like that, Paula. Don't! Eugh.' She shielded her eyes and backed away. Her face was sore with spit and tears; she was crying in hiccoughs. 'You look at me with this look – it's like *disgust*. You find me disgusting, don't you? Admit it. Admit it, Paula. I've got curves and I menstruate. Admit it, I disgust you, don't I?'

'Stop it!' shouted Paula. 'You're hysterical.' She reached out.

'No!' screamed Eleanor. She flinched automatically. 'Don't hit me. Please.' She was sobbing.

'Elea*nor*,' said Paula. 'I wasn't going to, I was trying to hug you.'

And Eleanor suddenly saw herself, again as she had as a child, in a grey institutional nightdress in some kind of mental hospital, an adult woman sucking her thumb. Because of Paula. Because she was not welcome in her own home, and it had turned her mad. Paula visiting, and Eleanor backing off, frantic, clutching for a nurse, afraid that Paula with her strong freckled body would hit her. And dying, dying. A slick of human fat kicked to one side. She had turned her whole being inside out for Paula. What more could she do? And then she could have her revenge, by dying, uncared for, taking slow joy in doing what was expected of her. Selma again. She damped it down before she saw madness.

She had chosen to sit in cafés reading comics alone while the others ate at another table, and stared at the print, tightening her throat against a lump. She was silly and obstinate, Paula said. Eleanor forced herself. There was anger, as well as self-efface-ment, in being an unequal person. Slow panic. Would they leave her when they went out to the car park? Then what would she do? Did she give herself up to the social services immediately, or stay in the café hoping someone might find her? Her mind always leapt several steps into the future. Rolf and Paula were an easy laughing team at a table across the room. She was tight with panic. She had secret powers. Lonely secret powers. All on her own.

She faced Paula, her features swollen and chafed and ugly. Paula was beside her before she could bolt or recoil. She held her to her, solid. She stroked her hair. Eleanor pulled away slightly, then flopped.

'My lovely, beautiful daughter, my beautiful daughter,' she was saying. 'Why do we do this to each other? How did you get so hurt?' Paula sat down on the bed and held her, heavy against her. 'I loved you so, so much.'

'You didn't,' said Eleanor. She still hiccoughed.

'I did. I did. So clever and pretty and loving. You were my first born!' She stroked wet strands of hair off her forehead. 'How could I not have loved you?'

'But you didn't, though,' said Eleanor, losing her voice.

Paula hesitated. 'You know, we felt we had to build Rolf up. You were so bright, and he had problems at school – we encouraged him whenever we could. Maybe we *over*-encouraged,' she said, surprise in her voice. 'He was such a slow little boy, he needed protecting and defending.'

'See? Still the same.'

'Perhaps from what you're saying – maybe we did over-do it,' said Paula.

Eleanor was silent. Paula hugged her tighter.

'But,' said Eleanor eventually. She yawned suddenly, her eyes puffed holes. 'I know . . . that we're taught to undervalue women, and so mothers really do respect their sons more. It's common. You award him a higher place in the world. But . . . there's more. I don't know –'

'If mothers undervalue daughters, daughters can undervalue mothers,' said Paula gently. 'But your theories don't extend to me, do they, Eleanor? You see me only as a mother.'

'I'm sorry,' said Eleanor, leaning her head briefly against Paula's arm. Paula hugged her tighter to her.

'I'll tell you quite, quite honestly,' said Paula looking down on Eleanor's brown head, still stroking the wet hair. 'Oh . . . how can I say this? I loved you, I really did, but you – irked me. You irritated me. Maybe I saw my own failings in you – I didn't have very much self-esteem, you know, Eleanor, whatever you might think. And you had so much, so easily. And you played up to Tim. Or,' she sighed, 'maybe it seemed to me you did. Perhaps I was just jealous. I was jealous.'

'Jealous of me with Tim? That's obscene. Obscene.'

'How could I help it if I felt it? He loved you so, and talked to you for hours and read you books. And I felt more and more unattractive and fat. And I thought Rolf needed making up to for it, so I gave him more attention. And occasionally, yes, it is true, I'd see myself being hard on you, maybe I took things out on you, and I'd try to stop myself. And then when you were fourteen or fifteen, and – oh, you had grown up to be so beautiful, and I'd see you larking around with Tim in your swimming costume or something, and I felt past it. You were so slim and lively.'

'Oh,' said Eleanor. 'Oh God, why couldn't you have said that before? I'd never have thought that. I was just a showing-off teenager, that's all. But,' she paused. They sat in silence for moments. 'I can only say I only felt judged and disliked.'

'How can I tell you it enough, then?' said Paula. She pulled Eleanor's face against her neck, and held her hard, pressed against the warm freckled beating of her skin, and Eleanor was alarmed and resisted, Paula so large and fleshy beside her, and she felt weighted and drowsy and flopped against her.

'I'll tell you,' said Paula, now threading the ends of Eleanor's hair and rocking her and holding her. 'I was pregnant with you before we were married – did you know that?' Eleanor shook her head against Paula's neck. 'And anyway, everyone – mum and my sister and even Tim – they all thought it was too early, they thought we should have some years together first, earn some money, they thought I should have an abortion. We didn't mean to get married yet, you see. There was so much pressure on me, immense pressure really, Tim worrying about having a baby then and everyone else going on and on. And all I wanted was to have a baby, this thing inside me that I loved already. I loved my baby – you – so much. Even then. And I fought, and I insisted, it was like I was left alone while I was pregnant, just me and the baby battling it out together. And then you were born, and you were so beautiful, so lovely, my little baby lying there, and I just loved you right away. So much. So much. I always did. I do.'

The night darkened the room, and Paula finally left to collect Poppy from Jason's house, and Eleanor thought suddenly of Selma, and Selma had somehow altered. Selma flirting with Ben, or talking with a note of hysteria, or loving and caressing, and tormenting and admiring her, but at a distance, an image once removed. Eleanor waiting, clinging: she lay on the bed, the coverings hard against her eyelids, and was disturbed by it, and saw herself no longer in a little room, the little room frozen with dust motes and fevered distortions, but in some larger place, a world like Selma's own of space and brightness.

They passed and greeted each other, and touched, and separated, and touched again. This woman was her myth. The myth of these years. But none of that mattered either, Selma was herself beyond all that, whether Eleanor passed her and touched her hand or not: the Selma who would go on walking, with others, and eat dinners in restaurants Eleanor would never see, please others with her talk, and disturb them, and lull them with her voice. Rich colour behind ivory features.

Eleanor sat by her tree in the garden. She sat until gnats gathered in patches between the branches. She scratched at her hair and neck. Mrs Gormer passed by on the lane on her way to evening milking and flashed her scarlety smile. The wood pigeons were distant; big black birds clattered in the fields; it grew darker and chill, and Eleanor sat thinking her thoughts. Then the farm gates next door swung shut, and she raised her head and there was Paula looking for her through the window, and they waved to each other, and Eleanor got up and tumbled across the grass back home.